Look for More Titles by Cassandra Chandler

The Blades of Janus
PACK

The Department of Homeworld Security (novellas)
Gray Card
Resident Alien
Business or Pleasure
Tied up in Customs
Entry Visa
Duration of Stay
Duel Citizenship

The Summer Park Psychics
WANDERING SOUL
WHISPERING HEARTS
LINGERING TOUCH

Other Works
"Second Sight" (short story)
"Second Skin" (short story)

CRAFTING A WRITER'S LIFE: Building a Foundation

Coming Soon

Forbidden Knights
FORBIDDEN PLEASURE

Forbidden Instinct

Forbidden Knights
Book One

Cassandra Chandler

Copyright Page

Forbidden Instinct
Forbidden Knights, Book One
Copyright © 2017 by Cassandra Chandler
ISBN: 978-1-945702-71-6

First print edition: October 2017
10 9 8 7 6 5 4 3 2 1

cassandra-chandler.com
P.O. Box 91
Mission, Kansas 66201

Dedication

For my mom—who saw the future.

Chapter One

In five minutes, Miranda's car would be a crumpled wreck. She checked her seatbelt with a shaking hand—again—to make sure it was fastened tight, then gripped the wheel hard enough to make her knuckles turn white.

A familiar silver minivan came into view ahead. She hadn't met the driver, but recognized the soccer-mom's short bobbed haircut. Miranda would never forget the woman's face—or the faces of the three children inside. Two of them were on the passenger's side. One of those was an infant.

The SUV is going to hit them from that side.

Her vision had been absolutely certain on that point. She glanced at the clock, then stepped on the gas.

2:46 PM. She had three minutes to get in front of them and slow them down. Three minutes to beat them to the intersection and be the one in front of the SUV that was about to speed through a red light. If she did everything right, the accident would only take out her car.

Her heart pounded in her throat, making it hard to swallow. She couldn't let herself panic. She knew she would make it through this. She'd *seen* it.

How did mom do this, knowing she wouldn't *make it out?*

Miranda couldn't think about the past. If she started to cry, it would blur her vision, dull her reflexes, and facilitate a family reunion she wasn't ready for. The present—and the specific future she was trying to create—needed her full attention.

Her ancient car struggled to catch up as the minivan accelerated. She managed to get behind it, then swerved into the left lane, crossing the double lines. She jerked the wheel back to the right just in time to avoid a head-on collision with a blue pick-up truck.

"Beeeep! Beep-beep!" She sang along with the pick-up's horn, knowing precisely how it would sound. Other cars joined the chorus.

"Everybody's a critic," she muttered under her breath. "I'm trying to save lives here."

She slowed, herding the soccer-mom behind her. The minivan's horn persisted.

"Yes, I know. I'm being an ass." She glanced into her rear-view mirror, taking in the angry expression of the woman behind her. "But I'm also saving yours."

Almost time...

She knew she had to steer away from the SUV right before it crashed into her. Maybe that act was going to offset the force of its impact or something. If she didn't time it right...

She *would* time it right.

A dark shape loomed in her peripheral vision and she jerked the wheel hard to the left. The first crash of metal hit her ears as she was hit. The second followed a split-second later—the minivan plowing into the back end of the SUV that had struck Miranda's car.

The world was set to tumble-dry as the street rolled around and around through the front windshield. Her car balanced on two tires for a last moment of teetering suspense before finishing its final roll and falling to the ground, upside-down. The roof crunched ominously, several inches closer to her head than it used to be—or maybe it was that she was hanging from the driver's seat, her seatbelt the only thing that kept her in place.

Probably both.

Tires screeched. People screamed. Horns kept blaring.

She laughed. It sounded hysterical, even to her. Tears ran over her temples and into her hair. Her eyes burned. She wanted to unbuckle her seatbelt, but couldn't will herself to let go of the steering wheel. She felt oddly disconnected from her body.

Is this what shock feels like?

It didn't matter that she'd known she would walk away from the accident. She'd dreamt this version of the future over and over before waking. But the primal part of her brain had basically seen her chewed up and spit out by a saber-toothed tiger. It was still processing the events.

She hadn't bothered to count all the iterations of what could be. In the end, there was only one possibility that didn't end in death. Miranda had to be in that intersection at the exact moment of the accident. It had to be *her*.

Mom would be so proud...

Her tears came harder.

Why couldn't people believe? Miranda wished she could tell people about her visions and let them make their own decisions. She should be able to walk away. Maybe actually have a life of her own, find someone who could understand and support her.

Darren's face popped into her mind's eye.

If only...

Sweet, smart, gorgeous Darren—with his jet black hair and steel gray eyes—who laughed at her jokes, even if he didn't make many of his own.

Getting to know him had made her happy, which was terrifying. She never knew when her visions would call for a sacrifice, and he somehow seemed the type who would throw himself on a grenade for others. She didn't think she was strong enough to endure another vision that sent someone she cared about to their death.

She shouldn't let him get too close. But she couldn't stay away.

No one at the accident scene was having trouble staying away from her car. They probably thought she was dead, and no one wanted to be the one to find her gruesome remains. If she hadn't known to turn her wheel just before the moment of impact, they would have been right.

The surreal cast to her perception started to fade. Her skin tingled and her heart kept pounding in her throat. Each beat sent a spike of pain through her head. She needed to get out of her car.

All she could see through the cracked glass of the front windshield were people's feet as they hurried around the intersection. She noticed a pair heading straight toward her. Black dress shoes polished to a high sheen and nice slacks.

The man stopped just outside her door, probably bracing himself for the worst. She considered making a funny face to lighten the mood, and let out another semi-hysterical sounding laugh. She cut it short as he knelt next to her open window.

Oh, wow...

Steel gray eyes bored through her, surrounded by thick dark lashes. The man's hair was raven-black, skin tanned to a deep bronze, jaw strong, features flawless. She had memorized his face weeks ago.

His eyes widened as he recognized her, too.

"Miranda?" he said.

"Hi, Darren. I'd offer to take your order, but I'm a little hung up right now."

She laughed, but her eyes had filled with tears again. He didn't laugh at her joke this time. She wished he would at least smile. Seeing his dimples always made her feel better. She wanted—needed— something that at least gave her the illusion of normalcy.

"You're going to be okay," he said.

She already knew that. Still, his seriousness brought home what she had risked. It made everything feel more real. She'd liked it better when her perception had that lingering sense of dreaming.

"Can you assess yourself?" he asked. "Do you know if you hit your head?"

"I didn't. I mean, my head hurts, but I think it's from the adrenaline."

He didn't look at all relieved. His eyes flicked to the ground, then back to hers.

"I need you to listen to me very carefully," he said. "We can't wait for the EMTs to arrive to check you out. We need to get you out of the car. Now."

Her visions tended to jump around, leaving large swaths of time unseen. The universe didn't seem to want to spoil all of her surprises. Miranda took in the grim expression on Darren's face and figured this wasn't a good one. She took a deep breath to calm her nerves and finally registered what was making him look so worried.

Gasoline was spreading onto the street from underneath the roof of the car. Her heart started to pound again.

She had seen herself on the other side of this. Walking stiffly among the tables and booths at the diner, holding a carafe of coffee. She was *not* going to burn to death.

Please, don't let me burn to death…

"Stay calm," he said. "I'm right here with you. I won't leave."

She closed her eyes and took a shaky breath, then let it out. She believed him. It made her less afraid, but also brought home the sharp sting of her loneliness. She was usually better at keeping it at bay. It had been a long time since someone had helped her through the aftermath of a vision. A long time since she hadn't felt completely alone.

She opened her eyes as he stood. He tried the door handle a few times, but the metal frame was mangled. The world seemed to spin as fumes burned her lungs.

She wondered briefly why Darren didn't just rip the door off her car, then remembered he couldn't do that yet. No, that was wrong— people couldn't do things like that at all. Reality was warping— memory, dream, and vision bleeding together.

She heard fabric rustling, then Darren squatted next to her again. He'd taken off his jacket and wadded it into a ball that he placed under her head. Brown leather straps hugged his broad shoulders—and held a handgun in a holster. He'd never mentioned being a cop. All she knew about his job was that he kept late hours.

He squeezed as much of himself into the car as he could fit. He was kneeling in gasoline. "Let go of the steering wheel and put your hands on the roof of the car."

She *knew* that she would be okay and was still panicking. He had no assurances of safety and was trying to help her anyway. He was risking himself for her. Her eyes filled with tears again.

"It's okay." He placed his hand on hers. "I won't let anything happen to you."

She let him gently peel her fingers off of the wheel, grateful that the adrenaline flooding her system seemed to be blocking her ability to read futures through touch. His hands were warm, his skin smooth. He pressed her hands firmly on the roof of the car, then reached into his pocket and pulled out a knife.

"I can't reach the seatbelt release, so I'm going to cut it," he said. "When I do, you'll fall." He put one arm across her chest. "I'll slow your descent as best I can, but will need your help to make sure you don't get hurt, okay?"

She nodded, bracing herself. His knife cut the seatbelt easily and gravity took over. She'd barely touched the floor before he was pulling her into his arms. She grabbed his jacket as she passed by, clinging to it. Darren tucked her against his chest and started running away from the car.

"There's gas over here," he shouted. "Everyone needs to stay clear."

A few bystanders glanced over, their jaws dropping open. The soccer-mom was among them, holding her baby while her other kids clung to her legs. Her gaze met Miranda's briefly, and the mix of horror and gratitude etched into her eyes was one Miranda didn't think she'd ever forget. Whatever happened next—whatever Miranda had to deal with after this—it had been worth it.

She turned into Darren's chest, letting it block out the rest of the world for a moment. Either the fumes, his proximity, or the adrenaline firing through her system was messing with her sense of reality again. Nestling in his arms, she felt like she was remembering something that hadn't happened yet.

A normal person could write it off as déjà vu. For her, it held more significance and a hope she shouldn't let herself feel.

He was going to hold her in his arms again.

Chapter Two

Gasoline soaked through Darren's clothes. The fumes stung his nose and lungs as he ran from Miranda's car—what was left of it, anyway. He hadn't recognized it when he'd approached the scene of the accident. It looked like a soda can that had been repeatedly stepped on.

He couldn't believe she had survived. She didn't even seem to be hurt—just understandably shaken. His skin tingled as he kept watch for any sign of a spark. He needed to get out of his clothes as soon as possible. And to take about a dozen showers.

Miranda was gripping the front of his shirt, pressing her body against his. He'd imagined holding her so many times during their chats at the diner. His daydreams were never like this.

He slowed when he thought they were far enough away from her car to be safe if it exploded, then glanced back at it. He'd been so sure the driver would be dead. He'd braced himself for the worst before looking into the crumpled wreck.

And then he'd seen Miranda smiling at him, her brown eyes wide as saucers and her dark hair dangling from her ponytail toward the ceiling. She had even made that joke, though it was obvious that she was utterly terrified.

People died every day. He was very aware of that working in private security. But it had been a long time since that danger had hit so close to home.

"It looks a lot worse from out here," she said.

"Try not to think about it."

The wail of sirens grew louder. He turned so that she wouldn't be able to see what was left of her car.

"I didn't know you're a cop," she said.

"I'm not."

"I'm pretty sure there's a gun in that holster." She cast another pained smile at him. "Unless you're just happy to see me."

He couldn't believe she'd made another joke. But that was Miranda. Always trying to make other people feel better. He held her tighter against his chest.

"Hey, Darren. You okay, man?" Scott came running up to them, which meant he had left their car behind—and the package they were supposed to be guarding.

"I'm fine." Darren felt the muscles in his jaw tense. He tried to keep his tone calm. "You were supposed to stay with the car."

Scott shrugged. "You said the accident sounded pretty bad. I thought you might need some help."

"What I needed was for you to stay with the car, like we agreed," Darren said.

"Don't worry about it. The coins are safe."

Darren glanced around to make sure no one besides Miranda was in earshot. It was easier for Scott to not worry about massively screwing up the job. His mom ran Ford Security, and was unlikely to fire Scott since he was due to take over the company in a few years probably. Darren didn't have that safety net.

"Let's maybe not talk about that right now," Darren said.

Scott cast one of his patented charming smiles at Miranda. "I'm sure we can trust this lovely damsel in distress to keep our secret."

Darren bristled. Scott loved to flirt with every woman he met, and normally Darren couldn't care less. But Miranda... She was off-limits.

Before Darren could stalk off with her, she cast a cold glare at Scott.

"I'm not a damsel in distress," she said. "I *was* a damsel in a predicament."

Scott looked over Darren's shoulder at the crushed remains of her car. "Looks to me like you were a damsel in a pancake."

"Better than a pickle," she said.

The tightness in Darren's chest loosened as he let out a laugh. If she felt good enough to make jokes like this, she was going to be okay. He was sure of it.

She leaned against him, stray hairs from her ponytail tickling his chin.

"Do you two know each other?" Scott asked.

Before Darren could respond, a pair of EMTs approached them with a gurney. Darren set Miranda on it, then reluctantly backed away. The next few minutes were filled with questions. Darren answered as efficiently as he could, and listened intently to Miranda's take on what had happened.

From how she described what had happened to her, the person who'd been driving the SUV had caused the accident. Darren looked around, but didn't see anyone in cuffs, and the back of the police cruisers were empty. He made a mental note to check in with his dad's friends on the force and help track down the person responsible. Miranda had nearly been killed.

A wave of anger pounded through him, but he quickly suppressed it. He needed to stay clear-headed if he was going to be of any help.

The EMTs started to wheel her away, and Darren followed for a few paces.

"Do you need me to go with you?" he asked.

Her eyes filled with tears, but she smiled. "No, I'm fine. I'll be back at The Red Thread before you know it."

"Don't rush it," he said. "I understand the urge to get back to work and throw yourself into the job so you don't have to think about what happened, but you need to take care of yourself. Listen to your doctors."

"Yes sir." She mock saluted him and laughed. She was still smiling at him as they wheeled her away.

A heavy dread settled into his stomach as he watched them close the ambulance doors. He hadn't realized just how much he'd grown to care about her until that moment. And the last time he'd watched ambulance doors shut like that—

Scott clapped Darren on the back, startling him out of his worst memory.

"Now I understand why you've been so dodgy about having dinner with me lately," Scott said. "If I was working a sweet little number like that, I'd keep the competition away, too."

Darren glared at Scott, then turned and started toward their car. He should be focusing on their assignment, but kept thinking about Miranda.

The first time Darren went to the odd diner where she worked, it was because he was hungry and it was the only place that was open at one o'clock in the morning. Then he had chatted with her and decided to go back the next night. And the next.

He hadn't wanted it to seem like he was only going to hit on her, so he'd kept going every night—even when she was off—acting like any good regular. But now he knew the truth about his visits. It was clearer than ever.

As soon as she was back at work, Darren was going to ask her out. For real—not just in his head. That decided, it was easier to get his mind back on the job.

"You shouldn't have left the package unguarded," Darren said.

The silver sedan the company had tricked out for transport jobs came into view. The doors were closed, windows up. When they reached the car, Darren tested the handle. Locked.

He let out a little breath, allowing himself to feel a small bit of relief. It vanished when he noticed that the passenger's side floor mat was out of place.

"Did you check on the package while I was gone?" Darren was already punching in the code to unlock the door. He pressed his thumb against the sensor that would read his print and heard the click of the latch.

"Relax," Scott said. "The doors were locked when we got here."

Darren lifted the rug, then used his key to open the trap door in the floorboard. He pulled out the metal case that held the package—a set of rare silver coins from Ancient Greece. The museum had loaned them to a professor of Antiquities at the local University, and Ford Security was handling their transportation.

"Keep an eye out," Darren said.

"I'm telling you, everything's fine." Scott wasn't even trying to check out the area. He was just staring at Darren with a weirdly blank expression.

Darren turned back to the case, his dread growing. He entered the combination, then used another key to open it. He lifted the foam that kept the coins in place and his stomach dropped.

"What the hell?" Scott pushed against Darren's side, trying to get a better view of the case—the *empty* case.

"Calm down." Darren forced himself to follow his own advice, even though his mouth was bone dry and his heart was pounding. "Take me through it. What happened after I left?"

Scott ran his fingers through his spiky brown hair. "Nothing. I sat there for a minute, thought you might need some help, made sure the compartment was secure, locked up the car, and left."

"No one approached you? No one was lingering in the area?"

"No. Dammit, Darren. I've had the same training as you. I know I don't always act like it, but I know what I'm doing."

Theory isn't the same as practice.

Darren kept the thought to himself. The other guys they worked with were mostly ex-military and used that phrase to taunt Darren all the time. He wouldn't use it against Scott.

"Maybe somebody cut through the bottom of the car." Scott bent over the footwell of the passenger's seat, feeling around in the secret compartment. He sat down heavily when he saw that the floorboard was intact.

"Those coins didn't walk off by themselves. Somebody took them." Darren scanned the nearby buildings.

The case had been secured to either Scott's wrist or the lock bar in the secret compartment ever since the coins were in their possession. And Scott hadn't been out of Darren's sight in that time—until the accident. An accident that suddenly seemed very suspiciously timed.

Darren spotted an electronics store across the street. It was a long shot, but if the owner was trying to get a view of their front door, the angle might be wide enough to capture their car through the front window. The image would be too grainy for a solid ID, but it would give them a clue about what had happened.

Darren tapped his partner on the shoulder. Scott seemed disoriented. Almost dazed.

"Are you okay?" Darren said.

Scott blinked a few times, then shook his head. "Of course not. My mom is going to kill me. I've finally proven I'm the fuck-up she always thought I was."

"Let's focus on trying to fix this." Darren nodded toward the electronics store. "They might have surveillance footage that can help." Scott slammed the door shut, then locked it. He stalked across the street next to Darren.

An electronic buzzer sounded as they entered the store. The guy behind the counter looked half-asleep. He didn't even move until Scott threw a hundred-dollar bill on the counter.

"Can I...help you?" The guy stood straighter, eyeing the cash.

"Show us the recordings from your security cameras for the last thirty minutes," Darren said.

The guy nodded, then snatched up the money and crammed it into his pocket. He turned around and started typing on the computer behind the counter. A monitor was mounted on the ceiling with three views displayed. As Darren had hoped, the street outside was visible. The camera views froze for a moment, then skipped before winding back.

"That's far enough," Darren said.

Scott's gaze was stuck to the monitor. They watched as Darren emerged from the car, then ran off toward the accident. Moments later, a man appeared next to the car, appearing out of thin air.

"The footage is glitchy," Scott said.

The cashier shrugged. "It's all we've got."

Darren focused on the image, memorizing everything he could. The man was about five seven, with a slender build and blond hair. He was wearing an overcoat that obscured the rest of his clothes. He leaned down to talk to Scott through the window. The details were too blurry to see exactly what was happening in the car, but after about a minute, Scott got out and closed the door.

The guy was holding out a small black pouch. Scott dropped something into it. Several somethings that caught and reflected the sunlight back at the camera.

"No way. No fucking way!" Scott turned to Darren. "I didn't do that. I swear, I didn't. That can't be me."

Darren ignored him—and the nauseated feeling rising up through his guts. He didn't want to believe it either, but the guy in the footage who had stepped out of their car was wearing the same dark blue jacket and pale gray shirt that Scott was wearing. He had the same haircut, height, and build.

Scott looked back at the monitor in time to see the blond man tuck the black pouch into his jacket pocket and put his hand on Scott's shoulder. He said something, then the footage glitched again. One second the guy was there and the next he was gone.

In the footage, Scott stood completely still for long enough that Darren wondered if the camera had hung. But then Scott started moving again suddenly. He put the case back in the car, closed the door, and walked off toward the accident site.

"I don't understand." The fight had gone out of Scott's tone.

Neither did Darren. He shook his head. "Let me think for a minute."

The blond guy had been waiting for them. He had shown up too quickly to not be expecting them. That meant he knew their route. All information about the assignment was confidential. Only a few people in their company should have known the details.

Which meant this was an inside job.

Darren couldn't believe Scott was involved. Maybe the man who had taken the coins could perform some sort of hypnosis. Darren had never heard of any techniques that gave so much control that quickly, though.

"What the hell was that?" Scott said. He looked like he was in shock.

"We're going to figure it out." Darren walked around the counter.

The cashier finally perked up. "Hey, you're not allowed back here."

"It's a little late for that," Darren said.

He pulled a portable flash drive from his pocket and plugged it into the computer that ran the security cameras. The software was fairly standard. It only took him a few moments to find and copy the files he needed. He deleted the originals with a program he kept handy on the drive. No one would be recovering that data.

He walked back to Scott, pocketing the drive again, and said, "A little something for his trouble."

It took Scott a minute to catch on, but then he pulled out his wallet and handed the cashier another couple of hundreds. Business at Ford

Security was good, and the more than generous bankrolling from Scott's mom helped with situations like this.

Darren put his hand on Scott's shoulder and steered him toward the exit.

"We were never here." Darren gave the cashier his most menacing stare as they stepped outside.

Chapter Three

Miranda stood behind the counter, wrapping silverware in paper napkins for the next day's shifts and trying to steady her shaking hands.

Adrenaline is a harsh mistress...

She took a deep breath to try to calm her nerves. The bright scent of pine soothed her.

Glancing at the walls, she noticed that Jack had changed out the greens recently. He'd woven them into intricate patterns that she recognized from the fairy tales her dad would tell her when she was a child.

She didn't have to worry about trolls, goblins, or ghosts hanging out in the diner with those things hanging on the walls. Birds and squirrels could be a problem, though. She snorted at the thought.

Jack went all-out with the old world theme in the place. Each door had a set of antique bells hanging above it made from bamboo, silver, gold, bronze, and other things she wasn't quite sure about. He'd matched their timbre so that they could tell which door had been opened. The front door bells had high, tinkly sounds. The back door's set were deeper, and the side door that led from the kitchen was kind of in between.

One of the bells above the front door rang. The dinner rush was well past over and the sky had turned dark. Since it was too early for Darren—if he was even coming in tonight—it was probably Eden. Miranda smiled as she turned to greet her best friend.

"Hi." Eden waved across the empty space, then sat at her favorite booth. She was dressed in her usual landscaping clothes—jeans, a T-shirt, and boots. Her curly hair was held back in a messy ponytail, looking jet black against her almost colorless skin.

Miranda grabbed a glass of water before heading over.

Halfway there, Eden stood up. "What's wrong?"

"What do you mean?" Miranda said.

"You're walking funny."

She shrugged. Eden had troubles of her own. Miranda didn't want to add to them by telling her about the accident, even though Eden was the only person Miranda could speak with openly. At least for a little while.

Miranda fought back sudden tears. There was nothing she could do about Eden's future, but she could at least try to make her present more pleasant.

When Miranda reached the table, she laughed. "Maybe I had a date last night."

Eden took the water and set it down, then gently gripped Miranda's elbow, guiding her to slide into the booth across from her at the two-seater table.

"Stop trying to protect me," Eden said.

Miranda wiped at her eyes. "I thought I was the psychic."

"I don't need to be psychic. Anyone paying attention can see you're hurting."

"I'm fine."

Eden cocked her head to the side. She scrutinized Miranda more closely, blue eyes sharp as a hawk's.

"Forget about me," Miranda said. "How are you?"

"I'm fine."

Eden crossed her arms and leaned back against the booth. She lifted both eyebrows as if to say, "Two can play at this game."

Miranda shook her head. "Working all night on this garden doesn't seem healthy. Are your doctors okay with you exerting yourself so much?"

"I can spend my last few months how I want to."

"Months?" Miranda's voice came out high and tight. She coughed to clear her throat.

Eden didn't have months left. She had weeks—days, maybe.

It didn't make sense. She seemed to be doing relatively well at the moment. How could her illness escalate so quickly?

Eden shook her head and smiled. "This is my last project. I'm giving it my all, and it's turning out so beautiful."

"I have no doubt of that," Miranda said.

Eden was pouring her soul into it. How could it not be?

"The moonflowers started opening last night." Her eyes brightened as she went on, the unhealthy pallor of her skin receding a bit. "The full moon is in a few days. The river stones and Artemisia stelleriana are already catching the moonbeams and glowing with this soft silver light."

"Arte-what-now?"

"You probably know it better as Dusty Miller."

"I don't travel in those circles. The only plants I see are in the salad I bring you every night."

Eden laughed. "I'm so lucky Shade is letting me take my time with it."

"Shade?"

Her cheeks outright flushed and she looked away. "Mr. Reese."

"I see." Miranda grinned.

"I can ask him if you can visit some time," Eden said. "I'd love for you to see it."

"That would be nice. I'd never even heard of a moon garden till you started talking about this project."

"It's the first one I've worked on." Eden's smile grew huge.

Miranda had never met Shade, but she already loved the guy for making Eden so happy.

"I selected every plant based on its luminosity." Eden became even more animated as she continued her description of the garden. "The leaves, flowers—even the rocks we used to make the paths—they'll all catch and reflect the moonlight, glowing brighter as the moon grows full."

"It sounds beautiful."

"I have pictures!" Eden popped up in her seat. She pulled out her phone and messed with it for a moment, then turned it toward Miranda so she could see.

The pictures were kind of hard to make out. It looked like the only lighting came from work lights driven into the ground around the site. She could still get a feel for what Eden had described, with the leaves and flower petals reflecting the light a surprising amount.

"Wait a minute," Miranda said. "Back up."

Eden scrolled back a picture and her face turned pink.

It was a selfie with Eden standing next to a hottie who seemed like he couldn't get close enough to her. He had his arm around her shoulders and his head pressed tight to hers.

What really captured Miranda's attention were the smiles on both of their faces, though. She'd never seen Eden smile like that.

Both of them had little crinkles at the corners of their eyes. The guy had deep dimples that made it seem like he laughed a lot. Miranda couldn't make out the color of his eyes both from the weird flash lighting and how pinched they were from laughter. She could tell that he had straight teeth and a strong jaw and short brownish hair.

"Is that Shade?" Miranda asked.

"Yeah."

There had been another picture of him in there, Miranda was sure. She reached across the table to scroll back to it. Shade was standing with one hand against his chin, like he was deep in thought. He stared into the distance, enhancing the seriousness of the pose. Except he was wearing a plastic pot on his head.

"Wow, he's hot," Miranda said. "Even with the weird lighting."

Eden's blush was adorable. The pair were undeniably in love. Miranda's heart felt like it cracked a little, thinking of how little time they would have together.

"Shade has porphyria," Eden said.

Miranda tried to mask her grief with a funny movie reference. "You keep using these words…"

Eden laughed, then said, "It's a rare disease that makes him sensitive to light. That's another reason I've been working on the garden at night—so he can join me. He has to avoid sunlight at all costs. It makes it a little hard to take pictures."

Sounds like a vampire.

Miranda kept the thought to herself. She was trying to *lighten* the mood, not bring up horror movie monsters.

"And that's why he commissioned you to make him a *moon* garden," she said. "So he can enjoy it at night."

"Exactly."

Miranda grinned. "But how do you explain the pot on his head?"

"He's a very free spirit."

That's one word for it.

They both laughed, and Miranda found herself liking Shade even more.

"He's been more involved in the process than most clients," Eden said. "He works with me in the garden every night. The company has been...nice."

Eden's smile dimmed and a tiny furrow appeared between her eyebrows. Miranda had seen that grim look before. She figured it meant Eden was thinking about her illness.

Usually, Miranda would try to distract Eden with a funny story when it showed up. Based on the picture of Shade in the plastic pot hat, it looked like he'd been doing something similar.

Miranda's voice was low as she asked, "Does he know?"

Eden's smile vanished completely and she looked away. "He doesn't need to know. In a week, I'll be gone from his life."

Miranda bit her lip to hold back tears that yet again threatened to spill over. How soon would Eden be gone from Miranda's life as well? She'd known Eden would live to see the garden finished—and not much past it. From how the garden looked in the pictures, the work was almost done.

Miranda had a sick feeling in her stomach. Coupled with the stress from the accident, she could barely keep a lid on her emotions.

When Eden reached out and gently touched Miranda's hand, her future trickled into Miranda. Everything was gray. Eden's future was shrouded in a thick fog that Miranda couldn't see through.

The nausea increased. Her heart felt like her chest was collapsing in on it, the weight of her emotions crushing her. She had never known someone who was nearing death. She hated that it was Eden—one of the most beautiful people Miranda had ever met. Even more, she hated not being able to do anything about it.

Days. She only has days.

"It's okay," Eden said. "It really is okay."

Miranda pulled her hand away. She couldn't look at that fog any longer—couldn't think about losing Eden so soon.

"I'll call your order." Miranda started to stand, hoping to have a moment to get ahold of herself, but her joints locked up, muscles still stiff from the accident. She tried not to wince as she sat back down.

"You are not fine," Eden said. "I can tell you're in pain."

Thinking about her own troubles after Eden's made them seem small in comparison. Miranda just needed to work extra shifts to buy a new car and pay for her ambulance trip. She'd have the time to do so. But she knew her friend wouldn't stop until Miranda had explained what was wrong.

"Okay, I'm not fine," she said. "I had a prophetic dream this morning. There was going to be a bad accident, and people..." She shook her head, willing the memory of the family's original fate from her mind. "The only person who stood a chance of surviving was me, so I took their place."

Eden inhaled sharply. "Are you okay?"

"I'm just a little banged up. I wish I could say the same for my car. It was totaled."

Without a hint of hesitation, Eden said, "You can have my truck."

"What?" The word came out as a gasp.

"The garden is pretty much done," Eden said. "I'll be walking Shade through it tomorrow night." Her voice grew quieter. "I've wrapped up all my other business. If you're okay driving me around every once in a while for the next month or so... I won't need my truck after that."

Miranda's heart seemed to seize in her chest again.

"No." She shook her head. "No way."

"Why not? Please, Miranda. Let me do this for you."

It seemed like too much. It would be a constant reminder of Eden. Of her absence.

Or of what it's meant to have her in my life.

Miranda nodded, blinking away tears. Her throat was too thick to let words escape. She'd been driving her mother's car for years—until today. Now she'd be driving Eden's...

A shadow blocked out the lights above her. She looked over her shoulder. Jack was standing right next to her, leaning on the back of the booth and staring at her with his shielded obsidian eyes.

He was huge—tall and broad enough that his presence was like a cloud passing between the earth and the sun. His beard was decidedly salt-and-pepper, but the close-cut hair that hugged his scalp was still black. Lines were etched into his rich brown skin—some from age, and some scars that she had never worked up the courage to ask about, even though she'd known him for as long as she could remember.

He arched an eyebrow at her. "Did I hear you say you were in a car accident?"

"What? That's…" Miranda let her voice trail off and laughed.

Jack had been close friends with her parents and was sort of looking after her, even though she was absolutely old enough to look after herself. He kept a strong emotional distance, but still wouldn't be happy she hadn't told him about the accident.

He worked every night shift with her. Since neither of them had any other family, they even spent holidays together at the restaurant, giving the other wait-staff as much time off as possible. He always said The Red Thread needed to stay open so that everyone would have a place to go.

"Miranda." His voice was a low rumble, like thunder.

She sighed. "How could you possibly have heard me from the kitchen?"

"I keep up with what's happening in my place," he said. "And you haven't answered my question."

There was no point in trying to lie to him, even if she would have been comfortable with it—which she wasn't. She just hoped that was all he'd heard.

"Yes, I was in an accident," Miranda said. "But I'm fine. The hospital released me and everything."

He leaned closer and tapped the side of his nose as he sniffed. "Bullshit."

Eden snickered, picking up her napkin and covering her mouth as if that could mask the sound. Jack stood back up and shifted his hand so that it was on Miranda's shoulder.

He had never touched Miranda before. Not once. Her stomach

flipped like it was on a roller coaster as she felt his warmth and strength. Her eyes filled with tears again.

Darren rescuing her, Eden giving Miranda her truck, and now Jack's supportive gesture... Miranda had forgotten what it was like to not feel isolated.

I shouldn't let myself get used to it.

Jack's deep voice was yet another comfort. "I see you most nights when Miranda calls in your order, but we haven't been introduced."

"I'm Eden." Eden held out her hand and he shook it.

"Call me Jack. You want your usual?"

"Yes, please," she said.

"I'll have it right out."

Miranda shook her head. "I'll take care of it. I'm supposed to make the salads." She tried to stand, but his grip on her shoulder didn't budge.

"You forget, I'm the boss," he said. "Right now, your job is to sit here and keep your friend company."

"I can—"

"Miranda."

He rarely used her name. There was a weird thrum of power to it, like her dad had described when fairies used people's names to cast spells on them. A shiver passed through her at the thought.

"I work the night shifts because that's when the really weird stuff usually goes down." Jack's gaze was mesmerizing, along with the low, smooth cadence of his speech. "I want to be here in case I'm needed. So I can help."

She remembered the few times people had wandered in looking for trouble. All he had to do was walk out of the kitchen. Sometimes he'd be wiping his hands on a towel when he sensed trouble in the dining room, sometimes sharpening a knife.

Once he'd come out holding a heavy iron skillet filled with eggs and vegetables—the restaurant's specialty. Somehow, that had actually been the most menacing she'd ever seen him. The people looking to make trouble had always turned around and left. Immediately.

"People like feeling needed," Jack said. "They like to help others.

Let me take a turn. Okay?"

She nodded, too overwhelmed to speak. Jack sauntered off, leaving her alone with Eden. Miranda had been so caught up in her own mission to help people, she hadn't even noticed Jack and his.

The Red Thread was one of the only all-night restaurants in town. People often showed up who were struggling and needed help. Miranda would bring them coffee, read their futures when her intuition told her to, and sit and help them work through things. Sure, she wasn't using her powers to save the world, but—

Her stomach suddenly felt like the floor dropped out from under her. That...was a bad sign. She had a feeling that crashing her car was about to look like a walk in the park.

"It really is okay to let others help you," Eden said. "You don't have to do this alone."

Another shiver passed through Miranda. This one wasn't a chill, though. It felt more like a heavy weight falling away—like making room.

For what, she didn't know.

"Something big is coming." The words came out before Miranda realized she was speaking. She lowered her voice so Jack wouldn't hear.

"Another vision?" Eden asked.

"Not exactly. It's more a feeling." Miranda shook her head. "It could be leftover nerves from the accident."

"You would know if it was." Eden reached across the table and took both of Miranda's hands in hers. "Take a few deep breaths and relax. Close your eyes and let it come to you."

Eden was a natural at coaching Miranda through visions. And with so little future left, Eden's own fate didn't tend to distract Miranda from whatever vision was trying to come through.

She pushed away the morbid thought and relaxed her mind. Eden's future flitted on the outskirts of her awareness—the gray fog that was starting to feel familiar.

Whatever vision was trying to come through, it probably wasn't attached to any one person's future. It was too big for that. Maybe the biggest vision she'd ever had.

The fog wasn't retreating like it usually did when Eden helped Miranda like this. Why couldn't she see anything?

And then she felt it. Felt the fog touch her skin.

It caressed her, enveloped her—not cold, but warm.

She'd never had any physical sensations in a vision before. It wasn't unpleasant…at first.

Then the fog started to burn. Pain seared its way into her awareness, flooding her body, consuming her.

Is this what death feels like?

The pain suddenly vanished. Miranda still couldn't see anything past the gray, but she felt a sense of peace and belonging—like she was with family again.

Her eyes flew open and she jerked her hands back.

"What? What is it?" Eden's eyes were wide.

"I'm going to die," Miranda said.

"What? How?"

"I'm not sure." She'd never had such an obscure vision—aside from the ones about Eden. Before Miranda could think better of it, she said, "Your illness isn't contagious, is it?"

Eden's face hardened. Miranda had never seen that happen before. She regretted her question immediately.

"I'm sorry," Miranda said. "I didn't mean to—"

"It isn't something you can catch." Eden shook her head and let out a laugh. There was a trace of bitterness to it. "I've always trusted your visions. I believed you when you told me about what you saw and your abilities. But if you think I'm some sort of Typhoid Mary—"

"That's not it at all. But whatever's happening to you, it's going to happen to me, too."

"That's not possible."

"My visions are never wrong. I mean, sometimes I can change things, but I never figured out how with you. But now I see the fog coming for me as well."

Eden shook her head. She grabbed her purse as she stood. Miranda tried to jump up to follow her, but her hips sent stabbing pain through her as she tried to force them into quick action. By the time she rose, Eden was halfway to the door.

"Eden, wait! I know why you're not afraid now. The fog wasn't scary. The other side of it felt more like... I don't know, like home." Miranda was desperate, grasping at straws. "It's the same fog. I'm sure of it. If your illness isn't contagious, maybe the gray doesn't mean death after all. Maybe it means a cure. Maybe I can cure you somehow."

Eden paused, her hand gripping the handle of the door. She took a deep breath and let it out slowly. "I work really hard to be okay with what's going to happen to me. Every minute of every day. It's a struggle."

Eden looked over at Miranda with an expression so bleak that it sent a chill through her. She'd never seen such hopelessness before.

"There is no cure," Eden said. "There is no stopping this. And the only thing worse than that feeling of despair is false hope. I've been there before. I won't do it again."

"But my visions—"

Eden shook her head. "You *aren't* always right. I am absolutely terrified."

"Eden..."

"I can't deal with this right now. I'm sorry." One of the bells tinkled as she threw the door open and half-ran into the night.

Miranda wanted to run after her, but knew she couldn't catch up. Even if she did, what could she say after that? She slumped back into the booth.

How could she have been so wrong? The pain in Eden's face as she left would stay with Miranda until the day she died. Which, depending on what her vision really meant, might not be very long.

The gray that shrouded Eden was coming for Miranda, too. If it didn't mean a cure for Eden...it meant death for Miranda as well.

She thought of the feeling of warmth and belonging that waited for her on the other side and tried not to be afraid.

She really tried.

Chapter Four

Darren felt like he was walking into an execution as he walked with her partner down the hallway that led to the CEO's office. Scott barged through the door without knocking, too quickly for Darren to stop him. Mrs. Ford was sitting behind a sleek desk made of glass, chrome, and polished black plastic.

Something about her had changed.

She and Scott had the same gray-blue eyes and pale brown hair. Hers hung around her face in its usual carefully styled waves. It only took Darren a moment to realize what was different.

The streaks of gray that had been abundant in her hair were nearly gone and her skin had smoothed considerably. She looked ten years younger. He had seen her *yesterday*.

He filed that observation away for later. The current shitstorm required his full attention.

As always, Blake Morrison was standing within her arm's reach. His shoulders were squared and his hands clasped in front of him. The stance was casual, but Darren knew Morrison was ready to act in a split-second to defend his boss.

He was a head taller than Darren, and thick with muscle. The designer suit hid what it could, but Darren had seen Morrison sparring in the company's training centers and knew not to underestimate the guy.

Morrison looked different, too. He hadn't shaved his head or face in long enough that a layer of dark stubble was visible. Normally, he was impeccable in his grooming. His amber skin was blanched and his eyes had a haunted quality when he briefly met Darren's gaze. He pulled himself up straighter and stared over Darren's shoulder.

What the hell is going on?

Darren noticed that one of the chairs opposite her desk wasn't empty just as Scott said, "Mom, I swear to you, we're going to find out who did this and make them pay."

She silenced him with a glare, keeping her stiff smile firmly in place as she stood and smoothed a hand over her skirt. "I wasn't expecting you quite so soon."

The stranger slid from the chair with a grace that didn't seem to match his large form. Darren logged details quickly.

Brown hair, shorter on the sides than the top, made to look disheveled intentionally. Dark blue eyes. Crows feet, laugh lines, and a smile friendly enough that Darren found himself wanting to like the guy.

Probably a con man.

Expensive suit. *Very* expensive suit. Silk scarf and long jacket— loose enough to conceal weapons. Not bulky enough to conceal the size of the guy. If he'd been wearing jeans and a T-shirt, he would have fit right in at a construction site.

Maybe something else?

"I don't believe you've met Mr. Reece," Mrs. Ford said.

"No." Scott's tone was petulant, and her smile became even more strained.

Mr. Reece extended a hand to Scott, who ignored it. Darren stepped forward, accepting the greeting on Scott's behalf.

"Ambrose Reece." The man's smile deepened.

"Ambrose?" Scott said.

Mr. Reece's smile grew, like he was thinking of some private joke. "It's a family name."

"I'm Darren Calverton," Darren said. "That's Scott."

"Yes, Scott Ford." Mr. Reece released Darren's hand as he turned to Mrs. Ford, and said, "I see the resemblance to your lovely mother."

She cleared her throat a bit awkwardly while Morrison cast a baleful look at Mr. Reece.

Office gossip said Mrs. Ford and her personal bodyguard were a couple, and Darren was pretty sure that was accurate. They never did or said anything affectionate, but there was an unmistakable chemistry between them. A colleague had made a joke in front of Morrison about him liking older women, and Morrison had dislocated the guy's arm in their next sparring practice.

"Ambrose Reece," Darren said. "That name is familiar."

"Mr. Reece is one of the foremost experts regarding antiquities."

Mrs. Ford walked around her desk to stand next to the group. Morrison followed at a not-so-discreet distance. He was definitely rattled by something more than Mr. Reece's flirting.

Mr. Reece let out a huge yawn, holding a fisted hand up to his mouth to partially cover it. The guy had huge canine teeth. Sharp, too.

Con man, construction worker, or vampire?

Darren would have laughed at his thought, if he wasn't so worried that he was about to be fired. The stress must be getting to him.

"I'm sorry to call you in at this late hour," Mrs. Ford said.

Mr. Reece smiled and shook his head, but yawned again. He waved his hand briefly toward the track lighting for some reason, then said, "Not a problem. I usually keep late hours. But I do need to be on my way. I'll be in touch if I hear anything from my contacts."

"I appreciate it," Mrs. Ford said.

He leaned in to Mrs. Ford and kissed both cheeks. Morrison bristled, but Mr. Reece only smiled at the other man. He nodded to Darren and Scott as he left the room.

A fence, maybe? Or someone with connections to illicit antiquities trades?

Mrs. Ford walked back around to her seat behind her desk, smoothing her skirt again as she sat. Morrison took up his position standing behind her.

"I only asked to see Darren," she said. "Scott can go."

"That's crap," Scott said. "We were partners on this job. Anything you have to say to him, you can say in front of me."

Mrs. Ford just stared at Scott calmly. If he was considering throwing himself on the grenade to save Darren, it didn't look like it was going to work, even if Darren would allow it—which he wouldn't.

She let them stew for long enough that Scott started shifting his weight from one foot to another uneasily.

"Are you finished?" she finally said.

Scott kept quiet. Probably for the best.

"I've reviewed your reports and will be speaking with each of you separately." She looked pointedly at Scott. "If you would please step outside."

"It's okay, Scott," Darren said.

Scott cast one final glare over his shoulder at his mother, then stalked outside.

Mrs. Ford shook her head. She ignored Darren for another minute, signing a few documents before placing them in a neat stack on top of her desk. When she was done, she very deliberately clicked the cap in place on her pen, then leaned back in her chair.

"My husband started this company," she said. "He wanted to create a legacy for his family. I've worked hard to keep things running. To make the company even stronger than it was when he passed away."

Darren knew better than to say anything. He stared at a fixed point on the wall behind her shoulder, his gaze and stance mirroring Morrison's.

"My son is supposed to run this company someday. I had hoped someday soon. But to do that, he needs experience. Knowledge. Most of all, he needs to take our work seriously. I hired you to facilitate that, Mr. Calverton. And you have failed."

Darren sucked in a breath to launch a retort, but stopped himself. He let the breath out slowly instead, checking his temper.

"You hired me to provide security for specific high-level assignments," Darren said.

"*Scott* was your assignment."

Darren chose his words carefully, pushing against the rage that seethed inside of him. "Forgive me, but grooming Scott to take over the company wasn't in my job description."

"You have a business degree," she said. "Scott can gain field experience over time, but what he truly needs to develop to run this company is business acumen. Something I had hoped he would learn from you."

"You didn't hire me to tutor your son on business matters." Some of Darren's frustration was seeping through.

"Didn't I? Did it escape your notice that the majority of your peers have extensive military and combat experience? Tours and active duty?"

Darren tamped down tightly on the anger that surged up in him, keeping his voice low and calm. "All of us went through the same training when we came on board with the company. I passed all the same tests."

That didn't stop the other guys from constantly taunting him, but he'd thought that at least Mrs. Ford took him seriously. Apparently, he'd been wrong.

Yes, he had a business degree. But he studied the strategies, he worked out, trained. Every employee at Ford Security had been molded to fit how the company wanted their workers to perform, no matter what their backgrounds had been.

"You also have been given all of the lowest risk assignments," she said.

Darren's stomach turned sour. "Some of those assignments involved extreme danger. We placed ourselves in mortal jeopardy on multiple occasions."

"Things don't always turn out as we expect."

That was sure as hell right.

Darren had wanted to protect people for as long as he could remember. He would have been a cop—like his dad—if he hadn't watched the man struggle with two jobs to put Darren through school after his mom died.

Working private security was supposed to let him help people while also having the resources to take care of his family—if he ever came up with the time to start one. Based on what Mrs. Ford was saying, his career was probably over.

"I can't see the future, Mr. Calverton," she said. "I assure you, if I had known those assignments would be that dangerous, I would have given them to a more experienced team. A team that didn't contain my son."

She stood up and walked around the desk, glaring up at Darren as if he wasn't almost a foot taller than she was. Morrison dropped his arms to his sides, his hands balled into fists as he no doubt watched Darren closely for any sign of a threat—like they'd *all* been trained to do.

"The black eye our company suffered today will set us back," she said. "If it comes out that my son was involved, people won't trust his leadership. They'll stop trusting the company. And I can't have that."

"You're throwing me under the bus," Darren said.

"Who was the first to leave the package?" She fixed that stony gaze on him.

"Lives were at stake."

"That wasn't your concern. You had an assignment."

"Saving a life will always be my concern."

"Fine. That's your choice. And you're free to make as many more like it as you wish."

She picked up the paperwork from her desk and handed it to him. His eyes skimmed over the words, registering things like "non-disclosure reminder" and "severance".

"You're firing me." It didn't feel real, even when Darren said the words out loud.

"Our severance package is quite generous, especially considering the circumstances of your departure."

"Firing me and buying me off at the same time."

"You can condemn my decision all you like—in your own head. But if you leak one word of this to anyone else, I will sue you for breaking your non-disclosure agreement."

He didn't doubt it.

"Those are your copies." She walked back to her seat, smoothing her skirt as she sat. "I expect you to clear out your locker immediately. I'd rather not draw too much attention to this, so Mr. Morrison will be personally overseeing your activities through the surveillance cameras rather than escorting you out of the building. I trust that you'll conduct yourself in a professional manner."

The papers he was holding crunched as his hands flexed into fists. His head felt like it might explode into flames at any moment. He took a deep breath, suppressing the rage yet again.

There was more going on here than she knew. Darren was sure someone in the company was involved with the theft. He doubted Mrs. Ford would listen to him at the moment, and with Morrison in the room, it wasn't safe to voice any suspicions.

Whoever had staged the accident had been willing to put innocent lives at risk. They had almost killed Miranda. For that reason alone, Darren would see them brought to justice.

And he would clear his name.

"Send in Scott, would you?" Mrs. Ford said.

Her stare was cold, but there was an uneasiness to it. Maybe she was wondering if he was going to argue or make a scene. He had other ideas.

He would focus on his own investigation—on figuring out who stole those coins and who in the company had helped. He would see that person in jail. If Mrs. Ford didn't offer Darren his job back after that, he'd still be able to go to another company.

He turned around and walked out of her office.

Scott fairly pounced on him the moment Darren stepped into the hallway.

"What happened?" Scott said.

Darren shook his head. "That's for her to tell you. She's waiting."

Scott glanced back and forth between Darren and his mom's office door, uncertainty playing across his features.

"It's okay." Darren forced a smile onto his face somehow as he rolled up the papers in his hands.

"We'll meet later?" Scott said. "To talk about this."

"Yeah. Better not keep her waiting."

Reluctantly, Scott slipped into the office.

Darren didn't waste any time. He walked briskly to the locker room. Thankfully, it was empty. He was already wearing his back-up outfit. He'd showered to get the gas off of him and bagged up his other clothes—minus his jacket.

Miranda still had it. She'd been clutching it in her hands as the paramedics lifted her into the ambulance.

He didn't regret helping her. Would never regret it. If that gasoline had lit up, she would have burned to death.

Everyone had been ignoring her car, probably thinking that the driver had been pancaked. He had seen it before at accident sites. Once people thought they understood a situation, they stopped looking for new information.

Her having his jacket was a good thing, though. It gave him an excuse to check on her at the hospital. He would swing by the diner on his way home and see if anyone knew where she'd been taken. He needed to see her again—to know that she was okay.

Thank God she had let them take her to receive care. If his mom had called for help sooner...

He shook his head forcefully. Now was not the time to go down Miserable Memory Lane. He grabbed his things from his locker and headed for the building's exit. If he was fast enough, he could avoid talking to Scott until they'd both had more time to calm down.

Terry—the guard who monitored the foyer—was standing by the front door, blocking it. He was enormous. Six-foot-five and as big around as a century-old sequoia. He was also one of the friendliest people Darren had ever met.

"New haircut, Terry?"

Terry ran his hand over his gleaming scalp, then along the short cropped beard covering his chin. His brown eyes glittered, only a slightly darker shade of umber than his skin.

"The wife likes it," he said. "And what the wife likes..."

Darren finished Terry's standard statement. "The wife gets."

"You gotta know how to keep your partner happy."

Darren expected Terry to go into his usual, "When are you going to settle down? I want to come to your bachelor party. Our kids can play together." Instead, his smile faded.

"I hate to do this, but boss's orders." Terry glanced up at the camera, then cleared his throat. "I need your badge and keycard."

Another layer of reality crashed down on Darren. This was really happening.

He felt like worms were crawling through his guts. His skin prickled and his face heated.

He pulled his ID and keycard from his belt and handed them over. At least they didn't ask for his piece. Ford Security's workforce used their own sidearms after registering them with the company.

Terry leaned down and whispered, "Sorry, man."

Darren nodded briefly, feeling the weight of the cameras on his back. He held his head high as he walked out the door.

Chapter Five

Every night Miranda worked, Jack would make her dinner. She usually had one of his skillet meals. Tonight she was eating Eden's salad. Miranda didn't want it to go to waste and doubted Eden would come back for it—if she came back at all.

Miranda sniffed again, stabbing the lettuce and moving it around on her plate. She didn't have much of an appetite.

Eden only had a couple of days left. There probably wasn't enough time to set things right between them.

How much time was left for Miranda? Her hands started to shake as she thought about it—the fog in her vision and what it meant.

Maybe we can make up on the other side.

Her eyes filled with tears again. She had just covered them with her hands when one of the bells above the front door sounded. She wiped her face dry and stood up, sniffing. She'd told Jack she could handle working her shift. She wouldn't let him down.

She plastered a smile on her face and headed for the menus at the podium near the door, trying to avoid eye contact. She didn't want any awkward, well-meaning questions about why she was upset.

"Welcome to The Red Thread," she said.

"Miranda?"

Her heart started to pound. "Darren? What are you doing here?" He normally didn't show up until at least an hour after Eden left.

"That's a better question for you. Why aren't you at the hospital?"

"They released me."

His lips pulled into a frown. "They should still be observing you."

"I'm fine."

He took a step forward and reached out as if he was going to touch her. She *wanted* him to touch her again—to hold her in his arms like he had after the accident. But she didn't trust herself not to hug him back or even try to kiss him, like she'd imagined doing so many times. And starting something with him now seemed cruel when she didn't have much time left.

She stepped toward the podium—away from him—and picked up a

menu, even though she knew he didn't need it.

"Do you want your usual?" she asked.

Her heart lurched as she took in the flash of disappointment that crossed his face. He lowered his hands and shook his head.

"Actually, I wanted to ask about my jacket."

"Your... Oh right."

She had clung to his jacket in the ambulance—held it against her stomach while the EMTs attached things to her chest and arms. The nurses had barely managed to pry it away when they admitted her, stuffing it in a bag with her clothes.

"It's at my place," she said. "I was going to have it cleaned for you."

"That's not necessary."

He kept staring at her with more intensity than she'd ever seen from him before.

"Is something else wrong?" he asked.

She tried to tell him that everything was fine, but choked on the words. Her eyes filled with tears again.

"Miranda..."

This time, she couldn't shy away when he stepped toward her. She was rooted in place. All of her energy was going toward trying not to cry as the fear came crashing down on her.

She was going to die. Alone.

Just like I've lived...

She sucked in a breath, her body shaking as the knowledge of her own end sank in deeper. How would it happen? Would it hurt as bad as it did in the vision? Worse? Was the warmth and companionship she sensed on the other side wishful thinking, or was that actually what waited for her?

Darren lifted his arms again, as if he was going to hug her.

Please let him hug me.

Instead, he rested his hands on her elbows and gently guided her to sit at the nearest table. He pulled a chair close and sat next to her.

"You shouldn't be here," he said. "At the very least, you should be home resting."

"I know. But I'm going to need the money." She wiped her eyes. "Hospital bills. Buying a new car."

Oh wait. I don't need a car after all.

Miranda could walk or ride the bus for a month. She did still have hospital bills to pay, and didn't want to leave an unpaid debt. She also didn't want to leave her friendship with Eden where it was. They had so little time left. Miranda's tears started up again, rolling down her cheeks.

"I'm sorry." Miranda wiped at her face and tried to get herself back under control.

Darren unrolled a silverware set from the table and handed her the napkin. She buried her face in it, taking a few deep breaths in the illusion of privacy it provided. She clutched it in her lap when she had recovered a bit.

"Don't be sorry," he said. "Anyone who'd been through what happened to you this morning would be shaken up."

"It's not just that. I can handle that." She let out a dry laugh and shook her head. "In the last twelve hours, I've totaled my car, lost my best friend, and found out—"

She barely remembered to stop herself before telling him the truth.

"Found out what?"

I have about a month or so left before I die a painful death.

When she didn't answer, Darren said, "You can talk to me—tell me anything."

His voice was so gentle. He'd never spoken to her quite like this before.

She had noticed the way Darren looked at her. Maybe they could have dated—explored each other to see what might come of it. Now they would never have a chance.

"I found out some bad news." She pulled a smile up through the depths of her sorrow. "It's just a bad day. Tomorrow will be better."

He picked up both her hands, resting them on the crumpled napkin in her lap. His skin was cooler than she'd expected.

She could give herself this—and only this—offer of comfort. She could hold his hands for a few moments, and pretend that she was normal.

But she *wasn't* normal. His future flowed into her.

Derelict buildings surrounded Darren as he drove through a rough section of the city at night. The Old River district? Something huge ran in front of him. She saw strobes of white in the darkness, felt the weight of his gun held beneath a small flashlight.

Then suddenly teeth. Fur. Blood. So much blood. She heard Darren's scream as a huge animal bit into his arm and knocked him to the ground.

And then the fog. That damned fog. Was it going to take everyone she cared about? Was that the companionship she felt on the other side?

Her mom would be there, and soon Eden. Apparently, Darren was joining them, too.

There was no way she was leaving him to this fate. He deserved a chance at a normal life. At any kind of life. Miranda sucked in a breath, ready to tell him not to go to that place, to avoid driving at night, to stay in his car if he hit an animal.

The vision shifted into something that felt more like a waking dream. That had never happened before. The fog dissipated, leaving her standing in a church. She walked between the pews, heading toward a casket.

Was this Eden's funeral? Her own? Miranda peered inside.

It was Jack.

Her heart felt ready to pound out of her chest. She could barely breathe.

How was Darren's future tied in with Jack's? That didn't make any sense. She blinked and shook her head, but the vision remained. She looked around at the church, then back to the casket.

Instead of Jack, Eden rested on the satin that lined the coffin. Her features were smooth in a way Miranda had never seen before. Her heart sank as she realized she had never seen Eden free from pain.

Miranda willed her eyes to shut. She didn't want to see any more. She felt Darren squeeze her hands in reality, and wondered how much time was passing as the vision took over her mind. She opened her eyes again, expecting to see him. And she did—inside the coffin.

His long lashes were dark against bloodless cheeks. There was no ease in his expression. He looked worn, his cheeks sunken, as if whatever would happen between the present and this future had hollowed him out.

Miranda pushed away from the vision, but she was trapped. She turned from the casket and ran toward the doors that led from the church, throwing them open and stumbling into the darkness outside. Her chest worked like a bellows. Cold air laced with ash burned its way into her lungs.

She looked up at the sky, stars blazing bright—too bright—overhead. She saw a constellation she felt she should recognize, but then the lights jumbled and fell through the sky. Each place they landed erupted into fire. The wind carried the screams of the dying to her ears.

"Miranda? Miranda, are you okay?"

She blinked, the restaurant suddenly appearing around her. Her limbs felt leaden. Darren was clutching her arms, holding her upright. He had broken the connection—dropped her hands. That's what had freed her from the vision. The vision of an apocalypse.

An apocalypse.

How could warning him affect the lives of so many? How could letting him suffer save others from so much pain?

"This is the curse that comes along with your gift," her mother had told her more than once. *"Sacrifices must be made. Sometimes the only choice you'll have is the lesser of two evils."*

The fear and uncertainty Miranda had been feeling stopped. All of her emotions shut down. She was cold inside—numbed beyond feeling. Once again, she was sending someone she cared about to their death. Only this time, she was doing it intentionally.

She couldn't warn Darren. Too much was at stake. And no matter which path she chose, he was going to die.

"I'm fine," she lied.

She expected fresh tears to spring to her eyes, but none came. She felt disconnected. Glancing around the restaurant, everything seemed surreal. The greens on the walls, the horseshoes and Celtic crosses. She felt like she might float up out of her body, leaving everything behind.

"I'm taking you back to the hospital," Darren said.

"Why?"

"Because you're obviously still in shock."

"I don't need a doctor," she said.

"Like hell you don't." He had risen from his chair at some point and was now squatting down in front of her.

"I can't afford more hospital visits."

"Then I'll pay for it. I'm not going to let you—"

He cut himself off so abruptly that it helped to bring her attention back into focus. He looked terrified. As frightened as she would feel later when all of this finally registered as real.

"My mom died of a heart attack." Darren's face had grown pale and his lips were bloodless. A muscle in his jaw was started to twitch. "She didn't listen when I told her she needed to go to the hospital. She downplayed it and said she didn't want to cost the family money. If she'd gone in sooner…"

Now Miranda knew what it was about the situation that was triggering him so badly. She brought a hand up to his face and trailed her fingertips along the stubble covering his cheek. Déjà vu once again assaulted her senses, making her feel even less tethered to her body.

"I swear to you, I'm okay," she said.

The glower didn't leave his expression.

She could kiss him. Just once. What did it matter now that she knew they would both be gone so soon?

As she started to lean forward, a strong hand clamped onto her shoulder, pushing her back to earth. She felt like she'd slammed herself down into her chair, but knew she hadn't moved. The room stopped swirling as the scent of eucalyptus stung her nose.

She looked up into Jack's dark gaze. He was smiling, but the lines around his eyes were deeper than ever.

"Everything okay out here?" he asked.

"Yes," she said.

Darren spoke at the same time. "No."

She glared at him. The last thing she needed was the pair of them ganging up on her.

"I think Miranda's in shock." Darren stood, but didn't move away. "She should go back to the hospital."

Jack's grip on her shoulder tightened and loosened a few times.

"Bring your awareness to the bottoms of your feet," Jack said.

He moved his grip to the back of her neck and she closed her eyes, focusing on his touch. There was nothing sensual about it. It was just comforting and...grounding. Especially when she did as he suggested and thought about her feet. He worked on her other shoulder for a few seconds, then rested his hand there.

"Better?" he asked.

"Yeah," she said. "How did you do that?"

He shrugged. "I've been around a while. Picked up a few things."

He set a paper bag on the table and turned his attention to Darren.

"What's that?" Darren asked.

"Your dinner," Jack said. "It's on the house today, though I am going to ask you for a favor."

Darren arched an eyebrow. "Which is?"

"Miranda needs to rest. I can finish out the night shift, but I'd like you to take her home."

"I can work," she said.

"I'll swing by your place at six-thirty tomorrow night," Jack said. "You can work the tail end of the dinner rush before your shift to make up the time you lose tonight."

The dinner rush... Tips would be good. Even an hour of that shift would more than make up for her leaving the night shift a few hours early. It would be crowded, though. She'd have to be extra-careful not to touch anyone...

But she'd be sticking Jack with working the front and back of the place and asking Darren for a favor at the same time.

"I can't—" she began.

"Miranda." Jack squeezed her shoulder again. "We just went over this. You're not the only one who likes to help people out. Right, Mr. Calverton?"

"Yeah, I—" Darren stiffened, then slowly stood. "How do you know my name?"

Jack shook his head and smiled. "Let's just say, I was in a similar line of work before I retired and opened up this place. You come in here every night carrying a piece. That caught my attention, so I did some digging."

Darren's hands flexed and his arms seemed to loosen at his sides. Far from appearing more relaxed, it made him look ready for anything.

He'd said he wasn't a cop, but Miranda had seen his gun herself. He didn't seem military, so that left...private security?

She remembered what his friend Scott had said about the package they were delivering. It made sense. She'd seen movies and TV shows that talked about that.

Jack used to do something similar?

"What do you say?" Jack asked. "Can you see Miranda safely home?"

"Yeah," Darren said.

"Great." Jack patted Miranda's shoulder before heading back to the kitchen. He turned toward them one last time and said, "Oh, and Mr. Calverton? I am holding you responsible for her safety. Your name isn't the only thing I know about you."

He winked before walking through the swinging door.

"Wow, that was kind of cool," she said.

"That's one word for it. I might have gone with 'extremely intimidating'."

"That, too."

She did need to go home, but not to rest. This new vision was bigger than any other she'd ever had. Something huge was on the horizon.

She couldn't think about it now—not in front of Darren. It was too terrifying, and she didn't want him to sense her fear. There was no way she could explain it to him.

"Then shall we?" Darren offered her his hand.

After what she'd seen, she was afraid to take it. She didn't want to see anything else. Her visions were escalating too quickly.

Instead, she rose on her own and hooked her elbow through his. They stared into each other's eyes for a few moments.

He was so beautiful. She wanted to take the time to commit every feature to memory. The little divot in his chin, the straightness of his nose. She wanted to run her fingers through his hair so that she knew what it felt like before...

Before the fog came for him. Before he had to deal with the consequences of *her* choice—the death she had selected.

She couldn't let the world burn. Not even for him.

Chapter Six

Twenty-four hours after he'd been fired, Darren was driving through one of the worst sections of town. He cruised around slowly, keeping his eyes peeled for anything out of the ordinary.

Every once in a while, he would let himself glance over at the empty passenger's seat, remembering Miranda sitting there the night before.

She'd never been in his car before. They'd never spent time together outside of the diner. Even with everything else going on in his life, knowing that he'd been able to help her—to take care of her—made his chest flood with warmth.

As soon as this was over and his name was cleared, he was asking her out for real.

His car pinged to let him know a call was incoming. He checked the caller ID before answering.

"Hey, Scott."

"You won't fucking believe this." Scott sounded livid.

"What did you find?" Darren asked.

"You were right. The accident was staged."

Darren wanted to slam his fist on the steering wheel. He took a deep breath and held it for a second instead.

As calmly as he could manage, he said, "Did the traffic cameras give you anything to go on for us to track down the driver who abandoned the vehicle?" The *stolen* vehicle, as they'd discovered.

Scott was quiet for a moment before speaking. "Morrison. The guy driving the car—it was Morrison."

Darren's stomach clenched. Possibilities started to take shape. Darren tried to straighten them out while keeping his mind open so he didn't fixate on any single theory before he had more information.

"How sure are you?" Darren asked.

"One-hundred percent. Morrison isn't easy to mistake for someone else, even though he was trying. I used camera footage on side streets and followed him for several blocks before he took off his hat and got into his car."

Even thinking the theft was an inside job, Darren hadn't expected this.

"Is this as bad as I think it is?" Scott said. "I mean, my mom trusts him. If he set us up, there's no telling what else he'd do."

"Give me a minute." Darren parsed through the scenarios in his head.

Maybe Morrison wanted the company. He might think if he discredited Scott, Mrs. Ford would eventually put Morrison in charge.

That was unlikely. She would run the company from the grave before she'd see it in someone else's hands. Everyone knew she thought of Ford Security as a family business. She would make sure it stayed that way.

Morrison could have been corrupted by an outside offer. Someone wanted those coins, and could have paid him to work with the hypnotist to get them.

That scenario was more likely, but Morrison had always struck Darren as loyal to Mrs. Ford. Smitten, even. He remembered Morrison mentioning that he liked strong women and shutting others down when they said anything about her "holding up well".

Which reminded Darren of the work she'd had done. That was strange, too. She was already gorgeous by pretty much any standards. Why would she change her appearance? Unless she was trying to look closer to Morrison's age.

A new theory wormed its way into Darren's mind. One that made his stomach twist even more.

What if Morrison and Mrs. Ford were in it together? What if she'd been approached by someone who wanted the coins and knew their best bet was to get them in transit?

No. No way.

Even if she was the type to be swayed by money—which Darren was pretty sure she wasn't—she wouldn't risk torpedoing her company for a short-term gain. She always looked to the future.

Still, the theory was sticking in his head. Especially with what Darren had discovered while Scott was doing his digging.

"I'm going to confront him," Scott said. "Let everyone know it was him and not you that's responsible for this mess. I saved copies of the footage I used. I'll show it to my mom and—"

"We don't know if Morrison's working alone yet. We need to do more investigating."

"Shit. Well, shouldn't I at least send these to my mom?"

"No." Darren wasn't ready to explain that Mrs. Ford was one of his prime suspects. "Make backups and hide them, like I showed you. Don't send anything even hinting about this through email. Don't call your mom, don't act weird around Morrison. Can you do that?"

"Yeah." He was quiet for a moment, then said, "Listen, I want you to know that I'm all-in with this case. I'm not going to let this slide."

"I know. And I appreciate it."

"What do I do after I make the backups?" Scott asked.

"Hang tight. I'm tracking down a lead of my own. I'll call you later and catch you up on what I find."

"Okay. Watch your back."

"You, too." Darren ended the call.

He couldn't tell Scott about the lead just yet. When they'd met up earlier, Darren had been able to use Scott's account to check on the tracking records for the company's cars. The one trip that struck him as odd was one of the "meet-and-greet" vehicles being driven through the Old River district two days ago.

The car was used for the lowest risk activities the company was involved in. It didn't have bullet-proof windows or reinforced doors. The thing was probably more fiberglass than metal. Given the state of the neighborhood, it seemed an odd choice.

Even stranger, no driver, passenger, or contract had been logged. From the GPS records, the car had pulled over to a curb and stopped briefly, then cruised around for an hour before stopping for a moment again, and heading back to company headquarters. Darren had memorized the route and was tracing it to see if he could figure out exactly where the person had been and what they had done.

His hands clenched on the steering wheel as he scanned the buildings for... He didn't even know what he was looking for.

He had already driven the entire route twice. All he had seen were abandoned buildings, empty lots, and a small park. There weren't even any vagrants around. Not so much as a stray cat.

Which…was weird. There should have been movement. Some signs of life, even in the middle of the night. A possum. A raccoon. A stray d —

Something huge ran in front of his car. Darren swore and turned the wheel, slamming on his brakes. Whatever it was, it was moving too fast to avoid.

His car lurched as they collided, metal crashing into flesh with a sickening wet thunk. His entire windshield was covered in fur for a moment as the thing rolled up his hood and over the roof of his car. Darren looked in the rearview mirror as it tumbled down to the street behind him.

"Shit!"

He pulled his car to the curb and jumped out, running back to see what he had hit. Instinct and habit made him draw his gun. He held it pointed at the ground as he approached where the animal should have been. All he found was a pool of blood. A *large* pool of blood. Paw prints led away from it toward the nearest abandoned building.

Darren's arms dropped to his sides. He couldn't keep himself from saying, "Seriously?"

What's next?

He walked back to his car and grabbed his keys from the ignition, then slammed the door shut and armed the alarm. He stood there for a moment, wondering if he was really doing this. Following an unknown animal that would probably bite him as soon as look at him, on the off chance that he could help it.

Yeah, he was doing this. He had hurt it, and he would help it if he could. He pulled out his flashlight and held it above his weapon, just in case.

The trail of red led up some steps and into what had once been a grocery store. The front windows were boarded up, but the door had been knocked off its hinges. Fresh red was smeared on the doorknob.

Also weird.

Darren had seen videos of animals who'd been trained to open doors. But they'd had homes with people. Opportunities to observe and practice. Which meant he had probably just hit someone's pet.

He imagined a little kid crying because their dog had run off. Wondering if it was okay.

Dammit.

He was going to find Fido and drag it to the nearest animal hospital. As soon as he figured out where that was. He just hoped he didn't have to shoot it to get it to go along with him.

Soft whimpering and intermittent grunts greeted his ears as Darren stepped inside. He glanced down and saw a line of red blotches on the dusty floor. Large paw prints staggered alongside the blood trail. Their shape was a little strange, but then the dog was hurt and probably having trouble walking.

"Hey, buddy," Darren called softly.

The whimpering turned to a low growl. Not surprising.

He assessed his surroundings quickly. There were too many ambush points for his liking. Wooden shelves still filled some of the relatively small place, blocking his line-of-sight. Some had been smashed, boards strewn about the floor. The blood trail led around the last few free-standing rows.

Of course.

Adrenaline flooded his system, sharpening his senses and making his skin feel electrified. He took a few deep breaths to even himself out.

No matter how much Mrs. Ford tried to deny it, he and Scott *had* been in dangerous situations before. They had learned to pay attention to even the tiniest details in their surroundings, to listen to their instincts and trust that they knew when danger was near. Darren had faced down guns, kidnappers, and even a maniac with a bomb strapped to his chest.

He had never felt this much danger. The air was thick with it.

Keeping his voice as calm as he could, he said, "I'm not here to hurt you. I'd like to help if I can."

The growling stopped. The space became utterly quiet except for the sound of Darren's breathing. He took another step closer, grit and dirt crunching beneath his feet.

Hell burst out from around the corner.

A six-foot tidal wave of fur and claws and teeth launched itself at him. Darren had been aiming at the floor, watching for something near the ground, but this thing... Its face was on the same level as his. It swatted Darren's gun away before he could get off a shot. Swatted the gun with its *hand*.

The creature was on him almost too fast to track. Darren's arms shot up to protect him from the attack, bearing the brunt of it. Pain lanced up his forearm as the thing bit him, hitting Darren with its full weight and taking him to the ground.

The hard tile floor smacked the back of his head hard enough to make lights flicker across his eyes. He forced himself not to panic—to block out the pain and look around for anything that might help.

The flickering light he was seeing turned out to be from his flashlight, spinning crazily on the floor after he dropped it. No help there. A board from the broken shelving was nearby, but not close enough. Darren still reached out with his free hand—the one not being chewed on by the furry monster—clawing at the floor as he tried to grab it.

His flashlight slowly stopped its spin, the beam at just the right angle for him to get a better look at what was latched onto his arm. His brain logged details that didn't make sense. Panic must be clouding his senses.

It was hairy, huge, and had a long muzzle—like a wolf. But from the quick glimpse Darren had caught before the thing took him down, it was bipedal. It glared at Darren with bright green irises surrounded by white sclera.

A dog with human eyes.

The thing gave Darren's arm another jerk, the pain escalating to levels that were close to shutting down his capacity for rational thought. If that happened, he was done.

But the excruciating movement had shifted him far enough that his searching fingers latched onto the loose board laying nearby. He lifted it and smashed it into the side of the creature's head as hard as he could.

Maybe it was the adrenaline or maybe the thing was more messed up from his car than he realized, but his blow knocked the creature off of him. Darren rolled away and came up in a crouch, breathing heavy and still holding the piece of shelf. Blood dripped from his mauled arm and his muscles burned like his veins were filled with fire.

The thing slowly stood on its back legs, one of its clawed hands held against its stomach, where a large spot of fur was matted with what looked like blood. It made a hacking noise and took a stumbling step toward Darren, then fell onto all fours.

In the dim light from his flashlight, Darren watched as its fur retreated into its skin, its ears and muzzle shortened, and its body shrank down to the proportions of a normal person. The light was left reflecting off the pale skin of a man stretched naked on the tile floor.

He pushed himself up on his elbows and glanced around the room, eyes wild. His hair and beard were dark red. He looked over at Darren with the same green eyes as the creature.

"What happened?" The man's voice was barely a rasp, but thick with a Scottish accent.

"I have no idea."

That wasn't true, though. Darren had *one* idea. One absolutely bat-shit insane idea.

This guy is a werewolf. I'm talking to a werewolf.

A werewolf who had bitten him.

Darren pushed aside thoughts of fairy tales and focused on the very real man in front of him who needed his help. The man's gaze slid to Darren's arm and a look of unbridled anguish twisted his features into an even greater expression of agony.

"Oh God," he moaned. "I bit you. I'm sorry. I didn't mean—"

The man's voice broke off as he arched his back, a scream tearing through him as he rolled to his side. Darren could see a dark spot on the man's stomach just like the one that had been on the wolf. Blood trickled steadily onto the floor.

"We need to get you to a hospital," Darren said.

He took a few staggering steps, the room spinning around him. He must be losing more blood than he thought himself. His arm burned—

his shoulders, his back. He fell to his knees next to the stranger.

"No time," the man gasped, each breath an effort. He still managed to grab Darren's sleeve. "The nights will help you. Find the nights."

The man's eyes went blank. He took one more shuddering breath, and as he let it out his skin, his eyes, his hair, his entire body turned a dark charcoal gray, as if he was turning to ash.

Darren jerked his arm away, and that small action caused what remained of the man to crumble in on itself, leaving behind nothing more than a pile of dust. Darren tried to scramble back, but his limbs gave out and he sprawled onto his chest.

What the hell just happened?

It might have been a hallucination except for the pain in his... everything. The burning had spread to his chest, his legs, even his head. His arm was numb where he had been bitten. But then the burning started to fade in the rest of his body. It was almost like a wave of heat and pain that traveled through him and then just left.

From how charged up he felt, it was probably a huge adrenaline spike. And, God, was he hungry.

He pushed himself onto his hands and knees and crawled to his flashlight. He managed to sit, then picked it up and held it between his teeth. Very carefully, he pulled up the fabric of his sleeve, angling his head to aim the light.

Blood coated his arm, but he didn't see any punctures or lacerations. Darren cautiously wiped a finger over his skin and found a jagged pattern of red welts where he'd been bitten. That was all. The feeling had returned to his limb, but the pain was gone.

What the hell?

He pulled the flashlight from his teeth and stood up slowly, still fighting waves of dizziness. The floor seemed to shift beneath him, the walls of the store tilting in at funhouse angles.

Acrid smells burned his nose, dust and decay nearly choking him. He could hear the wind whistling through the front door, see each splinter of broken wood in sharp relief. The world felt surreal.

Definitely adrenaline. Not turning into a werewolf.

Darren took a few deep breaths, trying to reason things through. It had to be the stress of everything. A trick or hallucination. Someone was messing with his head.

He remembered the blond man and how Scott had simply handed over the coins. Darren looked all around, half expecting the guy to step out of the shadows, waving a watch on a chain or doing whatever else hypnotists did.

Darren had to get out of there. But first, he needed to find his gun.

It hadn't slid far after being knocked from his hand. He picked it up and checked it, then slid it back into its holster. As he turned toward the door, the light of his flashlight glinted off of something in the pile of dust that his 'hallucination' had left behind. He walked over to it and pulled out a handkerchief before reaching down to pick up the object.

A small silver coin. The light from his flashlight reflected off of several stars laid out in the constellation Orion on one side. He knew without turning it over what was on the other side. A scorpion. It was one of the stolen silver coins he and Scott had been delivering.

"Shit."

It was still warm to the touch. Probably from being in the man's body. It couldn't have been anywhere else—the man had been naked when he died. Darren remembered the gut-wound.

Doesn't silver kill werewolves?

He shook his head, wrapping up the coin and stuffing it in his jacket pocket. He and Scott could dust it for fingerprints and see if there was anything stuck to it that might give them a lead.

If any of this was real, anyway. Darren was still wondering if he was having some sort of psychotic break. Maybe he'd been drugged. It could all be part of discrediting him, of laying the blame for everything at Darren's feet. What he had seen couldn't be real.

He headed back to his car, wondering where he could go that would be safe. Not his apartment. If Morrison and the blond man were going to these lengths to mess with Darren, they'd certainly be watching his house.

No, he needed neutral territory. Someplace no one would think to look for him, but where he might be able to get some backup if he needed it. He climbed into the driver's seat, his options playing through his head until one rose to the forefront of his mind.

Jack had said he'd been in a similar line of work. He had connections, if his veiled threat about knowing Darren's personal information was more than a bluff.

And Darren wanted to see Miranda again. He *needed* to see her.

He kicked the car into drive and headed for The Red Thread.

Chapter Seven

One of the bells above the back door rang out as Miranda stepped into the night air. The first few hours of her shift—working the dinner rush—had been busy enough to keep her mind off of her visions. Her usual shift...not so much.

She felt like she was about to crawl out of her skin. When would she die? How would it happen?

The only thing that helped was focusing on the less-personal vision —of the stars falling from the sky. It had to be a metaphor for something. She'd never had a vision like it, though. The damned fog was making everything hard to see. Maybe it was because she wouldn't be around to see it with her own eyes. Her own *physical* eyes, anyway.

She glanced around the mostly-empty parking lot and froze. Darren's dark blue muscle car was sitting in the corner spot farthest from the restaurant. The windows were fogged up so she couldn't see inside. There was a huge dent in the front bumper, and one of the headlights was broken. It had been fine the last time she'd seen it.

Her heart started to race. The attack must have already happened. How had he managed to drive afterwards?

She didn't know what she would find in his car. Part of her didn't want to find out. But he had headed straight to her car when he'd thought he was walking up to a nightmare. She would do the same for him. She hurried to his car.

If he had been able to drive himself to the restaurant, he couldn't have been hurt as badly as her vision led her to believe. She'd thought he was going to be killed.

She could barely make out a dark figure slouched in the driver's seat. Holding her breath, she rapped on the glass.

Darren stirred—at least, she hoped it was Darren. He jerked forward and glanced around, then fiddled with the key and rolled down his window. He stared up at her with those steel gray eyes.

"Are you okay?" he asked.

She laughed. "I find you passed out in your car in the parking lot, and you're asking me if *I'm* okay?"

"I wasn't passed out. I was just…thinking." He ran his hand over his face, then shook his head. "It was a long night."

"Tell me about it."

He laughed.

"No, really. What happened?"

He shook his head. "Long story."

"I don't have any customers and my break is just starting. Come in and have a cup of coffee."

He stared at her for a few moments, mouth opening and closing as if he was fighting to keep the words in.

Something had happened. She was sure of it. She wanted to help if she could. He didn't strike her as the sort who would ask, so she figured she'd give him a little nudge.

"I'm actually really bored and could use the company," she said. "Can you come to my rescue one more time?"

"Always."

He responded instantly, with an intensity that made her breath catch in her chest. Her heart seemed to stop. Her excitement was quickly drowned in sadness. Nothing could ever come of a relationship with him. She was going to die.

Then again, she'd been wrong about *him* dying in the attack she'd foreseen.

She had to know what was going on—and what would happen next.

Reaching her hand through his window, she rested it on his shoulder, pulling a vision of his future from him. All it usually took was a few seconds of a light touch. She could scoop up people's futures, like dipping her hands into water and staring at the reflection of the sky in what she held.

He sucked in a breath, staring at her hand on his shoulder. She gave him her best smile and cocked her head toward the restaurant, even though he wasn't looking at her.

"Come on—the place is dead and the coffee's on me," she said. "It's the least I can do after you taking me home last night."

Slowly, his gaze travelled up her arm until his eyes locked with hers. The look in those eyes… It was possessive. Predatory. Unlike anything she'd seen from him before. It made her toes curl and set her tingling in places that had been dormant for too long.

And it absolutely terrified her.

She stepped back, hand balled in a fist as she waited for an opportunity to read his future. If he would look away for a moment, she could take a peek. He didn't seem interested in dropping their eye contact, though. He managed to hold her gaze as he slid out of his car and closed the door.

She hadn't moved away as far as she'd thought, and he ended up standing right next to her, his body putting off an incredible amount of heat. He leaned a little closer and she thought he might be about to kiss her. Worse, she wasn't sure she could bring herself to stop him.

Instead, he took a deep breath through his nose, like he was... smelling her.

The Red Thread was a diner. A nice diner, but still a diner. She knew she smelled like grease and bleach. What she didn't understand was why his eyes drifted shut and he inched even closer, as if the scent was as sweet as fresh-baked cookies.

It was weird enough to break through the temptation of the moment. She turned away and started walking toward the front of the restaurant. Jack wouldn't like it if she brought someone in through the side door. Plus, the slightly greater distance would give her more time to read the glimpse of the future she'd plucked from Darren's shoulder.

She glanced down at her hand. Finally, she was using her powers as usual. Except all she saw was fog. That damned fog.

Whatever it was, whatever it meant, Darren was in the middle of it. Since she couldn't see anything, she was going to have to rely on conversation to try to figure out what was going on.

Flicking her fingers as discreetly as she could, she cleansed her hands of the energy from the reading, just in case she decided to try again.

"You said you've had a long night?" she asked.

"It was just...strange. I haven't slept in a while. I guess it caught up with me."

"Are you okay? I noticed the front of your car is banged up."

"I hit a dog."

The attack had already happened? And that *thing* had just been a dog? He didn't even seem to be injured at all.

"Oh no." She did her best to sound genuinely surprised. "Is it okay?"

"No."

She had a feeling conversation was going to be a dead end as well. Darren didn't seem in a talkative mood.

The dog had been huge in her visions. If it wasn't for its long, pointed muzzle, she might have thought it was a bear. At the very least, his arm should have been crushed. Bones broken, muscles torn. She turned so she could see his face again, searching for any signs of pain. He just looked...angry.

It was hard to make out details from the dim lights in the back lot, but his hair was dusty, especially in the back. And his clothes were a mess. She could see something dark staining his shirt. Blood?

The fog enshrouded his future. Like Eden's and Miranda's. She had thought that meant the attack would kill him. Yet here he was. It didn't make sense.

Even if her visions had suddenly become metaphors, the fog was the same for all three of them. With Eden's sickness, Miranda was sure that meant they were all going to die soon. Darren first—like immediately—then Eden, then Miranda not long after.

And then there was the vision with the falling stars. Miranda didn't need to see the casualties of whatever event that represented. She could feel the dead pressing on her in that future.

A crazy theory popped into her head. Zombie apocalypse. Not with actual zombies, of course, but maybe a sickness. A plague that would spread like wildfire throughout the planet. Something that dog had carried and passed on to Darren when he was bitten.

If he *had* been bitten. It didn't seem possible that the attack had already occurred. Unless one of the symptoms was...a lack of symptoms?

She needed more information. A little touch wouldn't do. Darren was at the center of the vision with the falling stars. Too much was at stake for her to hold back.

He started to open the door for her. She heard one of the bells let out a tinkling chime, a higher pitch than she was used to. She glanced up and saw the silver bell dancing on its string. That was another mystery for another time.

Instead of walking inside, she paused and angled her body toward his. She took his hand in hers, going so far as to interlace their fingers.

"You should take better care of yourself." She smiled at him when their gazes met again. She hoped that made the contact feel less out of place.

She didn't know how long Darren would indulge her before finding it weird that she was just holding his hand and staring at him, but holding hands was the best conduit for reading someone's future. If she held on long enough, maybe she could pierce the fog surrounding him and see what was on the other side.

It actually seemed to be working. The fog thinned, as if it was being burned away. Finally, an image formed.

Darren. Naked. Above her.

His head was thrown back, eyes clenched shut in an expression that was unmistakable.

She felt her heart quicken at the sight, her body responding. He was so gorgeous. For a brief moment, she wished she was the one conjuring up that expression of ecstasy on his face.

She couldn't see the person he was with. The vision was from their point of view for some reason.

The explanation came quickly, as she saw the woman's hand rise, caressing Darren's cheek, then trailing down his chest before he bent down to kiss her. Miranda knew the back of that hand like…the back of her hand. Because it was the back of *her* hand.

Her mouth went dry and the tingling that had started deep in her belly burst into full-blown fireworks. That could be her. That *would* be her.

But how could she start something with Darren when she thought they might be in the middle of a world-changing event? When she knew it was going to end in death for them both?

Unless she'd been wrong about the fog. Unless she was wrong about…everything.

The vision faded, but she found herself still staring into those steel gray eyes. His brows had lowered and the predatory expression was back. It didn't bother her a bit this time. She wanted him just as much, her body thrumming from the energy of the vision.

The look of rapture on his face… She wanted to be part of that, even if it seemed like a bad idea.

"Miranda…" He leaned in, absolutely planning to kiss her. She stood on her toes to meet him half way.

His lips touched hers gently at first, then harder as he gripped her arms and pulled her tight against his chest. The fireworks in her belly went lower, tingling energy spreading between her legs. It had been a long time since she had kissed someone at all. She had *never* kissed someone like this.

She put her arms around his waist, wanting to be closer. She parted her lips to run her tongue across the velvet surface of his mouth. He moaned, letting her in, then he plunged into her, his tongue thrusting against hers.

They needed to find a bed. The back seat of his car would do. She could find out what she needed to know before, during, and after sex. But right now, she needed this most of all. She needed him.

He let go of her arms, but only to grab a fistful of her hair, his other hand lowering to her ass and pressing her tighter to his body. Heat blazed from him.

He tilted her head to the side, his kisses trailing along her cheek to her neck. He nuzzled her ear, nipping her earlobe and pressing his hips against hers. The fireworks intensified as he ground his hard length against her.

At this rate, they'd end up having sex on the sidewalk in front of the restaurant. She wasn't sure she even cared. She was on the edge of the end of the world, after all.

"Step away from her."

Miranda jerked her head toward the strong voice that had broken through their moment. Whoever it was had better—

Her thoughts cut off as she saw Jack standing on the sidewalk, his placid expression severely out of place with the gun he was pointing at them. It was an old-fashioned revolver, like in a western. She thought of the modern version tucked under Darren's jacket.

"Jack, what are you doing?" she said.

Darren let out a deep rumbling growl, moving to stand in front of her. If Jack had snapped, he was more likely to kill Darren, though. Right?

She tried to move back in front of Darren, but he blocked her with his left arm. She glanced at it and saw that his jacket was shredded. His hand was coated in blood that had dried and darkened.

"Oh my God. Darren…"

He didn't seem to register that she had spoken. How was he upright? He must be in agony.

He let out another low growl, his weight shifting as if he was about to leap at Jack.

"Don't you dare." Jack pulled back the hammer on his gun. "If you have any humanity left, you'll step away from her. I'm a little rusty, and I don't want to hit Miranda if you jump away too fast."

"No one is getting shot." She wrapped her arms around Darren's chest, managing to slide around so she was at least standing next to him.

He was so hot. Even through his clothes, his skin felt like it was almost burning her. Weren't there some zombie stories about the person having a fever as they changed?

She shoved the thought away. She was being ridiculous. Zombies weren't real. Guns were very, very real. She needed to get Jack to back off so she could figure out what was going on with Darren.

"Miranda, you're not helping," Jack said.

"I'm not trying to help," she said. "Not you, anyway. What are you doing, Jack?"

He sighed, then reached into his pocket and pulled something out that was too small for her to see. He tossed it toward them. Darren plucked it out of the air with his right hand, then yelped and dropped it. It landed on the sidewalk with a *tink*, rolling in a circle until gravity made it stop.

A bullet.

"I have a full magazine in here just like that one," Jack said. "Silver. More than enough to put you down."

Darren still had his arm around her and his grip tightened. He was so strong, it was getting hard to breathe.

"Careful," Jack said. "She's only human. And judging from the look of things, you're pretty new to what you can do now."

Darren loosened his embrace and glanced down at her. His eyes glittered in the light cast from the streetlamps and the sconce above the door.

It wasn't moisture. Maybe the fever?

"It's going to be okay," she said, even though she knew it was a lie.

Neither of them was escaping their fate. She suddenly understood how they could start a relationship in the middle of this. He'd already been bitten and she had managed to infect herself doing her psychic detective work. They were both doomed, so why not seek comfort from each other while they could?

She latched onto the thought, reassured by feeling that she might finally understand what was going on.

"Jack, you have to stay away from us," she said. "I don't want you to get sick, too."

For the first time, Jack seemed to be thrown. His forehead crinkled up and he shook his head.

"What are you..." His features relaxed briefly, but then his jaw tensed and his eyes narrowed. "Pick up the bullet, Miranda."

"What?"

"Pick it up." His gaze hardened as he pointed the gun at *her*. "Now."

Darren started to lean forward. She pressed her hand against his chest and shook her head when he looked down at her. The glittering in his eyes was brighter. Almost like they were lit from within.

She was imagining things. It had to be from the stress—or from the illness already germinating within her.

"It's okay," she said. She looked back at Jack and repeated, "It's okay."

Slowly, she squatted down and picked up the bullet, then stood next to Darren. He draped his arm across her shoulders again and she wrapped hers around his waist. Well, the one not at all connected to the bullet.

She didn't understand what was so special about it, but when she brought her hand closer to her chest, Darren started to growl.

"Open your hand," Jack said. "Let me see you holding it."

"For Pete's sake." She held out her arm and opened her hand, the bullet rolling over her palm.

Jack nodded at her. "Okay. He hasn't changed you yet. But you still need to step away from him."

"What, so you can shoot him?" She tightened her grip on Darren's waist.

"Miranda, that's not Darren anymore," Jack said.

She looked up at Darren. His jaw was clenched, his lips tight, and his nostrils flaring. He looked super-pissed, which made sense, given the situation. But even staring down a gun, he'd tried to stand in front of her, to shield her from danger.

No. This was Darren. And as long as he was still himself, she would stand by him.

"He's not a zombie," she said.

She was mostly trying to reassure herself—to ground herself firmly in reality—but she spoke a little louder than she expected. Darren looked down at her, surprise softening the edges of his anger.

"You're not a zombie," she repeated, looking up at Darren.

Not yet, anyway.

Jack let out a snort. "I know. If he was a zombie, I'd have brought out my shotgun or a machete. Instead I brought silver—same as the bell he set off when he stepped close enough to the front door."

Miranda tore her gaze away from Darren's and looked over at Jack. Was he seriously talking about zombies as if they were real?

Jack lifted his free hand briefly, then let it drop to his side. "He's a werewolf."

Chapter Eight

This was nuts. Darren was looking down the barrel of a revolver that was wielded by a man who planned to put him down with silver bullets. Because he thought Darren was a werewolf.

The *really* crazy part was that Darren sort of believed him.

Darren's hand still itched where he had touched the bullet. He could hear Jack's heart—and Miranda's. Both thumping out quick beats, like drums before battle. The sound pounded in his ears and made his head ache.

He wanted to rip Jack's heart out of his chest to make it stop. He had a feeling he could, if it wasn't for the silver bullets in that gun—a gun Jack was pointing at Miranda. She had all but wrapped herself around Darren in an effort to protect him.

And Jack was threatening her.

Darren could smell the sweat and grease on Jack's skin. The gunpowder on his hands. Jack had fired a gun recently. Probably at a range to keep up his skills, no matter what he said about being "retired".

It didn't matter how sharp Jack kept his skills. If he tried to shoot Darren—or if Darren tried to get the gun away from him—there was a chance Miranda would get hurt. Darren couldn't risk that.

But for putting Miranda in danger, Jack was going to die.

The thought repeated in Darren's head, his vision going red. He could see the blood flowing in Jack's veins, the vital areas where the arteries were nearest the surface, and the bright red point in the center of his chest feeding it all. Darren would rip Jack apart, tear out his throat, and drape him over the Red Thread's sign as a warning to anyone who dared to endanger the people Darren cared about.

Except Jack was ready for Darren. Armed with silver.

How could he have known?

"Miranda." Jack's voice had become deadly calm. "Step. Away."

"No," Miranda said.

She smelled like fear. Sugar-sweet and cloying. Darren much

preferred her scent a few moments ago, when he was kissing her. Her scent had blossomed around her then, light and pure as honeysuckle.

Now, her body was trembling against his. God, it felt so good. But he didn't want her afraid. He wanted her to tremble from his touch, to be as hungry for it as he was for hers. He wanted...her. Even more than he wanted to kill Jack.

Darren closed his eyes and took deep breaths, drinking in her scent, focusing on it. If he really was a werewolf, Miranda was in danger. In danger from *him*.

Shit, am I really considering this?

Jack wasn't threatening Miranda. He was protecting her.

Darren thought about the thing in the grocery store. The giant bipedal wolf who had nearly torn his arm off before turning into a man.

The red overlay was gone from his vision when Darren opened his eyes, leaving the night bathed in the washed-out sodium glare of the streetlamps. Jack was still staring at him, muscles tensing, ready to fight, but his cardiovascular system was hidden behind his flesh and clothes.

Darren held out both hands in surrender. If he could get Miranda clear, maybe he could...jump over the building or something. Werewolves were fast, right? That's what he'd seen in movies and read in books. He could dodge the bullet and run away.

"Do as he says." Darren tried to step away.

Miranda pressed herself even closer to him. "Are you crazy?"

"Probably." Why else would feeling her softness against him be able to turn him on even in this insane situation? "Then again, I seem to be in good company."

Miranda had mentioned zombies. Jack not only believed in werewolves, he was prepared to fight them. And after what Darren had seen—what he was currently experiencing—he was starting to believe as well.

This wasn't the result of being drugged. He couldn't even try to convince himself it was some sort of psychotic break.

This was real. Darren had been bitten by a werewolf and now he was facing down a man who seemed to be a werewolf hunter.

"So, this is your *similar profession*?" Darren asked.

Jack chuckled darkly. "It wasn't too much of a stretch."

Darren let out a laugh. He let his arms fall back around Miranda's shoulders, pulling her cool body closer to his as gently as he could. One last hug, and then he would push her away. Except he wasn't sure how he could without hurting her.

"Miranda, I need you to let me go," he said.

She glared up at him. "Not happening."

Warmth suffused his body as she clung to him. She was so insistent on putting herself in danger for him. He closed his eyes and took another deep, steadying breath.

Her fear was diminishing, morphing into something smoother. Concern. He nuzzled the top of her head, letting her hair tickle his nose.

What would have happened if he'd worked up the nerve to ask her out before this? He had noticed her...noticing him. And she was impossible to ignore.

She wasn't as thin as a stick and top-heavy like Scott seemed to prefer. She was shorter and rounder, with softness everywhere, matching her expressive eyes and warm smile.

Scott was right. Darren had been seriously crushing on Miranda for a long time. Even without realizing how he felt, he'd been keeping her to himself, worried that his more adventurous partner would swoop in and charm her away.

A growl rumbled up from his chest.

Don't think about that.

He focused instead on Miranda in his arms, Miranda wrapped around him.

Okay, don't think about that too much either.

Things were already starting to stir. He tried to find the razor's edge —the balance between anger that there was a gun pointed at them, and the peace that holding Miranda and thinking about what she was willing to do for him brought.

"How did you do that?" Jack's voice had lost some of the fire, but none of its sharpness.

When Darren opened his eyes, Jack was staring at them. He had lowered his gun a little.

"Do what?" Darren asked.

"Come back from the edge." Jack shook his head. "I've never seen a werewolf back himself down from a change like that. I didn't know it was possible."

"I didn't know *werewolves* were possible until about five minutes ago." Darren managed a smile.

Jack snorted.

"What are you guys talking about?" Miranda relaxed her hold a little.

"You can step away from him." Jack lowered his gun a little more. "I'm not going to shoot him. Yet."

"This is insane," Miranda said. "Werewolves aren't real."

Jack chuckled again. "You, of all people, are going to lecture us about what is and is not possible in this world?"

Miranda's heartbeat spiked and she sucked in a breath. Darren didn't understand what it meant, but it seemed to stop her argument.

"We have some things to talk about." Jack gestured toward the door with his gun. "Werewolves first."

Darren shook his head, but then opened the door to the restaurant and walked inside. Miranda trailed right after him, keeping herself close.

As he stepped over the threshold, one of the bells above the door started to chime again. The note was different than what he was used to. He glanced up to see the silver bell dancing frenetically above his head. The others were still.

"Neat trick," he said. "Werewolf alarm?"

Jack shrugged, then reached up to still the bell as he followed them inside. "Some of my friends are…crafty. Keep moving. Through the kitchen and on your right."

Miranda was keeping herself between them still. She looked over her shoulder as they walked through the kitchen and said, "Jack, could you please put away the gun?"

Jack shook his head. "Not yet. But you're welcome to walk beside me if you'd like."

She scowled, increasing her pace so she was right at Darren's back. He crossed the small room, noting piles of iron skillets everywhere—more than it seemed the restaurant could possibly need. He stopped in front of the door Jack indicated. A small sign read, "Office".

Jack started to lean past him, reaching for the handle. His gun was kept leveled at Darren's stomach.

"Close quarters here," Jack said. "Hard to miss. I wouldn't try anything."

"I wasn't planning to," Darren said.

Jack had information Darren needed. He just had to figure out how to get it.

He wished he could get Miranda out of harm's way so he could put his full attention on finding those answers. Then again, having her to focus on was helping Darren control the rage simmering within him.

The door swung open on a dimly lit room. Darren's skin prickled as he stepped into it. Walking through the doorway was like pushing his body through air that felt substantial—almost like water.

Once he was in the room, his senses were muted. The glare of the lights dimmed, the harsh sounds of Miranda and Jack's breathing mellowed, and even the anger building inside of Darren seemed to quiet in the space. He let out a sigh, finally realizing how much the world had changed since he was bitten. In the office, he almost felt normal.

Another bell rang above the door. He knew before checking that it would be silver. He made a note of the other bells. Gold, brass, and several in dark shades that made it hard to tell what they were made of. There was one that might be bamboo and another that was unmistakably bone.

A round wooden table sat in the center of the room with seven chairs surrounding it. Engravings were carved all over its surface. Darren didn't recognize any of them. It looked like something he might see in a movie about wizards.

The rest of the room was even more interesting. Weapons of all descriptions hung on the walls. Axes, maces, swords, crossbows, rifles.

Then there was the really weird stuff. Boomerangs, staves carved into strange shapes, shields that had obviously seen more than one battle. Half a wall was taken up with wands made of different shades of wood. Some had wicked points, others were rounded or had stones attached to their ends.

"Next time I go to a Renaissance Festival, I'm stopping by here first," Miranda said.

Her eyes were wide as she turned in a circle, taking everything in. Apparently, she wasn't concerned for Darren's safety anymore. Which was fair, since Jack wasn't pointing his gun at either of them.

Jack headed to a cabinet filled with tiny drawers. It was sitting on top of a counter that held more stacks of iron skillets—the only reminder that they were still in a restaurant.

He pulled out a few speed loaders and set them on the table, then took another gun from the wall and set it next to them. The speed loaders were filled with shiny bullets that Darren was going to go ahead and assume were silver.

"Have a seat," Jack said.

Darren glanced at Miranda. She nodded, then walked to the table. He pulled out her chair for her, then sat at her side.

Jack let out another snort, shaking his head. "A werewolf with manners. Now I've seen everything."

He sat across from them and rested his gun on the table. He didn't take his hand off the trigger.

He was staring at Darren. Really staring. There was an unmistakable challenge in Jack's gaze that made the skin between Darren's shoulder blades itch.

The anger started to build again. His knee bobbed under the table as his foot bounced up and down. Miranda reached over and put her hand on his thigh.

Not even the muting quality of the room could dull the waves of electricity that travelled up his leg from her touch. His dick hardened as he imagined spreading her out on the table and fucking her until she screamed his name. He'd have to slit Jack's throat first…

Darren shook his head sharply, pushing the thought away.

That wasn't right. That wasn't what he wanted.

He focused on what was actually happening. Miranda's touch was gentle, her hand cool. He took a deep breath and let it out, looking for that razor's edge again.

"So, tell me about your night." Jack leaned back in his chair.

"You're the one with all the answers," Darren said. "Why don't you tell me what happened?"

Jack smirked. "My knowledge in this case is broad. I'd like to hear your particular details."

Miranda squeezed Darren's leg. He shifted uncomfortably in his chair as his pants became more restrictive. The distraction helped him stop thinking about leaping across the table and sinking his teeth into Jack's throat.

"I hit a dog," Darren said. "I got out of my car to help it and it bit me."

"A dog." Jack shook his head. "You're going to have to do better than that. Where were you?"

"I was driving through the Old River District."

"The Rath," Jack murmured.

Miranda leaned forward. "Wait, R-A-T-H? As in a fairy Rath?"

"Pretty much," Jack said.

"What's a Rath?" Darren felt like they were talking in code.

"It's a place where fairies live," she said. "My dad used to tell me stories about them. Raths are like little pockets of Faerie—the place where fairies live. Supposedly, they can be reached through natural landmarks, like a mound of earth or a copse of trees or river bend."

"Times have changed," Jack said. "The fey have had to adapt to modern environments to prey on humans. The Old River District is full of Faerie pockets. That's why we call it the Rath."

Miranda let out a laugh. "You can't seriously believe this."

"Let Darren finish his story." Jack turned his stony gaze back to Darren. "Then I'll tell you what I believe."

Darren shook his head. "I already told you what I know."

"You gave me a half-assed answer." Jack snorted. "'Hit a dog'. I need details. Where was the sun in the sky? What did the creature look like? Where did it bite you? Why were you there? And most importantly, how the hell did you get away?"

"Just lucky, I guess," Darren said.

Jack chuckled briefly. "Let me put it to you another way." He lifted his gun slightly. "*This* is a foregone conclusion. In my mind, that thing already killed you. I'm just finishing the job. Giving you a merciful end."

"Jack, please—" Miranda's voice crackled. The sugary scent of fear spread from her like a cloud.

Darren stifled a growl, knowing it wouldn't help his case any. He had to protect Miranda. Jack was after *Darren*. Maybe if he played his cards right, he could get her out of this nightmare.

Jack turned his attention to Miranda. "There's more at stake than just this one life. If he dies here and now, how many people will be spared in the future?"

Miranda's heartbeat skipped, then picked up. Whatever Jack was inferring, it had her terrified. Her pupils dilated and her fingers dug into Darren's leg. He tried to tell his body that it wasn't foreplay, but his dick wasn't listening. He forced his attention to what Jack was saying in an effort to distract himself.

"There are two types of werewolves," Jack said. "Those that run in packs and *rogues*. You get a pack in town, bodies pile up—in corners. They take out drifters, the homeless, or people on the outskirts of town. They find people in places where an animal taking them down and half-eating them is plausible."

Jack paused for a moment, probably waiting for what he'd said to sink in. Darren didn't want it to.

Werewolves eat people?

There was no way Darren would become a cannibal. He wouldn't let it happen.

"And that's the best case scenario," Jack continued. "The ones in packs are more controlled. They clean up after themselves to avoid being caught or cluing humanity in to their existence. You go up against a pack and you're dead. They never stay in one place too long, so you batten down the hatches and hang wolfsbane over your doors and try not to think about what they're doing."

He looked pointedly at Darren as he went on.

"Then there are rogues," Jack said. "Solo wolves. Ones that were turned, but not brought into a pack. Those are the ones you have to watch out for. They can't control themselves. They kill indiscriminately. They do *worse*. So I ask you again, Darren. What happened tonight?"

Darren glanced at Miranda. Her lips were parted, her eyes still wide. Her heart pounded in her chest. He could sense the blood flowing in her veins. He knew her skin would be soft under his touch. Under his claws.

He couldn't let himself hurt her or anyone else. But he had to believe there was hope for him. If werewolves could control themselves when they were in packs, maybe...

What? I could find a pack to run with? Only kill certain people? Only eat *certain people?*

No. There had to be another way. Unfortunately, Jack was the only person Darren knew of who might have a chance of helping him find it. He had to convince Jack that he wasn't a threat. The best way he knew to do that would be to cooperate.

"The sun had set maybe twenty minutes before." Darren took a deep breath and let it out. "The thing that attacked me... It looked like a monster. Like a cross between a wolf and a bear, except it walked on two legs. And it had green eyes."

"Green eyes surrounded by white," Jack said.

Darren nodded. "It bit me on my left forearm. We were in an abandoned building. I managed to grab a chunk of wood and hit it in the head to get it off of me."

"Wood?" Jack's eyebrows lifted. "You hit a werewolf with a stick and it let you go?"

"I guess," Darren said.

Jack was quiet for a moment. Then he raised his gun, and said, "Bullshit."

Miranda leaned sideways and extended her free arm toward Jack as if she could ward off the bullets with her palm.

She can't ward off bullets with her hand, can she?

It had been such a weird night...

"Stop it," she said. "Even if Darren is a werewolf—and I'm not saying I believe he is—he's answering your questions. He's not threatening you."

Jack shook his head. "I know you like him. Hell, I do, too. But he is dangerous. The change is only just starting in him."

Jack turned back to Darren, and the look in his eyes was almost pitying.

"You angry?" Jack asked.

"You're holding a gun on me and threatening to kill me," Darren said. "Yeah, I'm angry."

"I'm not talking about that kind of mad." Jack leaned forward, narrowing his eyes. His voice rumbled through the room. "I'm talking about anger that burns in your bones. Rage flooding through your blood, curling your fists, making you want to do unspeakable things."

Darren wanted to look away, to hide the guilt that was no doubt in his eyes. But he couldn't. Because Jack was right.

Before being bitten, Darren would have strategized ways of disarming his foe. He wouldn't have thought about disemboweling Jack and hanging him above the door to his restaurant.

Remembering the thought made Darren sick to his stomach—and made his skin prickle with anticipation at the same time.

"Once the full moon gets here, the man we knew will be gone," Jack said. "It's on me to stop the thing that you're becoming. Any way I can."

Darren couldn't deny the urges he was feeling, but he was fighting them off. He wasn't ready to give up.

There was something about the room helping him keep those impulses at bay. That meant there had to be ways he could control himself—keep himself from killing.

The way the conversation was going, Darren wasn't sure he'd have a chance to find out. Jack didn't seem eager to let Darren live to see that first full moon. And after what Jack had told them, Darren couldn't even blame him.

Chapter Nine

"Jack, this is Darren you're talking about," Miranda said. "You know him. Please, don't do this. You're having a delusion—"

"You're going to lecture me about delusions? *You* are telling me that everything in this world can be scientifically explained?" Jack's gaze bored into her. "*I didn't see that coming.*"

Her stomach seemed to drop through the floor. Did he know about her power? The way he was glaring, and his comment about saving lives in the future made her wonder.

"I know you're sweet on him," Jack said. "But he is dangerous. Even if he manages to keep himself from outright killing you, he could hurt you without meaning to with his new strength. He could turn you."

Darren's leg started to bounce under the table again. "How is it transmitted?"

Jack turned his attention back to Darren. "Why?"

"We kissed," Darren said. "In front of the restaurant."

"I'm aware," Jack said.

"Did I..." Darren glanced over at Miranda, then quickly looked away.

"Relax," Jack said. "That little make-out session wasn't enough to turn her. The only way to make someone a werewolf is to bite them— and break their skin—while you're in your werewolf form. That's how the curse is transmitted. Not through coughs, or touch, or kissing. It's not an STD and you can't get anyone pregnant. Turning makes you sterile. Do you know how we know this, Darren?"

Darren's leg went still. He didn't even seem to be breathing.

"Rape kits." Jack paused, his eyes pinching at the corners. When he spoke again, his voice was even lower and rougher than usual. "In their altered form, all werewolves care about is the kill. When they're human, they have 'broader interests'. They're still dangerous—maybe worse, since they can hide among humans. Tell me, Darren. Since you were bitten, have you had any...out of character thoughts about Miranda?"

"Jack—" Miranda said.

Darren spoke at the same time. "I would never hurt anyone that way. *Anyone.*"

"The man you were wouldn't. How much longer will you be him?" Jack paused again. "This room is muting your abilities. Helping you hold on to your humanity. You have three nights after this one until the full moon. Nothing will help you then. You will change. And you will kill. There's only one way to stop it."

Jack pulled back the hammer on his gun and gently put it in what Miranda thought was the uncocked position, then turned it around with the handle toward Darren. Reaching across the table, Jack set it down within Darren's reach. He leaned back and picked up the other gun, using a circular device that held a ring of shiny silver-looking bullets to load the weapon incredibly quickly.

Darren stared at the gun in front of him. He couldn't be considering…

"This is insane." She turned to Darren and said, "You can't believe him. This can't be true."

"Tell her the rest," Jack said. "You got away somehow, and I do not for a moment believe it's just because you hit the thing on the head with some broken board you found lying around."

"It was already hurt," Darren said. "*He* was already hurt. I hit him with my car."

"A werewolf would shake that off," Jack said.

"He was hurt before that," Darren said. "Someone put silver in him. Not a bullet. A coin."

He reached into his pocket and pulled out a handkerchief. He seemed to be handling it very carefully. He tossed it in front of Jack. It made a *thunk* as it hit the table.

"It happened like I said." Darren let out a tight breath. "A giant wolf-thing bit me, and I hit him with a piece of shelving. The blow knocked him off of me. Then he…changed. He changed into a man."

Darren glanced over at Miranda. His dark brows were lowered over his pale gray eyes. She had never seen him look more serious—not even when he was pulling her from the wreckage of her car. He had looked terrified then. Now he looked…terrifying.

Is it possible? Are werewolves real?

She might be able to consider that possibility, but she would *never* believe that Darren would become the sort of creature that Jack had described.

Darren looked away from her, as if he couldn't hold her gaze. He cleared his throat, and said, "When he realized he had bitten me, I think he regretted it. He kept saying he was sorry."

Miranda squeezed Darren's thigh to bring his attention back to her. "Why would he apologize if he was a mindless monster?"

"He really was sorry." Darren's eyebrows drew together as he considered her question. "Seeing that he bit me seemed to wreck him."

"Lots of people have regrets when their number is up," Jack said.

Darren shook his head. "No, this was different."

Hope was seeping back into his expression. Miranda had to help him build on that.

"Did he say anything else?" she asked.

"He kept talking about the night," Darren said. "No, nights. He told me to 'find the nights', whatever that means."

"Maybe something about the full moon?" She turned back to Jack. "Werewolves are mostly active at night, right? That's the way it was in my dad's stories."

Jack winced slightly, but recovered himself quickly. "Werewolves are active whenever they want to be. It's vampires who can't move around during the day."

"Vampires?" Miranda nearly choked on the word. "Vampires are real too?"

"They're not as dangerous as werewolves," Jack said. "A hell of a lot more common, though."

"Do you think we can find some vampires who can help us?" Miranda said. "Is that what the man who bit you meant?"

"'Nights'…" Jack lowered his gun a bit, his brow furrowed. For the first time that evening, he seemed uncertain. "Then what?"

"Then he turned to ash and disintegrated." Darren pointed toward the handkerchief on the table. "I found that coin in the remains."

Jack cocked an eyebrow, then leaned forward and picked it up. He unwrapped it slowly.

"If werewolves in packs can pick specific targets, that means they can think," Miranda said. "Darren can find a way to control himself."

"Werewolves are driven by rage," Jack said. "By a hunger for violence."

Darren shook his head. "The one who turned me was driven by pain. That coin was burning a hole in his gut. I've felt silver now. It's like touching acid. The poor guy had to be in agony."

Jack held up the coin, then turned it over in his fingers. "This looks Grecian."

"It is," Darren said. "It's from a small city that was destroyed by a natural disaster millennia ago. Until recently, it was on loan to Olympus University from the museum."

Jack let out a sigh. "I sometimes wonder if our founders took it a little too far with the naming theme for our fair city."

Miranda remembered the conversation Darren had had with his partner, Scott, after the accident. They had spoken about coins.

"Was this one of the coins you and Scott were transporting?" she asked.

"Yes." Darren actually managed a slight smile as he looked at her. "I'm surprised you remember that."

Jack was staring intently at the coin. "Underestimate her at your peril."

He knows.

Somehow, his statement made her sure of it.

Her stomach started churning. How long had he known? How did he find out? Why had he never mentioned it to her?

"Orion and the Scorpion," Jack said.

The hair on the back of Miranda's neck stood on end. "What did you say?"

"Orion and the Scorpion," Jack repeated. "That's the design. Orion on one side, the scorpion on the other. It's from a Greek myth."

"Orion…" She remembered her vision, with the stars falling to earth—remembered the pattern of the constellation and finally recognized it.

Dread flooded her body, making bile rise up in her throat. She pulled her hand away from Darren and hugged her middle tight. She had let him be attacked to avoid the apocalyptic vision. She'd thought that would be the end of it. The end of *him*.

She shook her head and started rocking, feeling the weight of the vision pressing down on her. She didn't know what to do, but knew she was at the center of it.

Darren being attacked was only the beginning.

"What is it?" Jack leaned forward in his chair. "What did you see?"

She shook her head.

"He needs to know," Jack said.

Darren looked back and forth between them. "Know what?"

"If you really want to help him, you have to tell him," Jack said.

He was right.

She took a deep breath, and forced out the words, "I can see the future."

Hearing it out loud added a layer of reality to her ability—her life— that she hadn't felt since her mom was alive.

She glanced over at Darren. His eyebrows hiked up his forehead briefly, but then he sort of shook his head, his expression becoming neutral.

"Okay," he said.

"That's it?" Miranda expected questions, disbelief, *something* other than this calm acceptance.

"I don't really have room to be skeptical." He smiled at her and shrugged.

"I suppose not." Because *werewolf*. This was so crazy. She turned back to Jack, and asked, "How did you know?"

Jack stared at her for a long time. The crow's feet around his eyes deepened, like he was in pain. Finally, he said, "It's from your dad's side. He and I fought the fey together, along with your mom and some others."

"What?" Miranda felt like her world had shattered around her. She and her mom had always been open and honest with each other—at least, Miranda had thought so. She shook her head. "My mom would have told me."

"She wanted you to have a normal life," Jack said.

"But I wasn't normal," Miranda said. "I'm *not* normal."

"Not everyone in your bloodline develops the sight." Jack cleared his throat, but his voice was still raspy. "Your dad thought you'd been spared."

He'd died before Miranda's powers had manifested. But her mom hadn't told Miranda *any* of this.

"Mom knew," Miranda whispered. "Why didn't she tell me?"

"She didn't want this life for you," Jack said.

"That wasn't her choice to make." Miranda nearly choked on the words, her throat was so tight.

"It doesn't matter now anyway," Jack said. "Because this life has chosen you. I need to know what you saw."

"Is that why you offered me this job after mom's funeral?" she said. "To keep tabs on my visions?"

"Hell, no." He took a deep breath and then blew it out. She'd never seen him so upset.

Jack's gaze softened and he smiled. Miranda couldn't remember ever seeing such a sad smile.

"Your mom didn't want me anywhere near you." His eyes glittered in the dim light and his voice sounded strained. "Your dad and I... We were close. *You* are all that's left of him in this world. And I couldn't leave you to be alone in it."

The room seemed to be spinning. She wasn't sure what was real anymore. *Nothing* she'd thought she understood seemed certain.

Darren reached over to her and placed his hand on her back. She took a deep, calming breath and let his warmth seep into her.

This she did understand. Darren wasn't a monster. He would *never* be a monster.

Apparently, Jack didn't agree. He lifted that damned gun again.

"Careful, there," he said.

"Enough," Miranda snapped. She shifted closer to Darren, pressing her hands to her thighs to keep from reaching for him. "Too many lives are at stake for you to throw away Darren's just because you *think* you know his future. I've *seen* it, and he will not be a threat."

At least, not to me.

Jack leaned back and tapped his fingers on the table. "Tell me."

She wasn't about to share her visions of her and Darren in bed. She focused on the more important issue.

"An apocalypse," she said. "But I think I prevented it already."

Jack waved his hand in a circle, encouraging her to go on.

"I've never had a vision like this one," Miranda said. "It was shrouded in metaphors." *And that stupid fog.* "Details kept changing, even while I was in it."

"What kind of details?" Jack said.

"Mostly who was in the coffin." She took a shaky breath, glancing up at Jack. "First it was you. Then Darren." She skipped over Eden. There was only so much Miranda could take at the moment.

If Jack was disturbed by learning of his imminent demise, he didn't show it. Darren was another matter.

"Wait, we're going to die?" he said.

"I don't know." Miranda shook her head. "I was in a church, and I saw Jack in a coffin. I looked away, and when I looked back, it was you. So I turned around and ran away. But when I made it outside, the stars were shining so bright it almost hurt to look at them. I didn't recognize the constellation until you mentioned Orion just now. That's what it was, though. And the stars were falling from the sky, exploding where they hit."

"That sounds more like missiles than stars," Darren said.

Jack leveled a grim look at Darren. "Fairies don't need to use missiles."

"Fairies." Her stomach started doing flips. She felt like she might be sick.

Her dad had told her fairy tales when she was a little girl. He'd told her the books weren't always right, and she needed to remember his versions. He'd said it was important.

She'd always thought they were just stories.

Darren rested his hand on top of hers, his touch so gentle. He was supporting her, and he didn't know that she had thrown him to the wolves. Literally, as it turned out. How could she ever tell him what she'd done?

"How do your visions work?" he asked.

At least she could explain her powers. Maybe when she had a chance to confess the rest, it would help him understand her choice.

"Like this." She looked at him and turned her hand over in his so that their palms were touching. She let his future flow into her.

He was below her this time. She was straddling him, fingers buried in the fine dark hair that coated his chest. His eyes were pinched shut and his hands clutched the sheets—the same sheets that were currently on her bed at home. Right down to the mismatched pillowslip she had used because she'd spilled something on one of the matching set.

She felt a quickening between her legs, her face tingling and her breath hitching in her chest.

They were still going to become lovers. Even after what she was about to tell him. And it was going to happen soon.

"What are you seeing?" Jack said.

His question brought her back to her physical senses, to the dark room where she sat with her boss, the not quite retired fairy fighter, and her soon to be werewolf boyfriend. Darren stared at her intently, pupils wide.

"I see that Darren is not a threat to me," she said.

"That'd be a lot more reassuring if you two weren't staring at each other like that," Jack said.

Miranda forced herself to look away. She turned her hand back over, but rested it on Darren's thigh. She could feel the energy crackling off of him and briefly wondered if their chemistry was a byproduct of him becoming a werewolf or the attraction they'd felt before it happened.

"I've seen you reading people in the diner," Jack said. "A light touch on the shoulder, you space out for a few minutes, then you sit down and talk. Maybe steer them toward making better decisions. That's talk-show stuff. You need to be ready for this, Miranda. You're walking into a war that's been going on for thousands of years. A war between humanity and the fey. You have to accept that there will be casualties."

He looked pointedly at Darren.

"Not Darren." She had already sacrificed him once. She wouldn't do it again.

If Jack—or anybody—tried to take Darren from her, she was ready to fight for him and their future together.

Ready to fight...

Her stomach seemed to rise and then plummet, like she was on a roller-coaster. The air shifted.

"Something's coming." She heard the words escape her lips like they were spoken from someone else.

A bell above the door rang—hollow and wooden. Jack whipped his head around, his eyes widening. He leapt to his feet. So did Darren.

Miranda jumped up and put her hand on Darren's chest. This would be the perfect chance to escape, but she knew they had to stay. Whatever was about to happen, Jack needed their help.

Jack turned to Darren and said, "You want to prove to me you're still a man and not a monster—that you can control this curse? Now's your chance."

He opened the chamber of his gun and let the bullets fall into his hand, then ran to the small cabinet full of ammo again. He pulled out another ring of bullets and reloaded. The bullets weren't shiny this time. They were a dull gray.

Miranda grabbed one of the skillets off the counter. She wasn't sure why she wanted it, but she knew it was important that she have it. She backed up against a wall, holding the skillet in front of her.

Jack turned toward the room. He smiled when he noticed her weapon of choice. "Iron. Good thinking."

"I wasn't thinking," she said. "It was instinct."

He nodded. "Trust your instincts. Always." He backed up against a wall himself, holding his gun level and aimed at the door. He was also holding a skillet, brandishing it like a weapon.

Darren turned to Jack and said, "Can I draw my gun without you shooting me?"

"It'll be better if you're not armed when it shows up." Jack was scanning the room. "We might be able to take it by surprise."

"Take *what* by surprise?" Darren said.

Jack shook his head. "I don't know."

The chimes sounded again, stronger this time. Now that Miranda was watching the bells, she saw that it was the bamboo one. She couldn't remember ever hearing it before.

Whatever Jack was expecting, it had him scared. More scared than he'd been sitting across the table from Darren—ready to kill or be killed. The tension had escalated, too. Miranda's skin was crawling.

"Jack, what's going on?" she said.

"Jack?" A new voice sounded in the room. Smooth and lyrical, even in that one word.

Miranda had been staring at the door the whole time and it had never opened. She turned to look in the direction the voice had come from.

A handsome blond man stood right next to her, almost close enough to touch. She yelped and jumped away, moving to stand behind Darren.

Miranda had never seen such a beautiful man. His large eyes were the color of a perfect summer lawn. His skin was as flawless and smooth as fresh snow, and his hair floated around his face in a halo of gold.

"Humans startle so easily." He laughed, a cruel smile twisting his inhumanly gorgeous features. "Unless my eyes deceive me, you'll not find succor with that one, though."

"Forester." Jack's eyes were wide with fear. "How the hell did you get in here?"

Miranda wanted to know as well. As far as she could tell, "Forester" had just appeared in the room out of nowhere.

"It did take some doing, even with my beacon," Forester said. "I was surprised by the wards, but now it makes a bit more sense—*Jack*."

Forester smiled. His teeth gleamed in the light—bright and perfect. He tilted his head a bit, and his hair fell against his face, revealing the point of his ear. A fairy?

Please, don't let him be a fairy.

If he was a fairy, he wouldn't even see her as an animal. He'd see her as a chew-toy. He'd want to make her squeak.

Forester turned his attention to her. "And you are?"

The green of his eyes swirled with flickering lights. His irises were larger than a human's. She started to feel unfocused, and was about to mumble her name, when Jack cut in.

"Don't answer him," Jack said. "Never tell a fairy your name if they ask. It gives them power over you."

She knew that. Somewhere in the back of her mind. Stories dad had told her. A warning repeated again and again.

Her thoughts were muddled. She looked at Forester's chin, breaking eye contact, and her mind began to clear. She tightened her grip on the skillet.

"It's inconsequential," Forester said. "I've heard the name I need— even though it's not a *true* name. Infamous Jack, the fairy killer." His smile became even more predatory as he turned to face Jack. "Choosing that name was a very clever trick. But it looks like your luck has run out."

Chapter Ten

This guy wasn't human. Even with his senses dampened, Darren caught the scent of clover the…whatever Forester was…put off. There was cool air coming out of his mouth and Darren distinctly heard the beating of *three* hearts in Forester's chest.

How different was Darren's body now? Had his internal organs morphed without him even knowing it?

"We've been looking for you for a very long time." Forester was still focused on Jack. "The look of surprise on your face is priceless. I'll remember it for eons to come."

"You're not going to last that long, elf." Jack pulled back the hammer of his gun.

Forester shook his head. "If you fire, I'll blink away before the bullets hit me. They will, however, hit my friend behind me."

The only people behind him were Darren and Miranda—and Darren was blocking her body entirely. Was Forester talking about Darren? Because they were *not* friends.

Although, something about the guy was familiar. The way he stood. The cut of his hair…

Forester went on. "Of course, we know how temperamental his kind can be. I'm guessing the little thing standing next to him is your side-kick. You hero-types do love to have side-kicks. A pity you didn't train this one better. Standing within arm's reach of a werewolf is outright stupidity. Although, it promises to be highly entertaining when he turns and rips her apart."

If he thought Darren was on his side, Forester was in for a rude awakening. Maybe that was what Jack meant about taking him by surprise.

"You'd make an excellent tribute next cycle," Forester said. "But I doubt you'll last long enough. There are too many among us who simply wish to see you dead." Forester turned and smiled at Darren. "May I count you among them, brother?"

"I'm an only child," Darren said.

Forester cocked his head to the side for a moment. "A rogue? I'm surprised there isn't blood on the walls already. I'm glad you saved some fun for me."

"That coin led you to me," Jack said. "It's your beacon."

Forester pressed a hand to his chest. "Your grasp of the obvious astounds me."

"What I don't get is why it was in a werewolf's guts," Jack said. "That seems mean, even for a little prick like you."

Forester laughed. "Didn't he mention? Niall follows Antares. He's one of the *Knights*. A traitor—but a useful one."

Niall... Darren had a name for the man who had turned him, thrown his life into chaos. It made everything more real somehow.

Niall had been a person, just like Darren. He'd been bitten. Darren wondered what the circumstances were and if Niall fought the change as hard as Darren was fighting it.

"I see my coin," Forester said, "but not the courier."

Courier...

The pieces fell into place. The footage had been grainy, but this was the same man Darren had seen outside of the electronics store. This was the thief who had stolen the coins and destroyed Darren's career.

It seemed like such a small matter, with everything else going on. Still, his vision started to go red. Darren clenched his hands into fists, nails piercing his palms. He caught the scent of his own blood blossoming, heard the patter of drops as it hit the floor.

Blood. He needed more blood on his hands. Forester's blood.

Darren had thought Forester's sudden disappearance in the footage was a software glitch. After this guy popping into the room, he realized it wasn't. Apparently, elves could teleport.

Darren couldn't underestimate this opponent. And he had to stay in control.

"Who did you hire to help you steal the coins from Ford Security?" Subtlety was beyond him. All of Darren's willpower was being spent not tearing into the guy.

"Hire?" Forester's lip curled up in disgust. "I didn't hire anyone. I made a *deal*."

"I saw what you did to Scott." Darren's voice was lower than normal. "I know you were working with Morrison."

Forester let out a sudden laugh, the sound like discordant wind chimes. "You were the dark-haired human. The one who had to be distracted."

Dammit, it really had been a setup all along. One that had nearly cost Miranda her life.

"Who told you to wait for me to leave?" Darren's shoulders bunched up. No matter how hard he tried, he couldn't relax them. "Who arranged the accident?"

"The accident," Miranda said. "Wait, *my* accident?"

Darren couldn't answer. His focus existed solely with the elf.

Forester cocked his head to the side again in that birdlike fashion. "Why do you even care?"

"Because they got me fired, turned into a werewolf, and they very nearly killed Miranda." Each word became more guttural, until Darren had to force out the last.

Forester's eyes widened and his smile grew broader. He looked absolutely delighted.

"How wicked!" he said. "I underestimated her."

Her?

Shit. Darren was past sure now. Mrs. Ford was behind it all. Scott was going to go ballistic.

Darren was going to rip her throat out with his teeth.

"I see you've found the answers you sought," Forester said. "How about you help me with mine? The werewolf who bit you. Where is he?"

"You're too late." The words grated against the back of Darren's throat. "He's already dead."

"That's a problem." Forester glanced at the table. "We'll figure something out, though."

"There is no 'we'," Darren growled. He'd never felt his shoulder blades actually press against each other. His arms felt longer, too.

"Oh, don't be that way." Forester smiled and came a few steps closer.

The idiot was almost in Darren's reach. Darren wondered which was faster—the elf's teleporting ability, or Darren's werewolf reflexes.

"Let me guess," Forester said. "The intrepid 'Jack' and his lovely assistant rescued you from the beast, but not before you were bitten. Now, they're trying to convince you that you're cursed. A monster. Does that sound about right?"

Darren felt a muscle in his jaw start to twitch. Forester's three hearts glowed brightly—one in the center of his chest and two on his sides. Darren could see the veins and arteries connecting them, hear the whoosh of blood circulating in Forester's body.

Whatever this guy was, he was close enough to human for Darren to kill. He'd knock Forester to the floor and step on his chest, then rip out his side-hearts before stepping harder. Till he popped.

Darren imagined the floor covered in blood. He wondered what color it would be—and smiled.

Forester smiled back. "Relax, dear friend. You aren't alone anymore. I know how your kind hates that. Let me teach you about your gifts. Your strength, speed, and heightened senses."

Darren would accept Forester's help—as he practiced using all those skills to rip the guy's head off. He needed to get closer to make sure he could catch Forester before he teleported away.

"Humans have such narrow perceptions," Forester said. "You've moved beyond them now. In a few hundred years, you won't even remember what it was like to be one of them."

Miranda stepped forward, putting her closer to Forester. Too close.

"A few hundred years?" she said. "Is Darren immortal now?"

"And suddenly I have your interest." Forester's mouth pulled in what should have been a smile, except for the predatory gleam in his eyes. "Why don't we make a deal?"

Miranda shook her head. "I know better than to make a deal with a fairy."

"You could at least hear me out," Forester said. "Darren will change and bite you—under my supervision so he doesn't get carried away—and you can stay young and..." he sort of grimaced, "'beautiful' forever."

Darren growled. He couldn't stop himself. There was no way he was biting Miranda. No way he was turning her into this.

Instead, I'll watch her grow old and die.

His skin started to crawl. He couldn't lose her. But he couldn't have her either. She had felt like…home. Like a connection, when Darren was floating in a sea of chaos. There had been moments when it was the only thing holding him together. And he was going to lose her.

Unless he changed her. And Forester could help.

No.

The air whistled past Darren's ears as he launched himself at Forester, arms extended to grapple him. Their chests collided and Darren grabbed the back of Forester's coat to hold him in place. He went in for the kill, but his teeth clacked together where Forester's neck had just been.

Darren stumbled forward, holding nothing but tattered pieces of Forester's coat in his…claws.

He didn't recognize his hands. His skin was dark gray, his fingers distended, with sharp points sprouting from their tips.

A series of loud staccato pops hit his ears. He looked at the source of the sound. Outlined in red, Darren could make out Jack, holding up his gun.

Bright bursts of light nearly blinded Darren as he watched Jack fire round after round at nothing. He was keeping his back to the wall, firing directly in front of him and to the side away from Miranda— keeping her safe.

Forester appeared next to Jack, on the side closest to Miranda. He must have predicted the safe zone.

The moment Forester appeared, he backhanded Jack viciously. Jack was lifted into the air and hit the wall hard, then landed on the counter below it and rolled to the floor.

Forester grinned at Darren, then vanished again.

The fairy reappeared standing on a counter near the swords. He grabbed one from the wall—one that gleamed silver even through the red clouding Darren's vision. Then he vanished again.

Shit.

Miranda was still in the room. Where was she?

Darren turned, a sound coming out of him that was more roar than growl. The red haze rippled on his left just before Forester reappeared at Darren's side. Darren was able to leap out of the way a fraction of a second before the silver blade would have reached him.

Forester kept swinging, his face pulled in a broad smile. He was laughing while he tried to cut Darren to pieces.

The speed Forester had mentioned was kicking in, but Darren didn't know how to control it. He jumped and hit his head on the ceiling, the wood paneling cracking from the impact.

Forester was too busy laughing to deliver a killing blow. His laughter ended abruptly as Miranda swung her skillet at him.

He caught her arm before it could connect. "You humans and your iron. You think you can best me when a werewolf can't? Ridiculous mortals."

Miranda let out a yelp of pain and dropped the skillet as Forester shook her arm. Rage burned through Darren's guts, through his muscles, soaking into his bones. He grabbed Forester's shoulder before he could even think and felt sinew tear beneath his grip.

Forester grunted and let go of Miranda. Darren lifted Forester into the air and slammed him onto the table, then grabbed his throat and started to squeeze. His huge elf-eyes bugged out of his head.

As he clawed at the table, his hand touched the gun Jack had loaded for Darren—the one with the silver bullets. Forester knocked it to the floor. He kept flailing, then suddenly slapped his hand onto the back of Darren's.

Pain arced through Darren, his skin burning. He let out a yowl and leapt back, shaking his hand. Forester vanished. The coin he'd been holding against Darren's hand fell to the ground.

Darren was going to kill Forester. Find him and kill him. For using silver. For touching Miranda.

Miranda...

Darren wheeled around, looking for her. He had to be sure she was safe. She was standing behind him. The gun Forester had knocked from the table was at her feet.

Had he changed? Was she facing the monster Darren had first seen in that dark grocery store?

She stared at him, eyes wide and mouth open.

Yeah. Probably so.

She ducked down and picked up the gun, pointing it at him as she rose.

She had defended him, offered to help him. Whatever he had turned into was bad enough that she was going to put him down. Part of him wanted to let her.

Part of him wanted to rip out her throat.

He forced himself to stay still. He didn't let himself close his eyes. He wanted her to see that he was sorry while he was still able to feel remorse. His teeth felt strange, and he didn't think he could manage words that wouldn't frighten her.

Except she didn't look frightened anymore. She stared at him calmly, then lifted her hand and made a motion like she wanted him to sit.

If she thought she could treat him like a dog just because—

"Darren." Her voice was level. She lifted her fingers, her lips forming words, numbers, as she matched them with her gestures.

3...2...

He waited a beat after '1', then ducked. She opened fire.

He heard Forester scream, heard the bullets hit flesh, smelled the bright scent of fresh-cut clover. And then Forester was gone. Darren could sense it.

Miranda had saved him.

The relief that crashed through him left him light-headed. She still believed in him. At least for now.

Miranda dropped her gun and turned away. She was heading toward Jack. To *Jack.*

She didn't belong with him. She belonged with Darren.

He gripped the table and flung it out of his way. It crashed against the wall, the heavy wood splintering from the impact.

Gratifying.

Darren picked up two of the chairs and threw them against the wall, delighting in the way they practically disintegrated. There were only five more chairs to destroy, but then there was the building.

He could sense his power, just beyond his periphery—sense a strength he hadn't fully embraced. All he had to do was let go. The thickness he'd felt in the air earlier had all but vanished the more he had let the change sink into his bones.

"Darren."

He managed to hear the small voice over the sound of blood rushing through his ears. He could hear the heartbeat that went with it. Two heartbeats. Humans.

Wasn't he human too?

Not anymore.

He picked up another chair and threw it after the others. It wasn't as satisfying. He needed more. Something softer. With blood...

"Darren."

The voice intruded on his thoughts again. It wouldn't leave him alone.

"Please fight this. I know you can fight it. I know you'll win."

Miranda. She was still in the room—watching Darren toss furniture around like a child throwing a tantrum.

What am I doing?

He closed his eyes, taking deep breaths to try to calm himself. Another voice cut in. Harsher, irritating. Male.

"He's too far gone. Shoot him before he turns completely. Shoot him or we're both dead."

Darren felt a growl build in his chest, rumbling out through teeth that still felt strange in his head. Miranda's scent flowed around him. He felt her stand right in front of him. She probably didn't want to miss.

"Touch me," she said.

How could he without slashing her skin? Without breaking her bones? He opened his eyes and saw that her hands were empty and open at her sides.

"It's going to be okay." She spoke with such conviction... And she backed up her words with action. She pressed her cool hands to his cheeks, making soft, soothing noises.

He could smell her fear, sickly sweet, but there was another scent woven through it. Like the first breath of spring after a long winter.

Faith.

"It's going to be okay," she repeated.

He couldn't help but believe her.

Chapter Eleven

Miranda was pretty sure she was going to throw up. Her head was pounding, her skin felt electrified, and she wanted nothing more than to run screaming from the room.

Well, almost nothing.

She wanted to help Darren. He was fighting so hard to hold on to his humanity. He was stuck half-changed. His pupils were huge, his teeth… She couldn't think about his teeth. The muscles of his face and neck had distorted and his skin was ashen gray. But he was still Darren.

"Deep breaths," she said. "Slow your heart."

As if her own wasn't pounding so hard that every beat felt like being punched in the chest. She had to calm herself down, too. She took the same deep breaths, felt a fear that she saw reflected in his eyes.

"You're not going to hurt me," she said.

She'd better double-check that. The future was a fluid thing, every choice feeding into it. They'd gone through some significant events since the reading she'd done earlier.

She left one hand on his face, making sure he kept staring at her. It seemed to help him center himself. She let the other hand drop to his and very carefully slid her fingers across his palm.

His claws had looked sharp. She didn't want him to nick her. Jack had said only bites could change people, but she didn't want to risk—

His future hit her like a tidal wave the moment his fingers gently closed on hers. Clear as crystal, bright as sunlight on snow.

The fog was gone, and she sensed the wide horizon of decades—centuries—ahead of him. Whatever was heading their way, he was going to live. He was going to live for a very long time.

She smiled and felt herself laugh. At least there was that comfort. She hadn't doomed him when she'd let him be bitten. She had saved him.

She saw Darren running through a forest in his wild form. There was no other word for it. He wasn't a monster lurking in the shadows. The sun was shining overhead.

Another werewolf cut through the trees near him. Then another and another—four dark forms weaving in among the trees, lost in the bliss of the hunt.

She sensed their target close at hand and prayed it wasn't a human. When the biggest werewolf launched itself into the air, landing on a huge buck, she let out a sigh of relief. It snapped the deer's neck with a smooth and powerful motion, riding it to the ground.

The others caught up and began to…eat.

The ground was stained crimson, but she wasn't repulsed. It was almost like watching a bizarre nature documentary. And then Darren looked at her. Not in reality, but in the vision. He stood straight and walked over to her, as if he could see her. He held out his clawed hand and she took it in hers. In her own *clawed* hand.

Shit.

She was going to turn. That's what the fog meant. Not death, but transformation. The end of her human life and the beginning of… something else.

"The Veil," she murmured. "The Fairy Veil."

"What?"

Darren's voice helped pull her from the vision and back to her senses in reality. His eyes had returned to normal, as had the rest of his face. Aside from the somewhat terrified cast to his expression, he seemed fine.

She laughed and threw her arms around his neck.

"It really is going to be okay," she said.

At least for them. If some sort of apocalypse was coming—zombie or otherwise—they would at least survive. The world wouldn't burn like in her vision. Trees and animals would still be around.

She wasn't sure about the rest of humanity.

But she would do her best to save them. She was certain Darren would help.

"I'm still alive over here," Jack said. "In case anybody's wondering."

She pulled away from Darren, but he held onto her hand tightly. The possessive glare was back in his eyes.

"Jack needs our help." She pulled on Darren's hand, urging him to follow her.

Jack was sitting on the floor, leaning against the wall. Blood trickled from his nose. He was holding his ribs with one hand, and winced when he coughed. She fell to her knees beside him.

"What do we do?" She looked up at Darren, but Jack waved her off. He was holding a phone in his hand.

"Don't worry about me," he said. "I've already called in reinforcements. And you need to be gone when they get here."

"More fairy-fighters?" Darren said.

Jack laughed, then coughed again. "You could say that."

He pointed to a cabinet and said, "Darren. Top row, far right. You'll find a small iron box. Get it."

Darren hesitated for a moment, but then headed toward the cabinet. Jack turned his head toward Miranda.

"Get my gun," he said. "That one there. It's still loaded with silver."

Miranda let out a frustrated breath. "You can't seriously still be thinking of—"

"If you wouldn't mind," Darren said. "I'd rather have you holding it than him."

That was a good point. She quickly rose to her feet, scanning the ground for the gun. It had fallen a few feet away. By the time she retrieved it, Darren was already squatting next to Jack. She joined them, doing her best to keep the gun out of Jack's reach.

"This is a magical tracker." Jack held up the silver coin briefly. He took the box from Darren and dropped the coin inside, then handed it to Miranda. "Keep it sealed. Iron blocks the Foresters' magic. They won't be able to track you."

"'They?'" Darren said.

Jack nodded. "*Forester* is what we call elves. They tend to live in wooded areas that they've turned into Raths. That's where they're strongest. I snapped a couple of pics of the coin. I'll see what we can find out."

"So suddenly you're helping me?" Darren said. "I thought I was a lost cause."

"I did, too. Until you pulled yourself back from the edge. Twice."

Jack shook his head. "I've fought a couple of rogues in my day. Lost some good friends to them, too. We'd track them as humans and try to kill them before they fully turned. I have *never* seen one come back from a transformation like that."

"Did they even try?" Darren said.

Jack smirked at him. "I never asked."

"That elf—the Forester—he was working really hard to convince me to side with him," Darren said. "Which means werewolves *don't* always side with the fey."

"That's a really good point." Miranda's excitement was building. Jack seemed to be softening toward Darren, and his argument would further their cause. "If all werewolves are vicious killers, why would Forester need to convince Darren to join him?"

"All werewolves *are* vicious killers," Jack said. "It's instinct. It can't be overwritten."

"But maybe it can be redirected," Miranda said. "Forester called the werewolf who bit Darren a traitor. Maybe he was killing the fey instead of humans."

Darren nodded. "Before Niall died, he told me to 'find the nights'. I thought he was talking about a time of day, but now I'm sure he meant the Knights who follow Antares. Like *he* did, from what Forester said. If we can find them, maybe they can help me."

"The Knights of Antares are a legend even among the people who fight fairy tales," Jack said. "We always thought the fey made them up to try to get us to hesitate before killing vampires and werewolves."

"So there might be individuals out there who can control themselves," Miranda said.

"Not that I've ever encountered—before now." Jack smiled at Darren. "I don't know if I can convince my friends to help. But I'm going to try."

Miranda felt as if a weight had been lifted from her shoulders. She let out a sigh, then leaned forward and carefully hugged him. "Thank you."

Jack patted her back. "Thank me when it's done. But in the meantime, you two need to get out of here. If my friends show up and find a werewolf hanging around, they won't give me a chance to explain what's going on. Lay low. I'll call you when I have something."

Darren suddenly stiffened, then said, "We have to go."

Miranda nodded, then stood. She led them through the kitchen. The side door seemed a better bet than either the front or back exits. It was closest to Darren's car, at the least.

Her purse was in a small closet that was on the way. She grabbed it and stuffed Jack's gun and the box that held the coin inside, then looped the strap over her shoulder. They stepped into the warm night air.

She looked at the dent on his front bumper and shivered. So much was happening in such a short span of time.

Darren unlocked the doors and held hers open. She wished she could smile at the gesture, but was too tense.

There could be werewolf hunters around. People who didn't know that Darren wasn't a threat. People he probably actually *was* a threat to.

Just because he wouldn't hurt her, that didn't mean he wouldn't hurt other humans. She didn't deceive herself on that point.

Darren would fight his urges as much as he could, but if someone threatened her… She didn't need her powers to know that it wouldn't end well for them.

She breathed a little easier when they pulled out of the parking lot, and easier still when they had several blocks between them and the restaurant. She took off her purse and put it in the foot well.

"That'll be more useful if you keep it handy," Darren said.

"What, the gun? I'm not going to need it."

He snorted and shook his head. "I wish I had as much faith in myself as you do."

"It's easier with my abilities."

"I suppose so. You should know…" His hands tightened on the steering wheel. "I'm struggling with it. I want to do…things."

They were going to do things, all right. She felt her face flush again. With all the adrenaline from the fight and just…everything…her body reacted to her visions of the two of them having sex as if it was happening in that moment.

"Not those kind of things," he said. "At least, that's not what I was talking about just now."

"I'm confused."

He let out a sigh. "When you have *those* thoughts, I can smell it."

"Oh. Oops." She rolled down her window, letting in the warm night air.

He laughed and shook his head. "It isn't that I mind. It's actually... There isn't a strong enough word for how much I like it. But it makes me want to do 'other' other things. Honestly, those urges are even harder to control than wanting to tear into people."

"Well, we did talk about redirecting your impulses." She grinned at him.

Darren was quiet for a moment, his knuckles still white on the wheel. He cleared his throat, then said, "If it ever comes near to that, use the gun."

"It won't."

"Have you seen every moment of my future?"

"No, but—"

He cut her off. "Redirecting me to kill asshole fairies like that Forester guy is one thing. But I will never force myself on anyone. If that happens, Jack's right. The Darren you knew will be dead."

"It. Won't. Happen." She glared at him, even though he was still looking at the road.

If they were going to get involved, he was going to remain 'the Darren that she knew'. She was sure of it.

"I'm just trying to make sense out of this," he said. "What I'm experiencing and thinking. The feelings I have surrounding you are..."

"Scary?"

"Intense." He sort of half-shrugged. "And yeah. Scary."

"So far, I've only seen you protect me. That doesn't seem so bad."

"You can't hear what I'm thinking." He glanced over at her, his eyes narrowed. "You can't hear what I'm thinking, right?"

She laughed. "That's not among my skill set."

Darren let out a huge sigh. "Thank God."

He cast another glance at her, but was smiling that time.

"Where are we going to go?" she asked.

"I don't know. I can't go back to my apartment. I'm sure it's being watched."

"By who?"

"You heard me talking to Forester about the coins being stolen?"

She thought back over the last few minutes. Amid all the chaos and terror, she vaguely recalled Darren asking about the coins he'd been transporting.

"I remember," she said.

"My partner and I figured out it was an inside job. What I didn't know until now is that the president of the company is behind it."

"Oh."

"She and her right-hand guy are trying to pin this on me."

"And they're working with an elf to do it?" she asked.

"I guess so."

"It won't end well for them," Miranda said.

"I'll be sure of that." His voice was a low growl.

She glanced over at him and saw that his knuckles had turned white again. The wheel was going to shatter if he tightened his grip much more. His brow was lowered over his eyes and a muscle was jumping along his jaw.

She reached over to touch his cheek and he jerked away from her hand. His expression softened as he gazed at her.

"Sorry," he said.

"It's okay. It looked like you were heading into a dark place."

"I live there now." He shook his head and scoffed. "Sorry. I guess I'm still adjusting to my new circumstances."

"I understand. But it's not all going to be darkness. There will be moments of joy and…" She had been about to say, "love", but stopped herself.

Was that where they were heading? Love?

It would explain a lot. She couldn't deny that she felt something toward him. Warmth, tenderness, a connection that was getting stronger the more time she spent with him—the closer on the timeline she came to those visions of them in bed.

"It must be nice to know the future," he said.

"Not really."

"What, because you miss out on being surprised?"

She shook her head, a dull ache spreading through her chest.

"It's lonely."

He glanced at her briefly, but gave her a moment to gather her thoughts. Which was a good thing, because she hadn't meant to open that particular can of worms just yet. There were a slew of things they needed to talk about, and this didn't seem that important.

Then again, if he understood how lonely her abilities made her—how much of a burden they were—maybe it would be easier for him to forgive her when he found out she had let him be attacked.

She shivered at the thought of that conversation.

All of her visions showed them together eventually, so she figured it wouldn't go too terribly. Then again, maybe to reach that future, she shouldn't tell him at all.

He was using her as an anchor. If he stopped trusting her, that might be too much for him to handle. It could push him over the edge.

She shook her head. It wouldn't come to that. She wouldn't let it.

"I didn't mean to broach an uncomfortable subject," Darren said.

"It's okay. I haven't talked about this with anyone since my mom died a few years ago. She was the only one I ever talked to about it, actually."

"That does sound lonely."

"Are you close with your dad?"

Maybe if he thought about the people he loved who were still mortal, it would help him hold on to his humanity. And she just wanted to know more about him.

Darren shrugged. "We get together once a week. I wouldn't necessarily say we're close, though."

"My dad and I were." Her throat became tight and she coughed to clear it. "I was in elementary school when he died."

Darren glanced at her briefly, the most open expression she'd ever seen on his face. It was raw and filled with so much sorrow it made her ache for her own losses.

This was probably not the best topic.

She tried to shift the conversation in a more positive direction. "I haven't been completely alone. Jack has been really supportive. Although, I wish he'd come out and told me he knew about my powers. That would have been nice." She pulled herself back from her rambling, focusing on something she hoped would make him feel better about her situation. "But I had you and Eden to look forward to every night."

He glanced over at her again and opened his mouth as if to say something, then clamped it shut and turned back to the road.

"What?" she said.

"Just… You're saying that your only friends—besides your boss— are two regulars at the restaurant. One of whom is me."

Miranda shrugged. "A lot of people don't socialize much outside of work."

"Yeah, people who work with a team. Who see the same people every day and can form some sort of community. Don't you have anyone else?"

"The closer I am to people, the easier it is to see their futures. Even an accidental touch can show me things that most people wouldn't want me to know. And—being the busybody that I am—if I see something I can probably help them with, I don't sit on it."

Unless helping them means the world might end.

She shook her head, pushing the thought away.

"It's really hard to get close to people under those conditions," she said. "It's just… It's easier to be alone."

"And you've been living like this for years?"

"I met Eden a couple of months before I met you. Things have been better with you guys to talk to."

The energy in the car was getting tense. She didn't understand why he was fixating on this.

Forester had said something about werewolves hating to be alone. She wondered if that was part of why rogues were so dangerous. Still, it was *her* situation, not Darren's.

"It's not so bad." She forced out a laugh, scrambling to try to lighten the mood. "I have one of those huge teddy bears they sell around Valentine's day. She gives great hugs."

Darren braked suddenly, then pulled the car over and parked next to a sidewalk. Miranda hadn't been paying much attention to where they were going. It looked like he had been heading toward downtown. He stopped in front of some dark storefronts.

"What's wrong?" she said.

"I need to touch you."

Chapter Twelve

The look on Miranda's face was about what Darren would expect after his statement. Eyes wide in shock, jaw slightly dropped.

Before the change, he would have thought he'd pushed too far and she was going to tell him to back off. Now, his senses told him anything but.

The sweet, rich scent of her arousal floated to him. He wished her window was up so he could saturate himself in it.

She wanted him. At least physically. Her body's response made his chest feel full and his body surge with energy.

It also made his pants way too tight.

But that wasn't why he had pulled over. The life she was describing would have made him sad before. Now, it made him ache. His head hurt, his heart pounded painfully in his chest, and his skin crawled with the need to hold her.

"You're not alone anymore," he said.

He reached over and cupped her cheek, pulling her closer. He didn't even have to kiss her. He just needed to touch her, to comfort her, to brush his head against hers, push her back in her seat and cover her body with his...

She unhooked her seatbelt and crawled into his lap.

Darren groaned as her weight settled across his legs, her thigh pressing against his erection. He wrapped his arms around her, pulling her closer.

It was awkward as hell, with her legs bent and her feet resting on the cushion of her seat. Straddling him would have been a more comfortable option for both of them. Especially once he unhooked his seatbelt...and his pants.

Then she kissed him, and he didn't give a damn how she sat. He just wanted her as close as he could get her.

Her mouth was warm and soft, her fingers cool as they burrowed through his hair. He slid his hand up along her side, lifting her breast and feeling its soft weight. Her breath hitched as he flicked his thumb across her nipple, and the honey-sweet scent of her intensified.

His dick was so hard. He needed to bury it in her, needed to feel her clench around him.

He moved his hand to her thigh, trying to pull her into his lap, but the emergency brake was in the way. She let out a little grunt, shifting her weight. He barely stifled a growl.

They were wearing too many clothes. And they were too constrictive. He was sure he could tear off her jeans without hurting her. He just needed to get the right angle.

He broke off the kiss as she struggled to reposition herself. Her hands were planted on his shoulders and she shifted again, exposing the softness of her throat.

He had never found throats very appealing before. Seeing her baring that skin to him—that vulnerable part of her body—ratcheted him up even higher.

He leaned forward and nipped at it, grabbing her shirt at her back and crushing her against his chest as he kissed the side of her neck. Her breasts were even softer, and larger than he'd realized. He imagined what they would look like if she rode him while he rocked into her as hard as he could.

"Darren…"

He let out a breath, kissing his way down the center of her chest. "I love it when you say my name like that."

He kissed her breast through her thin shirt, clamping his mouth over her nipple and sucking until the stiff peak pressed against the damp fabric. Her fingers curled in his hair, pressing him closer.

They needed to be in a bed. He pressed her back against the steering wheel to get more room to work…and set off the car's horn.

They both jumped, then stared breathlessly into each other's eyes.

Miranda broke eye contact first. She shifted in his lap and said, "We better go. Someone might call the police."

He tightened his grip on her. "I'll handle them."

"Handle them how?"

He imagined a stranger approaching—then tearing their innards out and throwing them over his car like garlands.

As appealing as that seemed, it was nothing compared to Miranda's warm body in his lap. He wouldn't let anything come between them.

"However it takes," he said.

He leaned in to kiss her again, but she backed away.

"Darren—"

He stifled a growl. Barely.

"Okay, you seem really worked up," she said.

He ran one of his hands down her back, cupping her ass and pressing her closer. "I thought we both were."

"Well, yes. But I have a feeling I'll have an easier time calming myself down."

"So, you don't want to…"

"Oh, I want to. Believe me, I want to do all kinds of things with you." She let out a sigh. "This doesn't seem like the time or the place, though."

Something shifted deep in his guts. Almost painful. He wanted her so much, it actually hurt. His skin started to burn and itch as he pulled his hands away. But she didn't want him as badly. She couldn't. No mere *human* could understand this glorious need.

What the fuck?

He closed his eyes and said, "I think you need to get out of the car."

"You can't be serious."

"Miranda, I can't… I need to calm down, and I can't risk hurting you. I feel like I'm about to burst out of my skin. Given my new circumstances, that's really alarming."

He was taking deep breaths, trying to calm himself down. He'd managed it before, but he hadn't been as worked up.

Well, in a way he had. But then it'd been about fighting and destruction. This had been about forging a connection—a lifeline to his humanity. To *Miranda*.

Her lips pressed against his again and he gasped. She nipped along his jaw, then down to his neck where she kissed and licked his skin.

"What are you doing?" he said.

"Giving you another outlet."

She slid her hand between them, her fingers raking his stomach as she felt for the fastener of his pants. His skin lit up as if her touch was silken fire. She reached into his pants and gripped his shaft.

An explosive burst of air rushed from his chest. He threw his head back against the headrest, eyes clenched shut. She kept kissing his throat as she moved her hand, squeezing him, pumping him.

"Miranda…"

She nipped his ear, then whispered, "You aren't alone either."

Something in him shifted, an energy he couldn't name. He couldn't speak at all, couldn't move. All he could do was feel her touch soaking into him, soul-deep.

She shifted off his lap, giving her more room to work. It meant she had to stop kissing his neck, but his attention was much lower at the moment. He felt her warm breath on his dick right before her lips closed over him.

His body convulsed as she increased the speed of her hand and tightened her mouth around him. His hips bucked against her, desperate for more. The seatbelt locked up, holding him in place. She kept up her pace, her head bobbing on his dick as she hungrily took him in.

Her scent. God, her scent…

He wanted to rip off her clothes and impale her on his shaft. She would be dripping wet, her pussy even hotter and softer than her mouth. He slammed his hands against the ceiling to keep from reaching for her, knowing it wouldn't be safe with him so worked up.

Her tongue pressed even more firmly against him, lips pulling on his skin. The metal of the car's roof started to give as he erupted into her mouth.

She kept up her fast strokes, moving her mouth, sucking him hard, taking everything he had to give. He could hear her heartbeat, the scent of her arousal pushing him even higher. He buried himself in her mouth as deep as she could take him, dick still pulsing as he was finally spent.

He could barely catch his breath. He couldn't think. All he could do was feel. Miranda close to him. An echo of her lips on his body. The warmth she put off. The odd feeling of safety and comfort being near her gave him.

She tucked his dick back into his pants, then fastened them. When he turned toward her, she smiled.

"Better?" she said.

"You have no idea."

He had been so close to going over the edge, but Miranda had brought him back—again. Maybe with her at his side he really could control himself. Maybe she could keep him from becoming the monster he feared.

Her smile broadened. She sat back in her seat, and said, "Then we'd better go."

"Yeah."

He pulled away from the curb, still not sure where to take them. There was a fair-sized park in the Old River district—the Rath—as Miranda and Jack had called it. But that seemed an ideal place for Forester to be hiding out. Darren wasn't up to facing him again just yet.

They could drive outside of town. Getting away from people might help. The only problem with that was that Miranda would be stuck with him. He didn't like the idea of her not having anyone to turn to for help if things went south.

He couldn't believe how well she was handling all of this.

She sure as hell handled me.

He shifted in his seat, his skin still electrified from what she had done to him. *For* him.

A chilling thought struck him. What if she had only done that to protect herself? She could have seen that he was losing it, and used sex to distract him.

He knew she was attracted to him, but things were moving ridiculously fast between them. They'd been thrown into this totally messed up, high stress situation, and it was escalating things.

He knew his change had increased his feelings toward her. The attachment he felt was...primal. But she was still human. What must this be like for her?

"You didn't have to do that." He spoke without thinking. He hoped to God it was true.

"I know. But I *wanted* to."

He let out a huge breath and closed his eyes briefly as relief crashed through him. He shook his head.

"What is it?" she asked.

"I can't stand the thought that you might do something you don't want to do to keep yourself safe. I don't want to turn into the monster Jack described."

"You won't."

"I wish I was as sure as you are."

"It helps that I can see the future."

He laughed.

"I suppose it would." He glanced over at her, wanting her to see how serious he was about his next words. "I meant what I said before, though. If it ever does come to that, I want you to use the gun. Don't have any second thoughts. Never feel bad about it. You'll be doing me a favor."

"It *won't* come to that."

"Miranda, I'm serious. I know you have this…power. But you can't have seen every moment of my future."

Forester had said that Darren was immortal now. That thought hadn't really sunk in. What would he do when Miranda wasn't around anymore to calm him down?

He might learn to control himself eventually, but given how strong his feelings for her already were and the urges he was fighting, he couldn't imagine making it through her death with his humanity intact. Just the thought of it made his guts twist and his skin start to crawl.

"Whatever you're thinking about, you need to stop it," she said. "Unless you're hoping for an encore."

He chuckled before he could stop himself—before the implications of her statement unfurled in his mind.

"Seriously. I don't want you to ever do something you don't want to." He tried to think of an alternative, but was coming up empty. "I would rather die than hurt you."

She sucked in a quick breath, then said, "Stop saying that."

He'd never heard her sound angry.

"I'm sorry, but it's true." He didn't know what else to say or why that had set her off so badly.

She reached into her purse and pulled out the gun, then opened his glove box and dropped it inside. She slammed it shut, then said, "I can take care of myself without anybody getting hurt. I'm done making sacrifices."

He wasn't sure what she meant by that, but it didn't seem like a good idea to press for more information.

She wrapped her arms around her middle. "If I wasn't concerned some kid might find it, I'd throw the stupid gun out the window."

"Wouldn't you know if that was going to happen?"

His lame attempt at humor went unnoticed.

"I can't see everything that's going to happen to everyone," she said.

"I wish you could see more of my future." From the corner of his eye, he saw her glance over at him, but kept his attention ahead. His grip on the wheel tightened. "You keep saying I won't turn into the psychopathic maniac Jack described, but you've also admitted there are gaps in your visions. And you don't know how dark my thoughts have become. How can you really be sure?"

"Because we're going to be together. A couple. And I wouldn't fall in love with that kind of person."

He did look at her then. He couldn't help himself. The sound of the wheels reflecting off the curbs helped him keep the car steady on the road, and his periphery let him see vehicles parked on the street even in the darkness between the streetlights.

Her eyes were relaxed and guileless, her jaw set and lips pressed in a thin line. There was more she knew and wasn't ready to share, but that had been enough of a bombshell.

"Love?" he said.

Her lips pulled into a slow, sultry smile. "Given the things I've seen us do, that's the only conclusion I can reach. Because I sure as heck wouldn't do all that with just anyone."

A deep crimson blush spread up her neck and across her cheeks. He really wanted to pull the car over again. Instead, he looked back out the front windshield.

Jack had said a werewolf could shake off being hit, but Miranda was still human. A crash could hurt or kill her.

Darren couldn't even think about that. But he would have to keep her mortality in mind. Especially if they were going to be lovers—to fall in love.

He'd been in relationships, but he'd never fallen in love before. It had always been too easy to walk away from his girlfriends or let them walk away from him when he wasn't attentive enough.

Miranda was different.

He could easily see himself falling for her, wanting to spend the rest of his life with her. But her life would be short. Measured in human years. Her presence was already keeping him stable. What would happen when she passed?

"You're doing it again," she said. "Thinking about something you shouldn't."

"I was wondering what I'll do without you."

"If I have anything to say about it, you'll never have to find out."

"Do your powers make you immortal like me? Because if they don't, you might not have much control over that."

"My powers aren't going to keep me alive. You are."

"How?"

"You're going to turn me."

Darren's stomach felt like it fell through the bottom of the car and then was run over by the back tires. How could she say that so flippantly?

"No." He shook his head. "No way."

"It's going to happen. And with everything I *have* seen, I want it to."

"You don't know what you're saying. The thoughts I have, the urges I'm fighting—"

"Can be dealt with pretty easily by us being...affectionate."

Affectionate? If the hummer she'd given him in the car was what she saw as *affection*, he couldn't imagine what actual sex with her would be like.

Actually, he could imagine it. His dick started to harden as scenarios played through his mind. He had a big bed at his place, soft sheets, a two-person tub they could soak in before, during, and-or after.

The kitchen island was pretty spacious, too.

"Okay, I like that look," she said. "Whatever you're thinking about now is much better than those other thoughts."

"Oh, I'm not sure you'd agree if you saw—"

"Me straddling you while you cup my breasts, holding me up? Or the time you'll bend me over the foot of my bed and... Well, you know."

His dick was at full attention, straining against his pants. He wished she had said something about the backseat of his car. He'd pull over immediately to bring that vision to life.

"What if I turn you and you have a violent episode when I'm not around?" he said.

Hell, what if *he* had an episode and *she* wasn't around to help him through it? It was getting easier for her to bring him back from the edge, but he was getting there more quickly and often.

"I'll duck into a broom closet or something and take care of business."

He turned to stare at her again.

"What?" She shrugged. "As if you've never done that before."

He laughed and shook his head, focusing back on the road. "I don't need your gift to know one thing about our future together."

"What's that?"

"It'll never be boring."

Chapter Thirteen

Hearing Darren laugh was one of the best sounds Miranda could remember. That he could do so even given his circumstances was even more reassuring than what her visions showed her.

She could tell that he was scared about the changes happening to him—as anyone would be. She was absolutely terrified.

Beyond the maybe-zombie apocalypse, her own impending transformation, and knowing that fairies were a very real threat, she was already falling in love with Darren. She could feel it—a weakness opening up in her heart, making her vulnerable to pain and loss.

"I really wish this car had a bigger back seat," Darren said.

"Why?"

She looked over her shoulder into the tiny bench in the back, then to Darren. He shifted in his seat. Her gaze dropped to his lap and the bulge straining against his pants.

If she hadn't been thinking such maudlin thoughts, she'd be all over him again. But her heart felt tender, and she didn't have it in her to… have him in her. She let out a nervous laugh at her horrible joke.

"What can I say?" He shrugged and smiled a little sheepishly. "You have a profound effect on me."

Will shutting him down now set him off?

She shook her head, refusing to see him that way or make any decisions at all based on fear. At least where Darren was concerned.

He had been so insistent that she only do what she wanted to do. He needed to get it through his head that she was actually attracted to him. Powers, werewolves, fairies, whatever else aside, she'd spent plenty of time indulging in carnal fantasies featuring Darren over the weeks they'd known each other.

If he kept thinking their feelings were just a byproduct of unfortunate circumstances, it would color their entire relationship. She could give in to the same doubts, if she let herself. For all she knew, he'd feel the same level of attraction to any woman now that he'd changed.

Crap. She really wished she hadn't thought of that. An altogether new vulnerability came to her awareness. Another chance to be hurt.

Darren was gorgeous. And yeah, she was pretty, but not in the supermodel way most guys liked. She was short and round and her cheekbones didn't look like they could cut glass.

Plus, she was a waitress, barely eking out a living, while he was a successful private security...guy. Whatever they were called.

She was so used to focusing on the end result. She never spent time thinking about the origin points, aside from strategizing which path would lead her to the best outcome.

She knew eventually she'd be a werewolf, and she and Darren would be in the same pack. What she didn't know was anything about the others. For all she knew, the other five were females—his many mates.

That wasn't a future she could be comfortable with. She wanted a one-on-one commitment based on mutual feelings, not a curse-based attraction heightened by proximity.

"What's wrong?" he said.

"Before things go any further, I have to know something."

"What?"

"Did you ever think about me? Before tonight. Did you ever have fantasies that involved me?"

His eyes widened and his jaw went slack. He stammered and looked away, his cheeks actually turning pink.

She'd made a werewolf blush. Miranda wanted to laugh again, but her question was too important.

"Of course I did," he said.

"There's no 'of course' about it. I need to know if what's happening between us is just a side-effect of your curse."

"Miranda..." He shook his head. "I don't really like eggs all that much."

"What does that have to do with anything?"

He sighed, but the corner of his mouth quirked up in a smile. A dimple appeared in his cheek.

"The first night I stopped by the Red Thread, it was because it was the only restaurant that was open," he said. "I ordered some skillet meal thing, and you chatted with me. I didn't come back the next day for the eggs, even though I order the same thing every time. I never really looked at the menu afterwards. I didn't care what I ate. I just wanted to see you. To spend time with you."

"Oh." It was the only word she could manage. The rest seemed to stick in her throat.

She'd been focusing on physical attraction. What he was describing sounded deeper. But then, she never let herself dream too big.

When she'd thought of him, the farthest she'd ever let her fantasies go was dinner, a movie, and then taking him back to her place. She'd loved spending time with him, but had thought nothing could ever come of it. It'd been too painful for her to dream about anything more.

"Scott is my best friend as well as my partner," Darren said. "We go to lunch together just about every work day. We used to go to dinner a lot, too, or out for drinks with the guys." He chuckled. "Ever since I started going to The Red Thread every night, I've had to come up with so many excuses. I thought about inviting him along, but then realized I wanted you all to myself."

There was so much about what he was sharing that she loved. Hearing about his life, his friends, his work. Knowing that he wanted to be with her before this all began. It was almost too much to process. She'd been part of his life without even realizing it.

"Wait a minute," she said. "I don't work every night."

Darren looked chagrined when he smiled. "I know. But it would have been weird if I only showed up when you were working. I didn't want to seem like a stalker. I figured if I went every night, people would just think I was a regular if word got back to you. Even when you weren't there, I thought of you. I couldn't help it."

"I… I don't know what to say."

"I was working up to asking you out. I wish I had before all of this happened."

She laughed and shook her head. "Before all this happened, I would have said no."

His face fell, then darkened. Her heart leapt to her throat—not because she was afraid, but because she realized that she'd hurt him.

She reached across the space between them, resting her hand on his thigh. His breath hitched.

"That's not what it sounds like," she said. "I would have wanted to say yes. More than anything. But my powers…"

Tears welled up in her eyes and her throat started to pinch shut. Dammit, she needed to fix this. She closed her eyes and coughed to clear her throat, then forced the words through.

"My powers make it dangerous for me to get close to people. I couldn't risk it. I wouldn't risk you."

She felt like a crack opened along her heart.

She had finally given in and taken the risk when this all started. She had touched him. And then she had sent him to his death. She had thought her worst fear had been realized.

And now he was here with her—alive, strong, *immortal*. But he was still so raw. He needed all the help he could get to hold on to his humanity.

Would finding out what she had done send him over the edge? Would she lose him after starting to connect in a way she had never let herself dream was possible?

"I don't understand how it would have been dangerous for me for us to become closer," he said.

"Because it would have made you another resource for my powers to draw on. If you were part of my life, you'd be written into my visions."

"That doesn't sound so bad."

"Until something comes up like that accident you pulled me from." It felt like so long ago, even though it had only been… Less than two days? That didn't seem possible.

"You had a vision about your accident?"

"Not *my* accident. Not originally." Her insides felt hollow as she remembered. "It was supposed to be the minivan that was behind me in the intersection. The one with the kids and the soccer mom."

Darren looked over at her, his eyes wide. She couldn't hold his gaze. She hugged herself as she looked out the window.

"I went through as many versions as I could handle, but the only way I could save everybody was to be the one who was hit."

"I can't believe you did that," he said.

"I was pretty sure I'd be okay."

"Pretty sure?"

He turned back to the road, his hands clenching the wheel. She heard a metallic clink.

"Darren, you need to ease up on—"

His skin had turned gray. A muscle was leaping on his cheek, which was…longer than she remembered. His cheekbones were higher and more prominent.

"It wasn't an *accident*," he said. "My boss and her goon set it up as a diversion so they could steal those goddamned coins."

Her stomach sank. How could they risk people's lives like that? They had almost killed a family. They had almost killed *her*. No wonder Darren was freaking out.

She started to unfasten her seat belt, planning to climb onto his lap if she had to. She was already reaching for him when he shook his head.

"If I'm going to live with this, I need to learn to control it," he said.

He took a few deep breaths, blowing the air out forcefully. His skin gradually turned pink again.

Miranda laughed. "That was amazing! How did you do that?"

"I thought of you. The future you say we're going to have. Getting to spend eternity with you."

"Oh." She tried to laugh it off, to shut down the reaching of her heart toward him. "I didn't know I was that good at blowjobs."

He let out a tiny snort, but shook his head. "Well, first of all, you are. But that's not what I was thinking about. I wasn't kidding when I said I loved spending time with you at the restaurant. You're quirky and fun and make me look at things differently. You care about people enough to put your own life on the line. I was thinking that I get to keep you safe—I *need* to keep you safe. And losing control wasn't going to help with that."

Her eyes filled with tears. They spilled down her cheeks as she clenched her eyes shut. No one had ever said anything like that to her before.

She needed to tell him. The truth had a way of getting out. And he deserved to know. The longer she waited, the worse it would be. She just had to time it right.

"I didn't mean to make you cry," he said.

"I'm sorry." She wiped the tears from her cheeks. "I just wasn't expecting that."

"What were you expecting?"

"From what you and Jack have told me about werewolves, I kind of thought your attraction would be more physical. When I asked about fantasies before, I was just thinking of sex."

He let out a huge laugh, smiling broadly enough that both dimples showed on his cheeks. "Is that all you ever think about?"

"It's all I felt *safe* letting myself think about."

"Wait a minute." He put on an expression like he was thinking really hard. "So, while you were wrapping silverware and glancing over at me..."

She started to nod. "I was usually thinking about you bending me over the counter or knocking everything off one of the tables or—"

He shifted in his seat, his smile fading. "I really wish I had known that sooner."

"I couldn't have told you."

"I still don't get that."

"Everybody dies. Everybody. And I can't... I can't watch people I care about..."

He reached across and grabbed her hand, squeezing it tight. His skin was warm.

"Don't," he said. "You don't need to worry about that with me. I'm stronger now, and... Hell, I can't believe it, but I guess I'm immortal. And I can control this. For that future with you, I will."

"Does that mean you're feeling better about turning me?"

"I don't think *better* is the right word for how I feel, but I'm going to do it."

Forever with Darren. She couldn't think of a better future. They'd find the Knights, learn how to use their abilities to help people. Heck, with a whole pack of super-powered werewolves to help her with her visions, she could make a real change. Starting with preventing that apocalypse.

Well, starting after...

"There's no way your boss is watching my apartment too, right?" she said.

"I can't see why she would."

"Then we should go there next."

"I don't know if I'm ready to change you yet. I mean, the full moon is so close, and we haven't figured out what that will be like and how to keep people safe."

"Relax," she said, casting what she hoped was a sultry smile at him. "That's not what I'm planning."

"Oh." He laughed. "Damn, that *is* all you think about."

Chapter Fourteen

Awkward barely scratched the surface of how Darren felt following Miranda into her apartment building. What they'd done in the car had been passionate and intense—not really thought out. This... This was purposeful.

It had been a long time since he'd gone home with anyone.

The building looked like it was over a hundred years old. The bricks were chipped, the stone worn from rain, and the stairs creaked loudly as they headed to the second floor. Every noise made him wince.

There were already newspapers laying on some of the welcome mats in front of people's doors, and the sun had risen before they'd arrived. Darren was afraid one of her neighbors would poke their head out and see him following Miranda with his raging hard-on. There was no point in even trying to hide it anymore. At least it didn't seem to be bothering her.

She opened the door to her place and walked inside. "Come on in."

He stepped across the threshold, wiping his hand on his pant leg. She seemed as nervous as he was. Her heart was beating fast, and her blood was pooling in her face and neck and...other places.

He could smell a mix of fear and arousal from her again. He didn't know if it was just anticipation about what they were about to do, or something else—something he was almost too afraid to ask about.

Finding out that she had risked her own life to save that family had nearly set him over the edge again. It was the first time that he had *wanted* to become like the thing that had turned him. Niall.

Darren couldn't believe how strong the urge had been to change—then track down Blake Morrison and Mrs. Ford and rip them to pieces.

But even more than that, Darren wanted to stay with Miranda. Both in the moment and in the future. If he killed someone who was innocent or coerced into action, he knew it would taint his relationship with Miranda forever.

Before he did anything, he needed the whole story. He had to stay in control. He couldn't risk hurting anyone.

Yet.

Once he had control of his powers, he was already forming plans for what to do with everyone involved in the theft. First on the list was to track down Forester and wring his neck.

The dark urges were getting easier to deal with. But they were still there.

"It's a nice place," he said.

"It's nice enough."

She locked her door and slowly slid the chain in place, keeping her back to him. Was he starting to scare her after all?

"I want you to know that I'm getting better at dealing with this," he said.

She turned around and smiled at him. "I'm glad."

"I know we've already…done things," he said. "But that doesn't mean anything else has to happen."

"I get that there's no *have to* here, but I think it'll be safer for us both if we don't fight our attraction."

"Safer?"

Her heartbeat picked up again as she took a deep breath. He thought she was about to say something, but she was keeping herself from speaking her mind.

"Miranda, you don't have to be afraid of me."

"I know. And you don't have to be afraid of me, either."

He laughed. How could he ever be afraid of her? She was human. She'd even left Jack's gun in the car. He could rip her to shreds without —

He shook his head, forcing the thought from his mind, the image of her in his bloody claws. There was no way he would ever hurt her.

But now he knew an important truth. On some level, part of him saw her as prey.

Only for now.

He reminded himself that she was going to become like him. The thought of eternity with her was compelling.

The more time that passed since his attack, the easier it was for him to handle the disturbing thoughts his new nature presented to him. If *he* could handle it, so could she. He just needed to be careful with her in the meantime. And he needed to turn her as soon as possible.

She closed the distance between them, grabbing his face and pulling him down for a kiss. He responded immediately, instinctively.

One hand went to the back of her head and the other her lower back, pulling her up against him. She wrapped her arms around his neck, meeting his tongue as he thrust it into her mouth. He slid his hands lower, cupping her backside and pressing her hips against his, grinding his erection against her heat.

When he shifted his kisses to her neck, nipping and suckling the skin, she groaned the word, "Bedroom."

He lifted her up off her feet. She wrapped her legs around his waist, smiling as he walked them into her room.

This was his future. It began now.

He wanted to set her on the bed and melt into her. He wouldn't even have to bother with a condom after what Jack had said.

He did need to strip off his clothes. His clothes…that were covered in dirt, grime, and his blood from when he'd still been human.

He noticed a bathroom connected to her bedroom, and turned toward it instead.

"Where are you taking me?" she said.

The breathless quality to her voice made him want to growl in triumph. Was that even a thing?

"The bathroom," he said. "I need a shower."

"That's a good idea. I stink like diner."

"You smell amazing."

She snorted, then nuzzled his neck. "You're biased."

"You smell like sex and honeysuckle."

"I've…never heard that before. But I have to also smell like grease and bleach."

"There's that, too."

She laughed as she slid down his body, keeping as much contact as possible. She leaned back a bit and pulled her shirt over her head, revealing her olive-gold skin. Her bra pushed her generous breasts up into soft mounds that he couldn't resist kissing.

He ran his hands over the smooth skin at her sides, lifting her breasts so he could suck more of them into his mouth, gently biting and then kissing them. She burrowed her fingers through his hair, groaning as he kneaded their heavy weight.

He couldn't take anymore. He lifted her from her feet and set her on the counter next to the sink. She wrapped her legs around his waist, pulling him close, opening herself for him to grind his dick against her.

She felt so good, even through their clothes. He could feel her heat, her wetness. Fucking her would be heaven.

She grabbed his hair again, turning him to face her. He'd never had a lover so sure of what she wanted, so willing to let him know. He gladly captured her lips again, delving into her mouth with his tongue.

Her legs tightened, increasing the pressure of their hips pushing together. He released her mouth and latched onto her neck, suckling the skin hard. She let out a groan, her hips moving against his.

His fingers curled against her back, digging into her soft flesh—but not too much. He had to be careful not to hurt her. He had to hold back.

Apparently, she didn't feel the same way.

For a moment, her pulse seemed to pause, then it pounded through her body. He could feel it in her pussy, her muscles clenching, reaching for something that was so close, but out of reach.

He thrust against her harder and faster, wanting to make this release as spectacular as he possibly could. She cried out his name, nearly pushing him over his own edge, but he held on. The next time he came with her, he was going to be buried deep in her flesh.

And it was going to be soon.

Her body went limp against his and he paused. He wanted to see her face after what they'd just shared.

A soft smile curved her lips and her eyes were heavy-lidded. She blinked a few times, as if she was disoriented, then she gave a brief laugh—almost a giggle.

"That sort of took me by surprise," she said.

"Don't worry, it happens to everyone."

She laughed harder, burying her face against his chest. The sound delighted him on yet another emotional level he had never reached. He was starting to acclimate, though. And he wanted more.

"Maybe I should have gone with, 'What, you didn't see that coming?'" he said.

She groaned, but laughed again.

He kissed the side of her head, then nuzzled her hair. He wanted to give his body a chance to calm down a little, but not completely. He wanted this to last. He wanted *them* to last. Forever.

He pulled back and cradled her face in his hands, his chest filling with a pressure that was similar to the urge to change, but much more pleasant. It was like his heart was trying to shift into her body. He didn't bother trying to fight it.

"I have to tell you something," she said. "Before anything else happens between us."

What could she possibly have to talk about during this perfect moment? And she didn't look happy. The nervous expression from earlier was creeping back onto her features.

"Okay."

She gripped his wrists and gently moved his hands away from her face, placing them on the counter on either side of her hips.

"Sometimes my visions call for sacrifices. Like me taking the place of that family in the accident."

His body tensed at the thought. From what she had told him already, her powers had made her so lonely. He wanted to kiss her and tell her that was all behind her. Something in the way she was looking at him made him wait.

"Sometimes I don't know what the sacrifices will be," she said. "Sometimes I only know the consequences of action...or inaction."

"That seems pretty vague."

"It can be. But I only receive visions that are really important. And I usually know what I need to do to save the most people."

"That's a lot of responsibility."

Her eyes filled with tears and she nodded. "But I can help people. More people than you can imagine, Darren. The vision I had of the apocalypse could affect the entire world. Billions of people suffering, dying..."

"You said you'd stopped it."

"I said I *think* I've stopped it. At least, I took the first step."

His skin started to crawl. He needed to change her, to give her the strength and speed he possessed. To give her a chance to survive *any* future ahead of them.

At the same time, her expression was making him uneasy. He already knew she was willing to risk her own life to help a handful of people. What would she do to protect billions?

"What did you do?" he said.

"It's what I *didn't* do." Her eyes were sparkling with unshed tears. "I didn't warn you."

"About what?"

"What would happen if you got out of your car. About…the attack."

"The…"

The attack. Being bitten by a werewolf.

She had seen it, had known it was going to happen—and she hadn't warned him. She hadn't even tried to explain, to prepare him for what was about to happen.

"Wait. You didn't know that werewolves were real until Jack told you. Until *I* told you." He voice was rising, but he couldn't bring himself to stop it.

"I know."

"What did you think was going to happen to me? What exactly did you see?"

She closed her eyes and the tears spilled over.

"I saw a giant animal bite your arm and take you to the ground." Her voice hitched. "I heard you scream and saw…blood."

His heart started to pound. "Did you even know I was going to make it?"

When she opened her eyes, he saw the truth in them. She hadn't known he would be okay.

She sent me to my death.

And the coldness in her gaze made it clear…she would do it again.

His blood was rushing in his ears. His fingers itched and his skin prickled.

He'd thought they were connecting, forming a bond unlike anything he'd ever been able to experience before. He'd thought she valued him, but she had thrown his life away.

He stepped back.

She followed, sliding from the sink to stand before him.

"Think of what was at stake," she said.

All he could think about was letting his claws burst out of his fingertips and flaying her neck. She would see blood then, too.

He grabbed his head and pressed his temples, as if he could squeeze the violent thoughts out of his mind. She had said something important. *Stakes.*

She had asked him to think of what was at stake. Billions of lives.

Dark thoughts rose up in him.

It shouldn't have mattered.

She'd said she already cared about Darren. That they would fall in love and be together forever.

It shouldn't have mattered that she *might* save billions of lives by letting him die. She should have chosen him.

"Please, Darren. Hold on. Please don't change."

"What *the fuck* do you care?"

He never swore at people.

This isn't me.

"I do care," she said. "Whether you believe me or not. Letting you go was one of the hardest things I've ever done."

He snorted and shook his head. She actually reached for him, putting her traitorous hands on his chest. As angry as he was, he still felt it jolt through his body. He still wanted her.

"I'm not asking you to forgive me or even to trust me," she said. "I'm asking you to let me help you."

Was she seriously still thinking something would happen between them after this? Had that been what she was doing all along? Working him up, getting him attached, just so she could safely drop this bombshell on him and not get killed from it?

His skin heated as rage swept over him. Maybe he *should* fuck her first. He could always rip her throat out later.

No... No. What the hell am I thinking?

He remembered Jack's warning. And that Miranda had left her gun in his glove box—far out of reach.

She went on, oblivious to the danger she was in. "The longer you hold on, the greater the chance you'll make it through this. And I need you to make it through this."

He clamped down his muscles, forcing himself to stay in place. He wouldn't let himself touch her. If it came to that, he would throw himself out a window to get away from her and keep her safe. But he still had to know where he stood with her.

She had been his anchor when he needed one most—the last thing connecting him to his humanity. He thought they were building a bridge to a new future together. A life beyond his wildest dreams. He tried to hold his words in, to make them gentler, but he was too raw.

"What, so you can use me as a pawn later? Send me out to die—again—if one of your visions calls for it?"

Her breath rushed out and her shoulders curled over her heart as if she'd been struck. Tears came from her eyes in a steady stream.

"It won't come to that," she said. "I've seen us in the future. I've seen us happy."

"After this?"

"I...don't know. Every action has consequences. Every choice. I may have changed things by telling you."

His voice rose even further. "You were thinking of *not* telling me?"

How the hell could they have a relationship if she was willing to use him like this? She couldn't keep something this important to herself if they were going to be together.

He wanted a partner. He wanted a...mate. He'd thought she wanted the same—not a tool she could use to shape the future as she saw fit.

"I've been doing everything I can to help you hold on to your humanity," she said. "I thought we were connecting enough that it would be safe to tell you before we took things to the next level."

"The level above selling me out, lying to me, stringing me along, and using me?"

"Stringing you along? I meant everything I said."

"You can give it a rest," he said. "I can control it now. You don't have to pretend to be interested in me to keep yourself safe."

He hoped.

"I'm not pretending. I never was. I may not have told you everything, but what I did tell you is the truth. You have to believe me."

"I don't have to believe anything you say."

Her face was twisted in such pain, he could barely stand it.

"Darren, please… We're friends."

Friends. That was all he was to her? She was so much more to him. Already so much more.

He didn't know what they were. 'Friends' had left the realm of possibility the first time they'd kissed.

"We are not friends," he said.

"Oh."

Her tears stopped. He might have thought that was a sign that his suspicions were right and she didn't give a damn about him and was using him, except the light seemed to leave her eyes as well. He felt more than half-sick, his heart a leaden weight in his chest.

She sniffed, letting her hands drop to her sides. She looked around the room as someone who was shell-shocked might. Then she bent down to pick up her shirt and pulled it back on.

"Miranda—"

Before he could say more, his phone made a trilling sound. Scott's ringtone.

It broke through the last of his rage, reminding him of his normal life outside of this madness and uncertainty. He still had Scott—and a case to work. But first, he needed to sort this out with Miranda. He needed to get his head out of his ass.

Darren pulled out his phone and hit the button to ignore the call.

She looked hollowed out. Their argument had done that to her. *He* had done that to her.

He'd managed not to hurt her physically, but emotionally…

If she doesn't give a damn about me, why does she look gutted?

His phone beeped to let him know Scott had left voicemail.

"It's okay." Her voice was flat. Emotionless.

Maybe taking a minute to cool off would be good for both of them.

Too bad Darren hadn't thought of that before he unloaded on her.

He hit play on the voicemail and held the phone up to his ear.

At first, all he heard was Scott breathing. Then he spoke. With each word, Darren's heart sank deeper.

"It was my mom," Scott said. "She and Morrison are working with the blond guy. I can't fucking believe they set you up."

More heavy breaths. Scott had a temper he had never really tried to control, no matter how much Darren encouraged him to. If Scott had been the one who was bitten, Darren didn't want to think of the carnage that would have ensued.

He couldn't believe he was grateful for anything about what had happened to him. But yeah, that.

And maybe the fact that billions of lives might be saved because of it?

Yeah. That, too.

He had tried to hold that thought in mind while arguing with Miranda.

Not hard enough.

"Fuck it," Scott said. "I'm dealing with this now."

The message ended.

Chapter Fifteen

"Shit."

Darren's expletive pulled Miranda back to her senses a bit. She still felt disconnected from her body, from life, from reality. She had been on the cusp of being part of something, of having a family again, and it had been torn away.

She shouldn't have told him. But she couldn't *not* tell him.

Now he was staring at his phone, looking about as angry with it as he had been at her moments ago.

She had never been so frightened. Not for her life—she somehow knew that he would never hurt her. But for her future. For *their* future. A future she had probably destroyed.

Darren punched a number into his phone, the grim set of his lips pulling into a deeper frown as he held it back up to his ear. His eyebrows were furrowed, lowering like a storm cloud descending around them.

He could still lose himself. Now she had no way of helping him pull back from the edge.

She was having trouble caring. All she felt was…numb.

Eden was gone. After the mess Miranda had made of her relationship with Darren, she doubted either of them would end up being turned. That meant not only had she lost Eden as a friend, she had ruined the only chance Eden had at living.

One life shouldn't matter so much. But Miranda was tired of making that choice. She didn't want to feel anything anymore. Didn't want to hurt.

One life for many is a fair deal. Her mother had drilled that into her. *Always be thinking of the greater good. Always think of the endgame.*

The endgame for Miranda was isolation. No wonder oracles secluded themselves. Forming attachments to people, letting herself care about them, only led to pain.

She needed to pull out of this. If she didn't, she wasn't sure what would happen the next time a major sacrifice came up. She wasn't sure she'd even bother trying to save anyone.

She shook her head. Too many lives were at stake. She would rededicate herself to her visions, to her calling.

She could team up with Jack and his crew—keeping them at a safe emotional distance, since she'd undoubtedly have to send them to their deaths eventually. She could use her powers to make a difference until the universe mercifully let her off the hook.

"Come on, Scott. Pick up." Darren covered his eyes with his hand. His skin had lost some of its color, but wasn't the gray cast she had noticed when he seemed to be fighting a change.

Concern edged into the corners of her awareness. She tried to steel herself against it, but it was hard. She cared about Darren more than she could admit to herself.

"What's wrong?" she said.

He lowered his hand and sighed. There was enough pain in his expression to pierce the coldness surrounding her heart. It was still reaching for him.

Idiot heart.

"Scott found out his mom was involved in the theft," Darren said. "He's going to confront her."

"Oh."

"He's not answering his phone. He must be with them right now."

"What can I do?" The words slipped out before she could stop them.

She wasn't sorry.

Darren shook his head. "If Scott was only dealing with Mrs. Ford and Morrison, it wouldn't be a big deal. But if Forester is there... Scott has no idea what he's getting himself into. Hell, I barely understand it."

"Fairies can't be trusted," Miranda said. "They make deals to see how badly they can screw people over. It's a game to them."

There was something in his expression—a softening, a look akin to regret—that made her feel hope, as stupid as that was. She wanted to believe that the future she had seen of them being together was still possible, even though she was terrified to believe it.

"Do you know where they are?" she asked.

"He didn't say. Can you read my future again? It might let you see where I'm about to go."

"It doesn't work that way."

"Please. Can you try?" He held his hand out to her.

She didn't want to read him. When she did, she'd know for sure if she had destroyed their chance for happiness.

Maybe that would be a blessing though. She could move on with her life on the new path that was before her.

Either way, they needed to help Scott. If this was the only way to do it, she wouldn't balk. She reached out and clasped Darren's hand.

The vision hit her immediately.

She saw a blond man standing with his back to her. It seemed like he could be Scott. He had the same build as the man she'd met after her accident.

But he was…wrong. She understood why when he turned around.

His skin was peeling in patches, part of an ear was gone, and there was a hole in his cheek big enough to show the teeth beneath. Scott reached out to her, opening his mouth to say something, but only a breathy groan escaped.

"Miranda. Miranda!"

Darren was holding her by her arms, crushing her against his chest. Her face was wet and her throat hurt.

She didn't care about their fight or that she'd torpedoed their future. She did care that there was a freaking zombie apocalypse coming.

"Christ, are you okay?" Darren said. "You started screaming."

"I didn't stop it," she said. "I didn't stop it."

"Stop what?"

"The apocalypse. The zombies."

His eyes widened. Once upon a time—two days ago—he probably would have thought she was nuts. Now she saw her own fear reflected in his face.

"You're kidding, right?" Darren said.

She pushed away from him. What was one ruined relationship next to this?

Eden would die, and Miranda would be devastated. But at least she could make sure Eden found peace. That all of the dead would find peace.

Miranda would make sure no one came back like Scott in her vision. She had to find a way to stop it. She had seen so many zombie movies...

The vision was the kick in the butt she needed. She couldn't believe she had let herself get so worked up over one man. Her heart clenched at the thought, but she shut down the pain mercilessly.

If they weren't going to fight this together, fine. But she wasn't going to just give up and let the world fall into that darkness.

Normally, her visions of the future wouldn't change unless she took some action herself. She'd thought letting Darren become a werewolf had somehow stopped the apocalypse. Or maybe it was them becoming a couple, since that was the only thing she thought her actions had changed.

That didn't seem possible, though. How could them falling in love prevent something this big?

"Listen to the voicemail message again," she said. "See if you can hear anything."

"You were kidding about the zombies, right?"

"I wish I was. I'll call Jack on the way. We need to get to Scott quickly."

Darren stepped back and let her cross in front of him to exit the small room. She'd half-hoped he would stop her. Maybe pull her into an embrace and kiss her and apologize for the terrible things he'd said.

Forget about her heart. *She* was the idiot.

She crushed the hope, stiffening her shoulders as she headed toward the door. There were more important things to worry about.

Darren followed her into the living room, pressing his phone against his ear. He held his hand against the other, blocking out the ambient noise around them. Miranda stood still, even holding her breath. She didn't want to distract him or accidentally cover any sounds that might give them a clue about where Scott was.

"I don't hear anything," Darren said. "Nothing that could tell me where he is."

He closed his eyes, his nostrils flaring as his breath quickened. She took a step toward him, but stopped herself. That wasn't going to work anymore.

Her stomach felt like it was twisting around on itself. She hadn't moved toward him to stop him from changing. She had wanted to comfort him. She still did.

"Maybe the nothing is the clue," she said.

His eyes snapped open. Glittering lights scattered across the pale gray of his irises. She tried to ignore it.

"At this time of day, would there be sounds at the office?" she said. "People walking around, shuffling papers, talking?"

"Yeah, there would."

"So he's not there. Where else might he be?"

"I don't know," he growled.

"Think, Darren. You said they're probably all together. Where would your boss meet with Forester?"

His face lit up. "I know where they are."

As he passed her, he reached out and grabbed her arm, pulling her along behind him. She wasn't sure if he even realized what he'd done.

It wasn't a forceful grip. There was nothing threatening about it. He had reached for her on instinct, his excitement probably making him forget how mad at her he was. He'd remember soon enough. She grabbed her purse as she passed the table near the door where it sat.

The hallway was blocked by the last person Miranda expected to see standing off against them. Her landlady.

"You let her go, you oaf!" Mrs. Elroy was holding a baseball bat as if she was about to take a swing at Darren.

He looked too startled to process what he was seeing.

Mrs. Elroy was even shorter than Miranda, with dyed red hair in short processed curls all over her head. Her green eyes were magnified to a huge degree by her thick glasses. She was wearing a bathrobe covered in a faded floral pattern, along with olive-green slippers.

Miranda almost laughed at the absurd picture before her. The teeny, ancient woman was trying to take on a werewolf. With a baseball bat.

"It's okay." Miranda tried to shrug off Darren's grip and step in front of him, but he wouldn't let her. Did he still feel protective of her?

She thought that had ended with their fight.

"I've seen my fill of guys like you," Mrs. Elroy said. "You let her go right now."

Wow. Miranda had to admit, the woman sounded intimidating. She was touched that Mrs. Elroy was willing to go to bat for her. Literally.

Darren dropped Miranda's arm and held his hands up. "I'm not a threat."

That's a bald-faced lie.

Miranda finally managed to get between the pair. "Darren is a friend."

Another lie.

She fought back the tears that tried to fill her eyes. If Mrs. Elroy saw that Miranda was upset, it would be harder to defuse the situation.

Mrs. Elroy didn't look convinced. "I heard you scream. If most of the tenants weren't already at work, everyone would have heard it. And I can see you've been crying."

She glared at Darren like she wanted to gut him. Miranda had no idea her landlady was so protective—or so fierce.

"I had a nightmare," Miranda said.

That was close enough to the truth.

Darren rested his hands on her shoulders. Mrs. Elroy's expression softened and she lowered her bat. Miranda wished she could see Darren's face. The shift in her landlady's demeanor was huge.

"Oh," Mrs. Elroy said. "Must've been a doozy."

"It was." Another truth.

Mrs. Elroy grinned. "Well, I'm glad you've got your *friend* to take your mind off it. Go out and get some fresh air. Maybe come back and…" She let out a huge laugh and grinned. "Well…just remember, the walls are pretty thin here. Ceilings and floors, too."

Miranda felt her eyebrows hike up her forehead. Darren's grip on her shoulders tightened. She could feel the tension radiating off of him.

Mrs. Elroy turned around, still chuckling, and headed down the stairs. The moment she was out of sight, Darren brushed past Miranda.

"Come on," he said. "We have to hurry."

Whatever Mrs. Elroy had seen in Darren's expression, it was gone, along with the moment. Miranda followed him out of the building.

Chapter Sixteen

The park in the Old River district was twenty minutes from Miranda's apartment—if Darren had been bothering with the posted speed limits. He wasn't.

He was terrified they wouldn't get there in time. Scott was Darren's closest friend. Honestly, he was Darren's only friend, aside from Miranda.

Darren wasn't sure if she'd call him that anymore. He wasn't sure he deserved her to.

She was holding the grab bar above her door, her other hand clutching her purse to her lap. He could smell her anxiety, but she hadn't said a word about his driving. She had gasped a few times, but that was it.

After what he had said to her, he was shocked she was still willing to help him. Maybe she was caught up in preventing the zombie apocalypse she had mentioned.

He couldn't believe that was real. It had to be a metaphor or something.

Like his turning into a werewolf was a metaphor for letting his temper loose on her earlier.

If he did let himself believe her vision—and if he was honest with himself, he wasn't in a position not to—he also had to face the fact that Miranda really was trying to stop an apocalypse. The billions of lives she was trying to protect suddenly became much more real. The lives she had chosen instead of his.

And now that he was rational again, he realized he would have done the same thing. He was *glad* she had made that choice.

The real kicker was that she had struggled with it so much. If she was only using him, it would have been a no-brainer.

"I'm sorry," he said.

"It's okay. I know time is a factor."

"I'm not talking about my driving."

He glanced over at her. She had shut her eyes tight and was biting her lips. He couldn't bring himself to slow down. If they were too late and something happened to Scott…

Darren couldn't even think about that. They would get there in time.

How horrible must Miranda have felt sending Darren to his death? If she cared about him half as much as he cared about her, it had to be hell. And then Darren had raked her across the coals for it.

"When Jack told us about what I am, what werewolves are like, I promised myself I wouldn't hurt anyone," Darren said.

"You might have to modify that," she said. "If we have to fight our way out of this."

Damn, he felt like an even bigger ass. She was ready to walk into the fire with him—again. Even after everything he'd said.

"I guess I should say I promised myself I wouldn't hurt anyone who doesn't deserve it," he said. "If Morrison and Mrs. Ford are working with Forester without a damned good reason, I won't have a problem protecting you."

"I can take care of myself. Focus on Scott. He doesn't know what he's walking in to."

Darren took a turn so fast that he heard her seatbelt lock up. She threw her hand out to the dashboard to stabilize herself.

"That isn't what I was trying to say." He tightened his grip on the wheel. "I'm sorry about what I said before. I told myself I wouldn't hurt anybody, but I did. I hurt you. I was so worked up about what we were about to do, and when you told me about the vision…"

He shook his head. "I've been so focused on not hurting anyone physically. I didn't give enough attention to not hurting you emotionally. And I'm truly sorry."

"Thanks." Her voice was thin and small.

"It won't happen again. I swear to you. I am not that guy and I won't let myself become like that. And you should know this absolutely qualifies as a 'shoot me next time' sort of situation."

She let out a brief laugh, but he wasn't joking. She had to understand how serious he was about this.

"My dad was a cop," he said. "I remember him talking about domestic calls and how rough they were. They almost always started with an argument. People don't think their words matter, but they do. Yelling at you like that... It's a gateway. And I'm not okay walking through it."

"I'm not going to shoot you because you hurt my feelings," she said.

"I did worse than hurt your feelings. I can see it when I look at you. I destroyed something between us."

The way she had looked at him before had made him feel amazing. Special. But he still wasn't sure if he was special to her because of how she felt about him or how he fit into her visions.

The way she made it sound, the apocalypse—the fate of the world —literally revolved around him. It didn't seem possible that one life could be so important.

Unless it's hers.

She was the one with the power to alter the course of the future. And if she wanted his help, who the hell was he to say no?

She had already done so much for him. He didn't think he would have made it through the night without going crazy or changing and killing someone without her constant presence, without her reassurances, without her touch. He would never feel that connection again, and it was his own damned fault.

His skin started to itch, his heartbeat picking up. He needed to stop thinking about that. He took another turn, feeling the wheels lift off the ground, and she gasped again.

"Let's focus on saving Scott," she said. "Then we can talk."

Shit.

Scott's life really was on the line. She hadn't come out and said it before—just talked about the apocalypse again. Now she was trying to save Scott. Because she *could.* She knew it wouldn't make the future worse.

She had told Jack that her vision of the apocalyptic future would result in his death, as well as Darren's. Not warning Darren about Niall had prevented at least that version of the future. Even though she'd thought she was sending Darren to his doom, she'd actually saved his life by letting him be bitten.

Darren focused on that. It wasn't a betrayal. She had done what she knew she had to do. What she knew was right. She hadn't threatened their future with her choice, she had *created* it. Or at least, the possibility of it existing.

Which Darren had then destroyed.

He couldn't think about that either. Instead, he did as she suggested and focused on Scott.

The park came into view. Scott's metallic gray sports car was parked across from it, in a neighborhood that should have seen it stripped for parts or stolen already—if it had been a neighborhood frequented by humans. Apparently, fairies didn't have a need for fancy cars.

Darren parked and leapt out. He wanted to tell Miranda to stay in the car, but knew she'd refuse. More than that, he would probably need her. He still wasn't sure how to handle what they were facing.

Packed dirt extended from the sidewalk, quickly giving way to lush grass. Darren was surprised the park was thriving so well within the city. There were no manmade paths leading deeper into the trees, and the spaces between them seemed darker than they should be given the time of day.

Miranda stopped at the tree line. "This park is too big for us to wander around looking for them. Do you think you can track him somehow?"

"Yeah." He felt ridiculous, but sniffed the air.

Interspersed with the dust and grass, he caught Scott's scent. Underneath, he detected the cloying sharpness of Morrison's cologne and Mrs. Ford's floral perfume.

"Okay, this could be really useful," he said.

He reached for Miranda's hand, but she pulled away. He felt it like being punched in the gut. But then she clasped his wrist and gave him a hesitant smile.

"Hands give the strongest visions. Remember?"

"I'd forgotten." His heart was pounding again. Had she maybe forgiven him? It wasn't the time to press the matter. They were walking into a dangerous situation.

"Stay close," he said.

The darkness under the trees didn't impact his vision in the slightest. It did creep him out, though. Darren looked up at the canopy and could see bright light between the leaves. It was as if the trees themselves were holding the light at bay.

Miranda walked closer, holding onto Darren's arm with both hands, almost hugging it to herself. She stumbled a few times, and he helped her along. When he glanced at her, her brown eyes were wide and staring around blankly.

"Can you see anything?" Darren asked.

"Not really. I know you won't let us get lost, though."

Her faith bolstered him. She still trusted him. At least he hadn't ruined that.

Voices carried toward them and the darkness faded as they neared a clearing in the trees. A ring of white birches grew at unnaturally equal intervals around the circle of immaculate emerald grass ahead. The light in the clearing was too bright, colors shifting in rainbow patterns that didn't make any sense.

Forester was facing off with Scott from the look of it, while Mrs. Ford and Morrison stood nearby.

He ran an SUV into Miranda's car.

Darren felt a growl building in his chest. He was about to step into the clearing, but Miranda dug her fingers into his arm to stop him. She shook her head when he glanced down at her.

"How much longer?" Mrs. Ford said.

"Humans. So impatient." Forester waved his hand in front of Scott's eyes, and said, "It's done. Your son will have no memory of finding us here."

"Thank you," she said.

A look of contempt flashed across Forester's features. He brushed the shoulders of his jacket, as if trying to swat away the words. Miranda's grip tightened again, her body tensing at Darren's side.

Forester cast his cruel smile at Mrs. Ford. "As I said, it was completely unnecessary."

"My son must have no knowledge about you or my involvement in this," Mrs. Ford said. "I'm doing all of this for him."

Forester grinned, his white teeth gleaming. "Is that what you're telling yourself? How entertaining."

"It's the truth," she said. "Scott isn't anywhere near being ready to run the company. He'll need my guidance even when he is. I have to be here for him."

Forester chuckled and turned to Morrison. "And what about you? You've broken your human laws to help her achieve this goal. What do you get out of it?"

"Fuck off," Morrison said.

The urge to kill Morrison lessened a tiny bit. Darren might have been amused, if his rage had left any room for other emotions.

"Blake." Mrs. Ford glared at him briefly.

"I asked for a boon in exchange for erasing your son's memories," Forester said. "This is what I want. Answer my question. And understand that I'll know if you're lying."

Morrison let out a sigh. "I get more years with her."

Mrs. Ford's expression softened in a way Darren had never seen before. Her lips parted and the lines between her eyebrows lessened. Morrison reached out and took her hand as she smiled at him—the most sincere and unguarded look Darren had ever seen her give.

"So, you want her to look young like you?" Forester said.

"I want her to be healthy and around for a long time," Morrison said. "I don't give a damn about the rest."

"My appearance can't change too drastically," she said. "The changes need to be internal. You said you can do that."

"I said in exchange for the coins I can give you fifty years of strength and health with none being the wiser," Forester said. "It's a simple matter to cast a spell and make your appearance match whatever age you'd like. There is one complication, however."

"What's that?" Mrs. Ford said.

"Her."

Darren felt Miranda tremble. Or maybe it was the ground beneath them. It seemed to buck and roll, spilling them into the light of the clearing.

"Darren?" Mrs. Ford's voice was high and tight, but carried across the space...that wasn't nearly as far as it had seemed when they stood at the tree line.

He looked over his shoulder and saw the trees a few feet away. The clearing somehow looked bigger from the outside. How was that possible?

At this point, Darren was surprised he could still be...surprised.

"Brother," Forester said. "How nice of you to come. And I see you've brought a treat."

Darren grabbed onto Miranda and pushed her behind him, away from Forester. "She's mine."

Forester rolled his eyes. "Werewolves. So territorial."

"Werewolf?" Morrison moved to stand in front of Mrs. Ford, his hand hovering over his jacket.

Darren snorted. Morrison may have had more time to adapt to knowing that the world was filled with fairies, but the look of surprise on his face told Darren that the gun under that jacket wasn't filled with silver.

He imagined charging at Morrison and ramming him in the gut. The look of shock that would surely be on the huge man's face as Darren easily lifted him into the air would be priceless.

The sound his guts would make when they hit the ground after Darren ripped him open would be even better. He was going to laugh and smile the whole time.

"I see you're getting into the spirit of things," Forester said. "But I need to finish my fun before you can have yours."

"I'm glad you find our business arrangement amusing," Mrs. Ford said. "But we need to finish this. Things have become complicated enough as it is. You can erase their memories when you're done."

"So impatient." Forester tsked. "Deals take time."

Mrs. Ford shook her head. "Enough stalling. You said Scott needs to be here because of his involvement earlier. He's here. We're where you told us to be. You have the coins. We've held up our end of the agreement. It's time you upheld yours."

Forester smiled at her again. How could Mrs. Ford not see the threat behind his eyes?

"You're right," he said. "It's time."

Chapter Seventeen

"Call it off," Miranda said. "Mrs. Ford, please call this off. You don't know what you're doing."

Mrs. Ford gave Miranda a condescending smile. "I've negotiated plenty of deals…whoever you are."

"Not with fairies." Miranda took a step forward, but the ground shifted beneath her feet. Vines and roots erupted from the grass, wrapping around her legs and torso.

She lifted her hands to her neck just in time to keep the vines from getting a chokehold. Her arms were trapped against her body. The plants tightened, strangling her with her own hands.

"Miranda!" Darren grabbed at the tendrils, trying to work his fingers between them and her flesh without hurting her. The panic in his eyes tore at her heart.

If he wasn't careful, he would change. She didn't know what would happen to any of them if he lost control.

"Well," Forester said. "Now that we've addressed that distraction, let's get on with it."

He lifted his arms, glowing green light emanating from his hands. The light dropped to the ground, rolling toward Mrs. Ford like a fog as Forester kept feeding it power. When the light reached her, it crawled up her body, like the plants had done to Miranda.

It seemed gentle at first, until it reached her face. The light engulfed her, striking at her eyes, nose, and mouth like snakes. Miranda heard a half-gasp, half-choking sound as it did.

"What the fuck are you doing to her?" Mr. Morrison took a step toward Forester, but the ground burst open under his feet, vines and roots wrapping around his arms and neck, pulling him to his knees.

"No interruptions, please," Forester said. "But I do want you to watch."

Forester's smile made Miranda's stomach lurch. The green light rolled toward Scott, engulfing him. Darren was so focused on Miranda, he didn't see. She tried to warn him, but the vines pulled tighter, cutting off her air.

He finally managed to get his hands between the plants and her neck, pushing her own hands out of the way. As soon as he did, he tore them apart.

Miranda sucked in air, trying to speak. The fog had almost reached Scott's face. He hadn't moved the entire time, as if he was in a trance.

"Scott..." she said.

Darren was busy ripping the roots from the rest of her body. He turned toward his friend just as the fog engulfed Scott's head. The light flashed, blinding her briefly.

Forester's right hand looked more like a claw as he curled his fingers, pulling on the energy around Scott. Darren looked back at Miranda, his face stricken.

"Go," she managed.

He ran toward Scott, but had only made it three steps before Forester lifted his free arm, holding his hand flat in the air, palm facing Darren.

A thick root reached through the ground and caught his ankle, tripping him. Dozens more tore from the earth, wrapping around his arms, legs, and neck, holding him prone.

"Darren!" Her heart pounded in her chest. Her legs were still tangled in the animated plants.

She clawed at the roots, but couldn't break them. She looked back to Scott, blinking away the tears that sprang to her eyes as she heard Darren's anguished cry.

Scott's flesh had folded in on itself. His eyes were sunken and his mouth hung open. His hair was white, his frame too large for his emaciated body.

Darren's cry ended abruptly as he started to cough and hack. At first Miranda was afraid the vines had started choking him as well. Then she saw that his skin had turned a dark gray.

Black fur sprouted everywhere she could see. His face distorted, his nose and mouth distending as they transformed into a muzzle. His teeth grew long and jagged, and his ears lengthened to tapered points that ended well above his head.

The light around Scott faded. His body fell to the ground.

Darren seemed to go berserk. He clawed at the roots still holding him to the ground, but more just sprang up to take their place. Miranda felt the ones around her ankles release her. The ground beneath her rippled as they joined the others holding Darren in place.

He pressed himself against the wooden cage, but couldn't break free. The roots pulled him closer and closer to the ground until he was lying absolutely flat on the earth, panting.

"That. Was. Impressive." Forester bit out each word, the strain of keeping Darren in place evident on his features and the way the arm extended toward Darren shook.

The last of the green light that surrounded Mrs. Ford flashed brightly again for a moment, then it faded as well.

Her features were transformed. Wrinkles gone, gray hairs vanished.

"It worked," she said. "I can feel it. It worked."

The roots around Mr. Morrison sank into the ground, retreating like snakes into their dens.

Mrs. Ford looked down at him and her smile intensified. "Blake, it worked!"

His face was a mask of shock and despair. He stayed on his knees.

"Edith…" he said.

"What is it?" She glanced around and saw Scott's body.

"No. Oh God, no!" She dropped to the ground, picking up Scott's body like it was a rag doll and cradling it against her chest. Her face was streaked with tears when she turned to Forester and shrieked, "What did you do?"

"Fifty years," he said. "Our deal was for fifty years. You never bothered to ask where I would get them."

"What?" she gasped.

Forester laughed. "Did you think I could just pull all that time and vitality out of thin air? I told you very clearly that we needed a blood-relative. You offered Scott."

"That was to get the coins," she said. "You told me you could only control someone if they were related to me."

"*And that they would be part of our arrangement.*" Forester made a tsking noise. "Really, such a savvy businesswoman as yourself should be much more careful in the wording of your contracts."

Mrs. Ford let out a sob. "I never would have agreed... I did this for him."

Mr. Morrison put his hands on her shoulders, helping her to stay upright. Miranda swayed on her feet, the grief and pain of the moment overwhelming her.

She had never felt so powerless. Scott was gone. Darren had almost completely changed. The form he was in now was only slightly more human than what she'd seen in her visions. She didn't know if he'd be able to pull himself back after this.

She didn't know how to help him.

"Please, take them," Mrs. Ford said. "Give the years back to Scott. I don't want them."

"Are you sure?" Forester said.

"Edith—" Mr. Morrison hugged her waist more tightly.

She ignored his warning. She clutched her son's body, and said, "I'm sure. Give them back. I just want him back."

Miranda felt a faint stirring of hope. Her dad had never told her stories about fairies bringing back the dead, but she'd read a few tales in books.

Bringing back the dead...

She remembered the vision of Scott as a walking corpse and her heart seemed to stutter.

This is where it starts. Something about this moment.

She had to stop Forester from bringing Darren's best friend back from the dead. As if she hadn't already put Darren through enough...

"What about the coins?" Forester said.

"Keep them," Mrs. Ford said. "I don't give a damn about them."

"Such a loving gesture." Forester smiled. "Don't worry. I'll reunite you with your son."

Reunite?

"Mrs. Ford, wait!" Miranda's warning was too late.

This time, instead of a slow fog, the green light shot out from Forester's hand. He pulled at Mrs. Ford's energy, fingers clawed, face illuminated with the macabre light as he laughed. Within seconds, Mrs.

Ford once more looked as Miranda had first seen her.

Except for the wide, staring eyes.

Her body slumped into Mr. Morrison's arms.

"Edith… No." He reached over and touched his fingers against Scott's neck. "You bastard. You said you'd bring him back."

"I said I'd restore the years to him," Forester said. "Look. He's just as he was when I started."

Miranda's stomach twisted. Scott's youthful appearance was restored. But not his life.

Part of her was relieved until she suddenly thought, '*It's just been set in motion.*'

"He's dead," Mr. Morrison yelled. "You killed them both!"

Forester shrugged. "Some humans just can't take losing that many years all at once. Now, if you want to make a deal—"

"No." Miranda was surprised at how calm her voice sounded. "No more deals. Mr. Morrison, you've seen what comes of them."

He looked completely broken. He stared at Miranda with blank eyes, then turned back to Mrs. Ford, rocking her body as he held her.

Forester cocked his head to the side as he looked at Miranda. "Curious. You seem a bit more…interesting than these other humans. Have you been with this werewolf during his entire night of transition?"

"That's none of your business," she said.

A slow smile creased his face. "You have. I've never heard of a human and a werewolf pairing before. Well, not where the human survived. How did you manage?"

"I'm resourceful." Miranda tightened her grip on her purse strap as she walked closer to Forester—which brought her closer to Darren. She had to have something she could use as a weapon. Some spare salt packets. Iron.

Wait…

She had the iron box that Jack had given them. But how could she get close enough to use it? If she threw it at Forester, he would blink away. If she tried to bludgeon him with it… That wouldn't go well.

Her best chance—the best chance for all of them—was if she could get Darren free.

He didn't even seem to be trying to escape anymore. He was lying still on the ground, almost completely covered in roots and vines.

She had reached Darren while speaking, and knelt at his side. He glanced over at her with the same gray eyes, sparkling lights shining in their depths. His pupils were hugely dilated.

She dared to reach out and touch the back of his head, gripping his...fur. He closed his eyes briefly. When he looked at her again, he seemed calmer.

"How did you survive, human?" Forester said.

In a quiet voice, she said, "I can see the future."

"An oracle." Forester angled his head to the side. He seemed to be talking mostly to himself as he continued. "An oracle would be an even better gift than the coins or even that fairy fighter."

Miranda took advantage of his introspection by setting her purse on the ground behind Darren—out of the elf's sight—and unzipping it.

"Tribute won't be coming up for another decade in mortal years." Forester smiled at her, revealing all those perfect teeth. Then he licked them. "What will we do with our time?"

"I guess I forgot to mention that I'm not available," Miranda said.

She reached into her bag without looking away from Forester, fingers feeling around for the box. It didn't take long to find. Her hand shook as she lifted it out, keeping her arm close to her body and trying to be discreet.

"Let me be clear as well," Forester said. "You belong to me now. My realm. My rules."

She felt Darren's muscles coiling beneath her, saw his claws dig into the earth for purchase. A low growl rumbled from his chest.

She wasn't entirely sure if it was directed at Forester or her. She hoped he'd forgiven her—and not just because he could easily kill her the moment he was freed.

"Take it up with my boyfriend." Tightening her grip on the iron box, she shoved it against the largest root holding Darren to the ground.

It worked better than she'd hoped. The root blackened and shriveled, the darkness spreading quickly along its length and even to the other roots touching it. They seemed to be turning to ash.

She let go of Darren just as he launched himself forward, clearing the space between him and Forester in one lightning-quick bound.

Forester stumbled back, but vanished right as Darren's jaws clacked shut where his face had been. Miranda held up the box, wondering where Forester would appear next, scanning the clearing.

Darren had locked onto Mr. Morrison.

"Darren, wait." She had taken two steps toward them when someone grabbed her by the front of her neck.

Forester pulled her against his chest hard enough to nearly knock the wind from her. He grabbed her wrist before she could smash him in the face with the iron box. His hand tightened on her neck, almost cutting off her air.

"None of that," he said.

She didn't know what to do. His Rath made him stronger…but it also had a weakness.

She let the iron box fall.

As soon as it hit the ground, the grass beneath it wilted. The air seemed to lose its luster, even as sunlight began to pierce its way into the clearing.

The plants a bit farther away returned to their normal green, which looked dull in comparison. The effect spread, destroying the magic that was making the park intersect with Faerie.

Forester tightened his grip on her neck. "What have you done?"

She couldn't have answered if she tried, pain lancing through her neck from where he squeezed it shut.

She looked over at Darren and saw that he had shifted his focus to them, his lips curled up in a snarl. His fangs were massive and sharp, especially in comparison with the rest of his face. He was much more than halfway through the transformation.

His skin had grayed completely and fur covered most of what she could see of him. His features were still a mix of human and wolf.

In her visions, he'd had the head of a wolf, but his body remained mostly human shaped. He'd be bigger and covered in fur, his hands would have longer claws, and his feet and legs would be wolf-like as well.

She hoped she would live long enough to see it.

He started toward them slowly, clawed hands flexed at his sides. Forester increased the pressure, tilting her head to the side. She tried not to show how much it hurt.

"One more step and I'll snap her neck," Forester said.

Darren froze, another deep growl echoing among the trees. Time seemed frozen as the two fey men glared at each other.

Two fey men. One forgotten human.

A human with a gun.

She saw Mr. Morrison draw his weapon and tilted her head to the side, trying to get her face as far from Forester's as possible. It was the only clear shot he would have, unless he was planning on trying to shoot Forester through her.

Pop.

Something hot and wet sprayed her neck. The sound was so loud it made her ears ring. Forester's grip loosened enough for her to pull away. Coughing and gasping for breath, she threw herself to the ground, turning to keep Forester in her sights.

Pop, pop.

The second bullet hit the elf in his shoulder. The third in the center of his chest. Blood trickled down from the first hole—in the middle of his forehead. Green blood.

Forester smiled, then started to laugh. "Not enough iron in those bullets."

Pop.

The fourth bullet hit him in the throat.

He coughed, more green leaking from the corners of his mouth. His brow actually furrowed as he lifted his hand to touch the bullet wound.

"Iron, massive tissue damage..." Miranda rasped. "We humans aren't picky. And I'm pretty sure Darren ripping your head off will shut you up permanently."

Forester glared down at her, then vanished. She doubted he'd be back anytime soon.

Miranda rolled onto her hands and knees, then pushed herself up on shaky legs. The immediate threat Forester had presented was gone, but that didn't mean they were out of danger. A rumbling growl punctuated her thought.

Across the clearing, Darren had turned his attention to Mr. Morrison again.

Mr. Morrison didn't look scared or sad anymore. He stared blankly at Mrs. Ford's body lying next to Scott's. His s dangled at his sides, as if his weapon was forgotten.

"Darren." Miranda approached Darren slowly, unsure of how he'd respond. Was he still in control?

He growled. Not a good sign. But he took a step toward Mr. Morrison, not her. If Darren was going to kill them both, she wasn't at the top of his list. She quickened her pace, putting herself between them.

"Please," she said. "Take a moment to think about this."

Lights glittered in his eyes. His lips were still curled back from the sharp teeth protruding from his mouth. He took another step closer, towering over her. Now she had his full attention.

She swallowed hard, wincing at the reminder of the bruised muscles in her throat.

"It's okay." Mr. Morrison's voice was stretched thin and laced with pain. "I don't care if he kills me."

Darren growled.

"It isn't okay." Miranda dared to put her hands on Darren's chest, felt the strange shape of the half-changed muscles as he breathed. The curl to his lips lessened.

"Darren, this isn't you," she said. "If you kill him, you'll be letting go of part of yourself. Part I need you to hold onto."

"For your *visions*?" Darren snarled.

She was amazed he managed to form words that she could pick out from among the rumbling growls. The hair on the nape of her neck pricked up at the menacing sound, the sense of his anger toward her. She pushed away her fear.

"Not just my visions." She lifted her shaking hand to his cheek, so close to those sharp-looking teeth. "I don't want to lose you. Any part of you. *I* need you. Not for my visions. For me. Please hold on."

His face relaxed a bit more. He closed his eyes and stood straighter. The color began to leech back into his face and his fur retracted.

He was doing it. Pulling himself back again—for her.

A breath of relief rushed out of her as a sob. She threw her arms around his neck and held him close. He hugged her back, burying his face in her neck.

It felt like they stayed that way for a long time. Miranda pulled back from Darren reluctantly.

He was himself again. Steel gray eyes, soft lips surrounded by stubble instead of fur.

Part of her wanted to laugh, she was so relieved. Most of her wanted to cry.

Mr. Morrison was staring down at Mrs. Ford and her son—at their bodies lying on the ground. He looked like he was in shock.

She checked on Darren to see how he was handling things. He stared at Scott's body for a few moments, then turned away. A muscle in his cheek twitched.

Miranda gripped Darren's hand tightly. She didn't dare let go. But she did reach out with her free hand and pluck Mr. Morrison's future from his shoulder.

She didn't bother trying to be discreet about it. Mr. Morrison was in his own world, his awareness flooded with grief. She was almost afraid of what his future would hold.

She looked anyway.

Crystal clear images ran through her mind. No fog or metaphors obscured anything. Compared to the futures she'd been reading, it was a cake walk. And the role he would play, how he would help support their fight… It was important.

She let out a sigh, then squeezed Darren's hand.

"Mr. Morrison, I need you to listen to me very carefully," Miranda said.

He shook his head. "I don't care if you can read my future. Edith was my world. I don't give a shit about anything else."

"Maybe right now," she said. "But that's going to change."

She had seen the near obsessive zeal in his eyes that would grow as time went on. And she was about to light the fuse.

"Giving up is easy," she said. "Fighting back—protecting other people from suffering the same sort of loss—that's hard. And that's what you're going to do."

That caught his interest.

"How?" He looked up at her, glanced at Darren. "I shot that guy right between the eyes, and it didn't slow him down. Four bullets, and he could just disappear from the battlefield, regroup, come back even stronger."

"You have a part to play in what's next," she said. "An important part."

Mr. Morrison shook his head.

"I hear sirens," Darren said. "We have five minutes."

"This is your first chance to fight back," she said. "When the police arrive, tell them that Mrs. Ford and her son were blackmailed into aiding with the theft of the coins. They met the blackmailer here and things went south. She made you wait in the car for the meeting. By the time you got here, it was too late."

Mr. Morrison's gaze became a little more focused. "Then what?"

"Then you do what you have to do," Miranda said. "Keep going, even when you want to quit. We'll be in touch soon."

She pulled on Darren's hand, leading him away. She only hoped that Mr. Morrison would listen to her. And that the vision of his future would come true.

Chapter Eighteen

Aside from Miranda telling Darren they should go back to her apartment, neither of them said a word until they were standing in her small living room again. Everything seemed slightly askew.

He felt that if he peeled back the wallpaper, the walls would be made of cardboard and he'd find that the entire apartment was fake. *Nothing* was real.

Except Miranda.

She hovered nearby, staring at him. Her eyes were red. Finally, she broke her silence.

"I'm so sorry," she said.

"Did you see it?" His words sounded brusque, even to him. He was trying to keep it together, but he had to know.

"See what?"

"Scott. Was he another sacrifice for your visions?"

"What? No." Her eyebrows pinched together above her nose.

"Did you see him die?"

She hesitated.

Fuck.

He stepped in close, but didn't dare let himself touch her. He was afraid he might hurt her in his rage.

And he was afraid it might make him forget how angry he was. He needed to be angry to fight off the despair.

"You're playing God, Miranda."

"I'm trying to help people." Her eyes filled with tears. "Do you have any idea what a burden this is? How terrifying it is to get close to people, knowing I may see them hurt or in pain or die and not be able to do anything about it?"

"You *can* do something about it. You can warn them. You choose not to."

"I don't get to pick my visions. If I trust them to be right about bad things happening to people, I have to trust them if they tell me an even worse future will result if I say something."

"You could at least try."

"What would you have done? If I told you I could see the future, and you were going to be attacked by a monster and I thought you would die, would it have changed anything? Would you have even believed me?"

He didn't want to admit it, but she had a point. He still would have gone to the Old River district. Still would have followed the dog into the abandoned store. He might have hesitated for a few moments, but he would have told himself he was being ridiculous.

And before he left The Red Thread, he would have made sure she was sent back to the hospital. Specifically, the psych ward.

"Warning people doesn't save everyone." The tears started streaming down her face. "If I hadn't told my mom about the Riverfront Skyway collapsing, she wouldn't have died."

Darren remembered reading about the Skyway collapse. It used to connect two of the tallest buildings in the city, crossing over the Olympus river. Some lunatic had planted a bomb on either side, but only one had gone off. It was enough to make the bridge crash into the water, but the buildings had been relatively unharmed.

No one was injured because someone had called in a bomb threat and police had cordoned off the area. Darren's dad had been on the scene. They had talked later about how lucky it was. His dad *still* talked about it. He always said it was a miracle.

"Did you call in the bomb threat so the police would know to close it down?" Darren asked.

If she had, she'd saved dozens of lives at least.

"My mom did. I told her about my vision, but it wasn't a bomb. The Skyway wasn't safe. One of the moorings had come loose and there was about to be a freak windstorm that was going to take it down." She pressed her hands against her eyes. "So many people... It was on a weekend."

She shook her head violently, then lowered her arms. Her hands were fists at her sides.

"I saw them all die. Men, women, children. Families. They crashed into the river. The ones that were lucky were impaled and died quickly. The ones that weren't drowned. I watched that, over and over as I slept, trying to find a way to make the dream change."

"Miranda—"

"There was nothing I could do. Nothing. So I called my mom and told her about it the moment I woke up. She said she would take care of it. That she had connections. And she did. They should have believed her, but they didn't. She called in the bomb threat, but knew that wouldn't be enough. So she—"

A sob cut her off. She shook her head again. Her voice cracked and she looked like she was close to hyperventilating, forcing the words out. "She hid in the skywalk while it was being evacuated. I never understood how she managed it. I guess with what Jack told me about her past..."

Miranda let out a hiccuping noise, but went on. "She wouldn't explain when she called me to say goodbye. I just knew she had barricaded herself in somewhere that she could see out so no police would be hurt when it...when it went down. She pretended to be the bomber, keeping them away until it happened."

Darren could barely breathe. He couldn't imagine what Miranda was feeling.

His dad had told him that the person behind the threat had been at the site, too. They had kept warning the police off when they would get too close. His dad said they's been furious at not being able to get to the suspect, and then amazed when the thing came down and nobody was in range to get injured. He always joked that the bad guy had actually saved them all.

Miranda's mom had saved countless lives. She had saved Darren's dad. And it had cost her own life.

Darren's heart pounded. Miranda had lost her mom—her only family—and then had sent Darren to what she thought was his doom after starting to develop feelings for him. It must have been her worst nightmare.

The whole time that she was helping him through his transition, helping him not feel alone, she was also working to stave off an apocalypse. By herself. He thought he had a handle on the rage that went along with his curse, but he was still being blinded by it.

"When they found her, they said it was suicide." Miranda's voice was shaking. "I couldn't tell anyone the truth. I was the only one who knew why her body showed up in the river days later."

She took a few quick breaths, then said, "So don't you tell me you think you know what I need to do when you're just stepping into the shitstorm that is my life. You don't know who or how or what I need to sacrifice. Or that I've given everything to my visions. *Everything* to keep people safe."

Darren had never seen her so angry. She was practically shouting at him. He deserved it.

"Letting you walk out that door was one of the hardest things I've ever done," she said. "And I would do it again to save the people you *get* to love from coming back as fucking zombies. *I* don't get to be close to anyone. I don't get to love anyone. Because the moment I do, I regret it."

"Do you regret me, then? Caring about me?"

Her breath rushed out of her and she sagged. In a small voice, she said, "No. Never."

He grabbed her arms before he realized what he was doing, then pulled her against his chest. His lips crushed hers, his tongue demanding entrance. She didn't hesitate at all, opening herself to him, meeting him with the same passion, the same molten *need.*

He moved his hands to her back, gripping her ass and lifting her from the ground. She wrapped her legs around his waist tightly.

Her fingers burrowed through his hair, nails scraping his skin and sending spirals of pleasure through him. He growled, walking them to the wall next to the door and pinning her body against it.

She gasped for breath when he released her lips, then groaned when he latched onto her neck, sucking her skin hard enough to leave his mark. He could tear her clothes off and be inside her in seconds. But her body wasn't ready, and he would never—could never—bring himself to hurt her.

He would never doubt her again.

He pressed his dick against her, feeling the heat and wetness of her pussy even through their clothes. She moaned, tightening her legs around him as if she was trying to pull him inside of her.

He nipped her ear and said, "I'm sorry... About everything. It took me too long to understand."

"I'm sorry I couldn't save Scott."

He froze for a moment, holding her close. "If there was a way to save him, you would have."

She buried her face in his neck. He could feel his shirt grow damp. He kept his body pressed against hers, but just held her.

On the other side of the wall, he could sense someone approaching her door. The person pounded a few times.

"Open up," Mrs. Elroy yelled.

Miranda actually laughed. It was thin and strained—filled with the stress they were both feeling—but Darren's heart felt lighter at the sound. He leaned back and kissed her until another pounding knock interrupted them.

He didn't bother setting her down. Instead, he reached over and opened the door a crack. Miranda had put the chain in place, and the door only opened a few inches.

"Can we help you?" he said.

Mrs. Elroy peered through the opening at him, then Miranda. "I heard yelling."

"Sorry, that was me," Miranda said.

"I know it was you," Mrs. Elroy snapped. "Otherwise, I'd have brought my bat. Listen, you guys want to have angry sex, fine. But I'm watching my shows, so keep it down."

Miranda was blushing furiously. "Um, okay."

"Sorry," Darren said.

"Hmph." Mrs. Elroy spun on her heel and headed down the hall.

Darren closed the door, then turned back to Miranda. Her eyes were red-rimmed, but she was smiling. It was a fragile smile. He didn't want it to leave.

"I don't want to have angry sex," he said.

"I don't either."

"When I changed in the clearing..."

How could he describe it? The rush of power, the unity with

everything around him as he sensed the world at a level he'd never imagined before. The urges to use that power in ways he also would never have thought of before. To destroy.

"I don't mind the physical changes," Darren said. "Now that I'm more used to the idea. But the emotional ones—the behavioral ones." He shook his head. "I won't be that guy."

"Are you expecting me to have a problem with that? Because I actually like it when people treat me with respect. Especially in bed. Most people do."

He laughed and nodded. "Everything feels so much more intense. Emotionally and physically. I'm having trouble keeping my equilibrium. That's the part that scares me more than anything else."

"We're both processing a lot right now. Things are happening fast. Big, huge, awful things. And some things that…aren't so bad."

There was too much to deal with. But being with Miranda— touching her, laughing with her… It was the most natural part of his new supernatural existence. The one thread from his old life that carried through and kept him sane.

"We can slow down," he said.

"I don't want to slow down. I just want us to understand each other. To help and support each other."

"That sounds great to me." He leaned back from the wall, starting toward the bathroom.

"Where are you taking me?" she said.

"The shower. The first thing I need you to understand about me is that I need to get clean." He smiled at her. "Plus the noise of the water will help muffle any sounds we make, since your landlady is watching her shows and she honestly kind of scares me."

"Oh." Miranda's cheeks pinked further, but she smiled back.

"And then we can move to the bed. Maybe the couch. That is, if you're interested."

"I'm very interested. I'm just kind of surprised you still are. A lot has happened."

Scott was dead. So was Mrs. Ford. And Darren hadn't been able to stop it, even with his new abilities. He would never joke around with his best friend again.

The thought made his skin prickle and his bones ache. His control started to slip.

If he couldn't protect them, how could he keep Miranda safe?

Darren shook his head, opening the bathroom door with his foot. He walked in and set her on the sink, but left his hands on her thighs.

"I can't think about that," he said. "If I do…"

He closed his eyes and took a deep breath. Miranda's scent filled his lungs—sweet as honeysuckle, warm as home.

"I don't want to talk or think or plan," he said. "I just want to feel."

Her smile faltered. "Okay. I'm happy to help."

"That's not what this is about."

He remembered everything she had said in the car the night before, when this was all just beginning. Especially about them loving each other.

Hope stirred in his chest.

"It isn't *touching* that helps me stay grounded and in control," he said. "It's that I'm touching *you*."

She closed her eyes and let out a slow breath. When she looked at him again, she smiled.

"You have no idea how much I needed to hear that," she said.

He put his hands on either side of her neck, running his thumbs along the lines of her jaw. "Forget the future. Forget the past. I want you focused in this moment. I want you. Now."

"I want you, too." She leaned forward and kissed him.

She helped him pull off his jacket and let it drop, her lips devouring his. The holster that held his gun required a little more care. He managed to slide it from his shoulders, then lowered it to the ground. After how it had bitten into his flesh during his near-change, he doubted he'd be putting it back on.

Miranda deepened the kiss as she grabbed his shirt, pulling it open hard enough that the buttons popped off. She dragged it down his back.

This was taking too much time. He stepped away from her, finishing with his dress shirt and pulling the T-shirt underneath over his head. He managed to step out of his shoes, and said, "Strip."

Miranda practically leapt off the sink. Her hands gripped the hem of her shirt before Darren realized he needed to turn away. If he watched her, he'd get too worked up. It was more important to control himself now than ever before.

He pulled off his socks and pants, listening to the soft hush of fabric as she did the same behind him. As soon as he lost his boxer-briefs, he jumped into the tub and started up the water.

He didn't bother trying to avoid the cold spray as he worked to adjust the temperature. It would help him to cool off a little before...

Before he turned around and saw Miranda standing naked right next to him.

Good God, she was beautiful.

Her breasts were beyond full. They curved on her chest, beckoning him to taste them. Her olive skin gleamed in the light. Her nipples were dark, already taut.

Her stomach had curves to it as well, and her hips... He groaned as he thought of what it would be like to hold onto those soft hips and ram his dick into her from behind.

"Miranda, I don't think I can move."

Her brow furrowed in concern. "What's wrong?"

"I don't think it's safe for me to let myself."

She smiled and stepped into the tub with him. "I can help with that."

She slid the glass door to the tub shut.

"I want to touch you," he said. "I *need* to touch you. To be sure you're ready for me. I don't want to hurt you."

She wrapped her arms around his neck and said, "You won't. I trust you."

He wished he trusted himself. But he was stronger, and he had never, ever, wanted someone like this before.

She ran her hands along his arms, then grasped his wrists gently and guided his hands to her breasts. He groaned again as she covered them with her own, cupping and kneading her soft flesh through his hands.

He flicked his thumbs over her nipples and she inhaled sharply. He searched her face for signs of pain, but all he saw was pleasure.

"You won't hurt me," she said.

He nodded. It didn't matter that she hadn't turned yet or how they had reached this point. What mattered was how they felt about each other.

The bond they shared, was new, but it had been tested. It was stronger than anything he'd ever felt before. He trusted it enough to keep her safe, and that was the purest form of knowledge he'd ever experienced. He was certain of it to the center of his soul.

He slid his hands to her back and pressed her body against his, bending to kiss her. His tongue slid into her mouth, dancing with hers as she eagerly joined him. He lifted one of her legs so her foot rested on the rim of her tub, then ran the backs of his fingers along her thigh until they reached the soft curls between her legs.

She was already slick. Her breath hitched as he explored her, caressing her before burying two of his fingers deep. She gasped against his mouth.

He pressed his other hand on her ass, keeping her pinned against him. Her breasts rubbed across his chest as she writhed in his hands.

His dick started to pulse. If he didn't calm down, he was going to come all over her stomach. He wanted to be inside her, he wanted to fill her. If it felt this good just touching her, what would it be like when he finally buried himself deep?

He spread his fingers, massaging her pussy, begging her body to be ready to accept him. He knew he was big, and he didn't want her to be uncomfortable for a second. He flicked his thumb across her clit, still pumping his fingers into her.

Her fingers dug into his back as she threw her head back, moaning his name. He could feel her body pulsing, her hips thrashing as she ground her clit against his palm.

The second she started to calm, he turned her around and braced her arms against the tile of the shower. He grabbed his dick, lining it up with her sweet center, and drove himself home.

"Oh God." Her voice was lower than he'd ever heard it, and it sent a shock of pleasure through him.

Hot. Wet. Tight.

His world became each feeling as he felt her body trembling around him. The aftershocks of her orgasm caused her sheath to rhythmically squeeze his dick.

He pulled himself almost out, then rammed into her again. She groaned, arching her back and standing on her tip-toes to give him better access.

He held onto her hips, loving the ampleness of them, their softness beneath his hands, against his body. He rocked into her over and over again.

"Darren…"

He was lost in the cadence of his thrusts. He leaned forward, covering her with his body, wanting more of their skin to touch.

He buried one hand in her hair, turning her to face him as he angled his head to kiss her. She wrapped her arm around his neck, holding herself up to reach his lips, to open herself to him in yet another way.

His tongue plunged into her mouth, his dick filled her, over and over again. He let go of her hair and placed his hand on top of hers on the wall, lacing their fingers together.

Energy shot along his nerves, lighting up his cells, reaching every part of him, until finally exploding into her.

She gasped, her body responding, echoing the pulse in his dick, taking everything he had to give, pulling on him, demanding more as he kept pounding into her.

The lights in the room seemed blinding, his senses alive, his skin buzzing with sensation. He could feel the hammering of her heart through his own chest, pressed tight against her back, the hum of her ecstasy spread through him.

With one last long thrust, he pressed himself against her, wrapping his arms around her stomach to hold her up as he kept himself buried as deep as he could get. Their heartbeats began to slow. She let out a soft cooing sound as she relaxed into his embrace.

His dick slid from her, satisfied for the moment. He doubted it would stay that way long. He already wanted her again—couldn't wait to bury himself in her heat.

He held her against his chest, turning them around so she faced the shower. She let out another coo as the warm water ran over her stomach.

There was a shower caddy hanging from the nozzle, and he squirted some liquid soap into his hands, then rubbed it into a rich lather. He took as much time as he dared exploring her, learning her body. His dick was already stirring. He wanted her in bed. Immediately.

She had other ideas.

"I'm sorry about Scott."

He froze for a moment, then went on rinsing her. "Did you really..." He wasn't sure if he wanted to ask, but he had to know. "Did you see it happen?"

"No."

"But you saw something."

She turned him so that he was the one in the water, encouraging him to tilt his head back to wet his hair.

Darren had never had a lover bathe him before. Then again, no one had ever tried to. She didn't say anything as she massaged the suds into his hair or rinsed it clean.

When she began spreading the soap over his body—slowly, lovingly, taking so much care with him that his heart ached from it—she spoke again.

"I saw what will happen to him if we fail."

Scott was already dead. What could happen to him now?

There was so much more to the world than Darren had ever suspected. Werewolves, vampires, elves... Maybe ghosts were real as well.

Something she'd said earlier popped into his head, making his stomach heavy with dread.

"Wait, when you said you're trying to stop a zombie apocalypse... You were kidding, right? About the zombie part?"

She stopped with her hands on his chest. Darren could feel them trembling.

There was so much that he was adjusting to, but even with everything he'd come to accept as real, a "zombie apocalypse" still seemed impossible to him. From the sharp scent of fear she started to put off, he knew for certain that she wasn't kidding.

He wanted to see Scott again. But not like that. They had to stop it. If they cremated Scott's body, he couldn't rise.

Then again, if he came back, who was to say how much of his self he would retain? Darren was a werewolf now, but he didn't feel that different. Well, except from the murderous rage. Maybe Scott would—

What the fuck am I thinking?

Darren shook his head.

No way. He couldn't wish that on his best friend.

Being a werewolf was one thing. Being a zombie? If it was anything like the books and movies, it had to be horrible. Darren could only pray that those unfortunate souls...didn't have souls. That the essence of who they were would remain safe and content in whatever "after" they had earned.

Wherever Scott was now, he needed to stay there.

Darren let out a breath as he turned his face to the ceiling. Grief flooded him, followed quickly by anger.

Forester had done this. And Forester would pay. Darren would track down the elf, dig out his spleen, and feed it to him. He would pry out his eyes and—

"Stop." Miranda gripped the sides of Darren's face and stared at him intently. "Whatever you're thinking about, you need to stop."

He growled. Dammit, why was he growling at her? Forester was the one who needed...

Her hands trailed down Darren's chest, interrupting his train of thought.

"Stay in the moment," she said. "Remember?"

Darren nodded.

They would take care of Forester later and stop the apocalypse. It was the only way they could truly be happy together. He had to believe they'd be successful, because he wanted more of this, more of her. He wanted them to reach the future she'd foreseen.

Chapter Nineteen

Walking to her bed after their amazing activities in the shower wasn't easy. Miranda could still feel Darren inside of her, like an afterimage burned onto her nerve endings. The movement of her legs brushing together was close to setting her off again.

They wanted to stay in the moment. They *needed* to stay in the moment. She was as bad off as him in that regard.

Well, maybe not quite.

His eyebrows were pinched together as he followed her, his grip tight on her hand. His dick was already stiff again, like it was straining to be inside her.

This time was their oasis in the storm that surrounded them. She was going to make the most of it.

"Sit down."

She waited for him to sit on the edge of the bed, then knelt in front of him. Running her fingers along the insides of his thighs, she watched his reaction.

His breath hitched and his eyes widened. He stared at her as if mesmerized, as if she was the only woman in the universe. She had never felt so desired before. She wanted him to feel the same.

She brought her hands to his chest, running her fingers over the firm muscles of his pecs, then down over his abdomen. She leaned forward and kissed his navel, not wasting any time in reaching for his dick.

He gasped as her fingers closed around its girth. How the heck had she managed *this?* No wonder she was still feeling its impact.

She'd never wanted anyone as much as Darren. Apparently, her body was in complete agreement with her heart.

She ran her cheek along the length of him, holding his dick steady as she trailed his crown across her lips.

"Miranda…"

"Did you want something, Darren?" She grinned up at him, but he didn't smile back. He was panting, still watching her with wide eyes.

She ran her tongue along his length. He tightened his grip on her sheets and grunted. She wetted his crown, then licked her lips before pulling him into her mouth.

She slid him in slowly, loving the low groan he let out that matched her movements. When she had him as deep as she could manage, she pressed her tongue against him, swirling it as she pulled him back out, squeezing the base of his dick with her hands.

"God, Miranda. That feels too good."

She sucked him in deep, repeating the motion. This time, when she reached his crown she let him slide from her mouth fully so she could say, "Do you want me to stop?"

"Never." He groaned as she wrapped her lips around him again. "Except…"

She hadn't expected that. She sat back so she could look up at him.

"Except what?"

His eyes were sparkling again, lights going off deep in their gray pools like fireworks. It was the first time she'd seen those lights when he wasn't angry or struggling against a change.

He smiled as he reached for her, clasping her waist and pulling her up on the bed. "*Except* I want to fuck you so much, it's driving me out of my mind."

Her pussy clenched, as if it had heard and understood his words—and was totally on board with that idea. She was, too.

She climbed over him so that she could lay down in the middle of the bed, then turned to smile back at him. "Then what are you waiting for?"

He grinned, but instead of crawling on top of her, he settled with his head between her legs. Before she could say anything else, he pressed a kiss against her curls.

More pleasure arced through her body, making her gasp. She wondered how much her body could take—if she could keep up with him.

His fingers joined his mouth, exploring her, filling her, bringing her back to the brink of ecstasy. She ran her nails over his scalp, encouraging him. He half-groaned, half-growled in response.

She was getting used to how he communicated, how he was

changing as his new nature took effect. She found she actually enjoyed it. Within a few weeks or months, she'd be joining him. She wouldn't be alone anymore.

She already wasn't.

Her eyes filled with tears at the thought, even as her body lit up further from his attentions.

Through his ordeal, he'd been so concerned with her. When she'd opened up to him, it had seemed to rock him to his soul. It may have taken him a while to understand why she'd made the choices she'd made and what they had cost her, but he seemed to truly understand now.

He wanted to help her. That was more precious to her than anything. Not being alone in all this.

"Darren."

She needed him closer. In her, filling her. Immediately.

He glanced up and must have seen the need in her eyes. He pulled himself up along her body, his dick resting just at her entrance.

Barely parting her flesh, he dusted her hair from her face and kissed her. Soft and lingering.

She slid her legs up along his thighs as he pressed himself deep. She felt her body welcoming him, every inch of movement as he joined with her. She wrapped her arms around his back and held him tight.

The path before them was still unclear. All she knew for certain was that they would face great danger—and they would face it together.

He rocked against her, shifted his weight to his elbows so he could look into her eyes. She let herself become lost in them, in the languid rhythm of his thrusts. His hard length filled her, each pull against her flesh sending pleasure spiraling through her body.

No thoughts of death or destruction. No wondering about the future or grieving the past. Just this moment.

His pace quickened, the force of his hips increasing. Warmth pooled in her belly, turning molten as he landed harder, deeper. He kept his gaze locked on hers. The emotional intimacy of it was almost as intense as the physical. She'd never felt more alive than when they touched.

Energy uncoiled through her, the heat building until it finally cascaded through her body, lighting up every part of her. She pulsed around him, his hips pounding against hers, never slowing, demanding every drop of ecstasy her body could give to her.

He finally closed his eyes, throwing his head back and shouting her name as his thrusts became frenzied. He pounded himself into her, over and over again, until finally stopping, pressing her to the mattress, his shaft buried deep in her heat.

He collapsed on top of her, their chests touching, breath mingling. He nuzzled her neck, then rolled to his side, keeping his arms around her. She snuggled close against him, holding onto him, too.

"Thank you." He pressed a kiss to her forehead.

"For what?"

"For not giving up on me. For giving us a chance."

"I could say the same thing to you," she said.

He ran his hand along her back. "I shouldn't have been upset in the first place. If I'd been thinking clearly, I would have seen the reasoning behind your choice."

"Knowing why doesn't always help. I felt like part of me died when I let you walk away."

"Miranda…"

He cradled her face, tilting it up to kiss her again. She let his warmth soak into her.

The desperate energy of his kisses from earlier had dissipated. There was still plenty of passion, but a relaxed contentment underlying them. He trailed his hand to her breast, caressing it as he deepened the kiss. He let out a sigh as he pulled back.

"I'm so glad I didn't lose you," she said.

He laughed. "You and me both. I wish you could feel what it's like from this side. Holding you. Hearing you say these things."

"I can. Well, in my own human way. And I will feel what it's like after I turn."

His smile faded. "When will that happen?"

She clasped his hand in hers, bringing it up to rest near her face. Willing herself to relax as she focused on that question, she let their shared future flow into her.

She could still feel the fog approaching her, but it wouldn't reach her for a while. A shimmering strand of gold glittered in front of it. She saw her hand stretch toward it, could feel Darren and others close by. More werewolves—his pack. A male and a female. But Miranda was still human.

Her attention returned to the room and the bed she shared with Darren. His body close to hers, warming her.

"There's something that I have to do first," she said. "As a human. Some reason that I can't turn yet."

"But you will turn."

"I'm sure of it."

He let out a breath, then kissed the back of her hand.

There was one more topic she wasn't sure how he'd react to, and waiting wasn't an option.

"You should know that I don't think I'm the only one you'll be turning," she said.

"What?" He leaned back, his body tensing next to hers.

"My friend Eden has the same fog surrounding her future. I think the fog is the Faerie Veil—the boundary between human existence and becoming fey. It's close to her. Almost as close as yours was. I think you're going to turn her."

"Why would I do that?"

"Because she's dying." Miranda's eyes filled with tears as the surety of Eden's future hit her. "If you don't, she won't make it to the end of the week."

"I don't even know if I *can* turn anyone yet. The full moon is right around the corner. Being with you is helping me adjust, but I don't know what will happen during that night. I might kill her instead of turning her. Jack made it sound like I'll completely lose control."

"Jack made it sound like you'd already be a homicidal maniac right now."

"True. I would still feel a lot safer if I had a place where you could lock me up to keep everyone safe."

"Are there any holding cells at your security company?"

"Yeah, actually, there are."

"We should call Mr. Morrison later and ask him about retrofitting one as a werewolf holding cell."

Darren laughed. When she didn't join in, he said, "Wait, you're serious?"

"Mr. Morrison is going to be instrumental for our fight," she said. "I saw it when I read his future. He's going to open a secret R&D department called the Daedalus Division and dedicate it to fighting fairies. He'll be a great ally."

She felt Darren stiffen next to her. "He almost got you killed."

"He was caught up in things he had no chance of understanding. He was in love."

"That's no excuse."

Miranda pushed herself up on her elbow so she could look into Darren's eyes. "What would you do to protect me?"

He answered without hesitating, without thinking. "Anything."

She lifted her eyebrows at him.

With a sigh, he seemed to sink deeper into the mattress. "Okay, I see your point."

"I see yours, too." She ran her fingertips over his erection, loving how his eyes softened at her touch.

"You have a powerful effect on me."

She crawled on top of him, straddling him. The look of delight on his face warmed her heart. The openness of his smile, the mixture of hope and longing. It almost seemed a reflection of how she felt about him.

She slid along his length, knowing her body was more than ready for another round. She lined him up and slowly lowered herself over him until their hips were flush. He gripped her thighs, smile fading as pleasure swept over his features.

"Werewolf lovers sure are voracious," she said.

He nodded, thrusting up into her. She gasped, pressing her hands against his chest so she could lean back and look at him while they made love.

"Can you imagine what it'll be like when I turn?" She laughed. "We'll never do anything else."

"I'm okay with that." He sat up, bringing their chests together, then wrapped his arms around her and pulled her closer for a kiss.

"There are a few things we'll need to take care of—saving the world and all." She gasped as they hit a particularly sensitive spot with their movements.

"Only that?"

He kissed her collarbone, then trailed a row of nips and bites to her breast, lifting it so he could suck her nipple into his mouth. Her breath hitched as he circled it with his tongue and ran his teeth gently over her skin.

"I don't remember what we were talking about," she said.

He let go of her breast and laughed. "Good. We'll figure it all out later. Right now, let's just enjoy this."

She nodded, then grabbed his face and kissed him.

They had time. Not much, but a little. She wanted to make every second count.

A shrill ring broke through her sleep. The sky outside the window was dark. Apparently, their last nap had taken them past sunset.

They had been in bed all day, except for brief trips to the bathroom or kitchen. Miranda vaguely remembered looking up the number for Eden's business at some point and leaving voicemail about not going to the restaurant due to "renovations".

She didn't care if they never actually spoke again. Well, okay, she cared, but it was most important that Eden stay safe. Going anywhere near The Red Thread right now didn't seem very conducive to that.

Darren stirred next to her as the phone rang again. Miranda reached for her phone on instinct, fumbling with it as she picked it up from the nightstand. She accepted the call without thinking to check who she'd be speaking to.

"Hello?" she said.

"It's Jack."

"Oh hey."

He paused for a moment. "You okay?"

"Yeah."

She was still groggy, her body relaxed on a level she hadn't experienced…well, ever. Darren draped his arm over her waist and pulled her closer.

"You don't sound okay," Jack said.

She muttered something blearily, then forced herself to sit up. Darren grunted in protest.

"I was asleep," she said.

"You let Darren out of your sight?"

"No, he's right here."

Crap. Adrenaline shot through her system, helping to wake her up. She didn't know how Jack would react, and didn't want to make the target on Darren's back any bigger.

There was another long pause.

"Are you all right?" Jack said each word crisply.

"I'm fine," she said. "Better than fine."

She smiled down at Darren. At some point, she had turned on the string lights she'd hung near the ceiling around the room. Everything was washed in soft colors. His eyes were closed, long lashes casting shadows on his cheekbones.

"You don't have to worry about Darren hurting me," she said.

Other people? Maybe.

Miranda? No.

"You can't let your guard down—" Jack said.

She pulled the sheets over her. It didn't matter that he couldn't see her. She'd feel better if she was covered.

"Let me stop you right there," she said. "So far, almost everything you've told me about werewolves is absolute bull. Frankly, I'm sick of hearing it."

"Did he bite you?"

"Not that it's any of your business, but no."

"It is entirely my business," Jack said. "I'm putting my neck out for you two. Asking questions about the Knights of Antares is sending up all kinds of red flags among my old crew. They want to know why I'm asking, and it is not a good thing to raise their curiosity. If they come looking for Darren, they won't care whether you've been turned or not. If you get in their way, they will kill you."

She heard Darren start to growl beside her—not as asleep as she thought. She reached out and stroked his hair. "I'll see them coming."

"Have you had more visions?" Jack asked.

This time, she was the one who paused. She didn't know how freely she could speak in front of Darren. She didn't want to upset him.

"A few," she said. "And I'm getting better at interpreting them."

"Did you see Forester?" Jack asked.

"Not in a vision."

She glanced down at Darren. He was staring at her now, furrows appearing between his brow. He wrapped his arms around her waist and buried his head in her lap.

She sighed, not seeing any way around just coming out and telling Jack about what had happened. "Darren received a call from his partner at Ford Security."

"Scott Ford?" Jack really had researched Darren thoroughly.

Miranda nodded out of habit, even though they were talking on the phone. "Yeah."

"Scott found out his mother was dealing with Forester and tried to confront them," Miranda said.

Jack let out a huff of air. "And?"

"We didn't get there in time," she said. "Forester killed them both."

"He *killed* them?" Jack sounded surprised.

"Yes."

"Miranda, this is important," Jack said. "Elves are part of the High Court of the Sidhe—of fairies. They have rules in place for how they prey on humans. Rules they love to dance around with and try to find loopholes through, but that they *do not break*." He emphasized each word at the end of his sentence. "One of the most important for us—the rule that keeps most of humanity blissfully ignorant and still breathing —is that fairies aren't allowed to outright kill us unless it's self-defense."

"Hooray for us," she said.

Jack went on as if he hadn't heard her. "Fairies can work incredible magic. They can make pocket dimensions and alter reality. Imagine if one of them became bored and decided to unleash that on us."

Her stomach seemed to crinkle up. She remembered the vision of zombie-Scott.

"Mrs. Ford made a deal with him," Miranda said. "Forester followed the letter of it, and managed to kill them both in the process."

Jack let out a sigh. He actually sounded relieved. At least, until he spoke again.

"How did Darren take it?" His voice was somber.

"How do you think?" she snapped.

Darren tightened his grip on her waist. With his werewolf senses, he could probably hear every word of the conversation.

She wished she could drop the phone and kiss him. She'd do that as soon as possible. In the meantime, she kept stroking his hair, hoping it soothed him somewhat.

"I've gotta tell you, I'm stunned," Jack said. "Darren is... He's not like any werewolf I've encountered. Even heard of. Which brings me to *my* bad news."

When he paused, she prompted, "Which is?"

"None of my sources has a lead on the Knights of Antares. They're all saying it's a legend."

"Great." There went her main string of hope.

"But they have reasons to *want* to believe that," Jack said. "Just like I keep wanting to believe—"

"Wanting to believe what?"

"I'm going to be honest with you, Miranda. Part of me wants to believe that Darren is going to become a mindless killer."

Darren let out another growl. He looked up at her, sparks kindling in the depths of his eyes.

"How can you say that?" she said.

Jack's sigh was clear over the phone. "I've killed a lot of monsters in my day. I didn't bother to get to know them. I couldn't take the chance. Darren has me thinking. Questioning my prior choices. Wondering if I might have...made mistakes. I don't like it." After a brief pause, he said, "But I like *him*. I'm trying to keep an open mind."

"Thanks." Her voice was dripping with sarcasm.

"I'm telling you this for a reason," Jack said. "You know me. You know I care about you. The others on my team don't know you from Adam—and they won't *want* to know Darren. They'll just want to put him down. I keep pushing this, someone's going to get too curious and try to figure out where my questions are coming from. They'll come for you both."

Her heart sank, but she tried to keep her voice strong. "I told you, I'll see them coming."

"I hope so."

So much for asking Jack to help them find a place for Darren during the full moon. Mr. Morrison was a much safer bet.

"I'll keep digging as much as I can," Jack said. "But we may need to look elsewhere for support for Darren. The Knights aren't an option."

She felt her shoulders sag as if a weight had been placed on them. Finding other werewolves who were fighting to keep their humanity—and winning—would help Darren so much.

At least she knew they would find others eventually. Sooner would definitely be better than later, though.

She sighed. "Thanks for trying."

"I have some more bad news," Jack said.

"Great."

He ignored her sarcastic comment. "That coin was used in a city-state in ancient Greece that was known to be ruled by a particularly volatile and powerful Fairy Lord—one of the High Court Sidhe. We don't know much beyond that because apparently he got bored one day and destroyed the whole place. No survivors. The only record we have is from people who happened to visit the town and left before it all went down."

"I really don't like where this is heading," Miranda said.

Jack plowed on. "Forester mentioned paying tribute."

Her heart started to pound. "You think that same being is here in Olympus?"

"It would make sense. Either him or some other Sidhe Lord that knew the guy."

Orion and the Scorpion...

So much of this kept coming back to Greek legends. She thought of her dad's stories again, and the importance of names among the fey.

"Our founding fathers really should have picked another name for this city," she said.

"Look, I'm coming around on the whole Darren thing. You have yourself a werewolf bodyguard. At the moment, I'm counting that as a blessing. You tell Darren... Tell him I have his back. For whatever that's worth."

She looked back to Darren. He was still frowning, but who wouldn't be after listening to this conversation? She smiled at him, knowing it probably looked a little forced, and ran her fingers through his hair again.

"Knowing we're not alone..." she said. "It's worth more than you think."

Chapter Twenty

Miranda kept playing with Darren's hair after she ended the call. He had buried his head in her lap again, feeling her warmth, taking in her scent. It was more comforting than anything after listening to her conversation with Jack. Remembering Scott.

Whenever Darren thought about what had happened in the park, he wanted to stand up and punch through the wall. Then tear the wall down and hurl the pieces through the window.

But this was Miranda's home. It was where they'd first made love. He didn't want to destroy it. He took a deep breath and let it out slowly, focusing on her.

"Are you doing okay?" Her voice was as gentle as her touch.

"I don't know how to answer that."

"I'm sorry you had to hear me talk to Jack about Scott. I didn't think you'd want me to leave."

He tightened his hold on her waist. "It would have bothered me more if you'd left the room."

"Do you need to talk about it?"

"I need to *not* talk about it. Or even think about it. I can't ignore that it happened forever—that he's gone. But I need time. I need to let my subconscious work on it for a while before I really think about it. If I try to right now, I feel like I'll lose it."

"Then don't think about it." She bent down and kissed his head.

"You can't imagine how much that helps."

"What, not thinking about it?"

"You touching me. Kissing me."

"If that's a line, it's a great one."

"I don't know how I would have made it through this without you. Thank you. For everything you've done for me."

"This isn't a chore for me." There was a bit of a bite to her tone. "Being with you…it's what I've wanted for a long time. I know we're dealing with awful stuff right now, and I feel kind of bad admitting this, but I'm happy. About us, at least. That we found our way to each other."

"I wish it had happened sooner. Starting a relationship in the middle of all this is kind of stressful."

"Maybe this is the way it had to be. Maybe our bond will grow even stronger because of all that's going on."

"I can't imagine feeling a stronger connection to you than this." Then again, she hadn't turned yet.

He thought of what it would be like to hold her, make love to her, with no fear of getting carried away and hurting her with his new strength. A wild feeling surged through him as he imagined her at his side as a werewolf.

He leaned up so he could kiss her. She wrapped her arms around his neck, pulling him close as she lay back against the pillows.

Her phone rang again.

"Would you mind terribly if I smashed that?" he said.

She laughed as she picked it up. Her heartbeat sped as she read the screen.

"What's wrong?" he said.

"It's Eden."

Miranda quickly answered the call, sitting back up as she did. "Eden?"

There was a pause before Eden said, "Hi."

Darren could hear every word as if they were both standing in the room with him. It'd been the same with Jack's call. He sat next to Miranda so he could offer his support, like she had supported him when talking to Jack earlier.

"Are you okay?" Miranda reached for Darren's arm, clasping his wrist gently.

"I don't know," Eden said. "It's a lot to ask, especially with the way I walked out before, but could we meet? I need to talk to you."

"Of course." Miranda's grip tightened. "Where are you?"

Eden let out a little sigh. "We can meet in front of my office. Do you know where my storefront is?"

Miranda nodded, the phone pressed tight to her ear. "Yes. We can be there in ten minutes."

Eden paused for a moment. "We?"

"Um…" Miranda smiled at Darren. "Yeah. Darren will be coming along. I hope that's okay."

Eden's voice picked up. Darren could hear the grin in it.

"Darren?" Eden repeated. "As in 'hunky Darren that you've been drooling over for weeks' Darren?"

He lifted his eyebrows at Miranda and mouthed, *drooling?*

"I'm pretty sure he can hear you," she said.

Eden paused for a moment. "Oops. Sorry."

Miranda shrugged. "It's okay. He's well aware of me drooling over him now."

"That brought…not the mental images I'd like to associate with you guys," Eden said.

Miranda laughed. "Well, you can see us with your own eyes shortly. We just need to get dressed."

"Not helping," Eden said.

"Sorry." Miranda swung her legs over the side of the bed, pulling on Darren's arm. "I don't live far away. We'll see you soon."

There was another pause. Darren could hear Eden's breath hitching, as if she was crying. Miranda was still smiling blithely. She must not be able to hear it. He touched her shoulder to get her attention.

As quietly as he could, he said, "Is she okay?"

Miranda's brow furrowed as she parroted his question to Eden. "Are you okay?"

"I don't know," Eden said. "I just need to see you."

Miranda's voice was filled with tension. "Okay. We're on our way."

"Thanks," Eden croaked out. "Bye."

"Bye." Miranda looked down at her phone. The call had already been ended. She gazed up at Darren with eyes full of worry.

"Something must have happened," she said.

He pulled her into a quick hug. "We'll find out what's going on faster if we hurry. Come on."

They were pulling up in front of Eden's business office within eight minutes. The streets had been empty this time of night, and Darren's car still had its speed, even if it had lost most of the front grill. A woman stood beneath a sign that read, *Landscapes by Eden*.

Darren chuckled. "I like the name."

"She told me once she's always loved plants and decided to put her name to good use," Miranda said.

They hopped out of the car and headed across the street. A woman Darren assumed was Eden turned as they approached. She had large blue eyes and curly black hair that hung past her shoulders.

Her skin was beyond pale—it looked almost bloodless. There was a purple tinge around her mouth and nose.

Her scent was even more distressing—a sharp cast to it that reminded Darren of the feeling he always had in hospitals. Beneath the sharpness, he caught a scent like rich potting soil mixed with blood.

And…sex.

He felt his cheeks heat. Miranda had mentioned that Eden was working on a "moon garden" for some rich client. That probably explained the soil smell. Maybe she'd cut herself and the guy had… comforted her?

He shook his head, as if that would rattle the speculations out of his brain. His werewolf senses were definitely giving him TMI.

Miranda had said Eden wouldn't live till the end of the week. After seeing and…*sensing* her, Darren wondered if she'd make it through the next day. He understood Miranda's urgency around the matter now. If they were going to save Eden by turning her, it needed to happen soon.

"Hi." Eden and Miranda spoke simultaneously as they embraced in a huge hug. Eden buried her face in Miranda's shoulder.

Darren didn't know what to do. He felt like a third wheel. Miranda glanced over at him, her face pinched with worry.

His heart started to pound. This was his potential pack—his future standing before him. If Eden was involved with someone, that might complicate matters.

"What happened?" Miranda said.

"I'm not even sure where to begin." Eden pulled back from the hug, but kept holding onto Miranda's arms. She looked unsteady.

Darren took a step closer so he could catch her if she fell.

"First off, I owe you an apology," Eden said.

Miranda shook her head. "There's no need."

"Yes, there is. I'm so sorry about how I left the other day."

"I understand," Miranda said. "It's okay."

Eden smiled, but then tears started streaming down her cheeks. Miranda pulled her back into a hug.

"Tell me," Miranda said.

"Shade lost his best friend yesterday. I told him about our fight, and he reminded me that none of us knows how much time we have and we can't waste it fighting. He didn't even know about...about my..." Eden gasped a huge breath, then said, "I'm so sorry."

"Oh, Eden." Miranda leaned back and kissed Eden's forehead.

Darren's heart lurched again. He wanted to protect them both. It was obvious how much they cared for each other in every gentle touch and gesture.

He couldn't help but think about how had always Scott kidded around with him. He'd had a habit of elbowing Darren in the ribs when he'd thought Darren was taking himself too seriously.

Darren hadn't been able to save Scott. But if Eden wanted Darren to try to turn her, he would. In that moment, his mind was made up.

"It's okay," Miranda said. "Really, it's okay. You're only human."

Eden let out a snort. "It's funny you should say that." She looked over at Darren. "Can Miranda and I talk privately?"

"Darren and I don't have secrets." Miranda smiled at him, gaze intense, letting him know she meant it.

He believed her.

He wanted to grab her and kiss her, but that would just be awkward. Luckily, she stepped over to him and put her arm around his waist. He held her close against his side.

"You can trust him," Miranda said.

"But I need to talk about your..." Eden cocked her head to the side and shrugged. "You know."

Darren felt his eyebrows hitch up his forehead. "Um, maybe I should give you guys a minute."

"She means my powers." Miranda cast a mocking scowl at him, then smiled. "Darren knows about what I can do."

"Wow. I guess if he's on board with that, then this won't be so weird." Eden paused for a moment, then said, "No, this is still going to be weird."

"Out with it," Miranda said.

"Okay." Eden took a deep breath, then let it out through pursed lips. "Have you ever had a vision that involved... How do I even say this? Non-humans. Like people who aren't—"

"You mean like werewolves?" Miranda asked.

Miranda had perked up, but Darren felt his stomach drop at her words.

Eden laughed. "No, not werewolves." Her expression turned serious suddenly. "Wait, are werewolves real?"

"Yes." Miranda nodded. "Werewolves, vampires...zombies." Miranda's voice trailed off at the end and she squeezed Darren's waist.

"Vampires." Eden closed her eyes and let out another breath. "Vampires are real."

She opened her eyes again. There were tears glittering in them, but she was smiling.

"That's what I needed to know," Eden said. "Thank you."

"Hold on a minute." Miranda cocked her head to the side. "You can't get away with calling us out here and asking us if vampires are real and then not explain. Where is this coming from?"

"I can't tell you," Eden said. "It's not my secret to share."

Eden smelled like freshly turned earth, but there wasn't a spot of dirt on her outfit. Wasn't there something about vampires sleeping in coffins filled with dirt? If that was the case, they would carry the scent with them. That plus the smells of sex and blood...

"Her boyfriend's a vampire," Darren said.

Miranda and Eden both turned to him and gasped.

"How did you know that?" Eden said.

He shrugged, feeling his cheeks tingle again. A blushing werewolf. Great.

Miranda wouldn't let it go. "Yeah, how?"

He sighed, then pretended to scratch his nose, hoping Miranda would get the message. She did, but her reaction wasn't what he expected.

"Oh, you could smell it with your werewolf senses," she said.

"Miranda—" He let out a sigh.

"What?" Miranda said. "We can know that her boyfriend is a vampire, but I can't tell her that mine's a werewolf?"

He glanced at Eden, trying to read her response. Her eyes were wide and her mouth hung open, but then she closed it and smiled.

"This is a really strange night," Eden said.

"Tell me about it." Miranda shifted closer to Eden. "I'm guessing the vampire boyfriend is Shade?"

"Yes." Eden smiled and her gaze became a little unfocused. There was wonder and affection and longing there.

Darren couldn't resist putting his arm around Miranda's waist and pulling her against his chest.

"He offered to turn me," Eden said. "But it was just too much to process. I've been so light-headed lately, I wasn't sure if I was hallucinating or not. That's why I wanted to talk to you. I figured if anyone would know about this, it would be you."

"Ask the oracle. I get it." Miranda laughed. "Wow, you're a woman in high demand. We were going to offer for Darren to turn you."

"Really?" Eden's eyes widened.

"We were going to try if you were interested," Darren said. "I'm not even sure if I could. I'm still new to this all."

"Do you have like a werewolf mentor who's helping you through it?" Eden asked.

Darren snorted. "If only."

"Maybe Shade can help," Eden said. "He says he's old. Like hundreds of years old. I bet he's come across werewolves before."

Darren wasn't sure if that would be a good thing. "Isn't there a rivalry or something between vampires and werewolves? That's how the movies usually show it."

Miranda shook her head. "I don't remember my dad telling me stories about werewolves and vampires interacting at all. If I'd known it would be this important, I would have paid more attention to them. I was always more into the fairies."

"I'm not complaining about that," Darren said.

Eden's face lit up. "Are fairies real too?"

Darren and Miranda shared a look.

"Yeah, but that's not a good thing," Miranda said.

"Oh." Eden actually looked disappointed.

He hoped she never had a chance to meet a fairy and find out just how wrong her apparent ideas about them were.

"If Shade is as old as Eden says, maybe he knows about fairies too," Miranda said. "We can ask him about the coin and the Fairy Lord. He might even be able to help us with the full moon."

Darren's misgivings were still there. "I don't know if that's a good idea."

"Why?" Miranda craned her neck to look up at him.

Darren stared at Eden, not wanting to voice his concerns in front of her. She must have read his doubts in his expression.

"Whatever else he is, Shade is a good man," Eden said. "If he can help you, he will."

Darren shook his head. "We're still learning about all this. For all we know, Shade could be working for the Fairy Lord."

"The full moon is in two days," Miranda said. "Jack can't help us. If Shade is willing to, I don't think we can shut that door."

Damn.

"I don't really understand everything you're talking about, but Shade did say that we might have to run after her turns me," Eden said. "I think he'd be breaking some sort of rule, but if it means we get to be together forever… We're both willing to risk it. If he's working for this Fairy Lord you guys are worried about, he's already open to leaving him."

That was only somewhat reassuring.

Miranda turned to Darren and said, "We need all the help we can get if we're going to stop the zombie apocalypse."

She was right. What they were facing was so much bigger than dealing with his own…issues.

"Zombie apocalypse?" Eden let out a laugh. "You're joking, right?"

He didn't know what to say. Miranda was uncharacteristically silent as well.

Eden's smile vanished. "I know the other night you said something big and bad was coming, but a *zombie* apocalypse?"

"I'm not one-hundred percent certain yet, but my visions have been...pretty horrific lately." Miranda shook her head. "At the moment, I'm most concerned about you."

Miranda held out her hand to Eden. With barely a pause, Eden took it. Miranda closed her eyes. They both took a deep breath, letting it out in synch. They must have done this before.

Even with all of Miranda's talk of Eden, Darren hadn't realized how close they were. Hopefully, that bond would last through their respective changes.

Part of him was disappointed that Eden wouldn't be joining their pack. That part was drowned out in how happy he was for her to have found someone to love. Like he loved Miranda.

Miranda sucked in a breath, her eyes flying open.

"What? What is it?" Eden said.

Miranda shook her head, then grabbed Eden's wrist, half-pulling her friend toward the car.

"We're leaving," Miranda said. "Now."

Darren fell in step beside them. When Eden stumbled, he put his arm around her waist to help her.

"What did you see?" Eden asked.

He looked at the grim expression on Miranda's face and knew before she answered.

"Nothing," Miranda said. "Nothing at all."

Chapter Twenty-One

The streets were empty this time of night. Miranda started to say a prayer of thanks, but thought better of it. She didn't know who was listening.

Her chest hurt from the way her heart was pounding. Her neck ached from constantly looking over her shoulder at Eden curled up on the backseat, watching her breathe—*willing* her to keep breathing.

There had been no encroaching fog in Eden's future. No signs of an impending change or important events. Just silence. Darkness.

Miranda could feel it pressing on her, like a bubble surrounding Eden's fate. A bubble that was about to pop.

Now she knew what the future looked like for someone who was moments away from death. She would never mistake it again.

Shade's house was on the outskirts of town. Darren blew through traffic lights, as if he could sense Miranda's fear. She didn't want to say anything out loud and upset Eden.

Outwardly, Eden seemed okay. Maybe a little winded, but no worse than Miranda had seen her before. Something had changed and was speeding her descent.

Following Eden's instructions, they drove up a long curved drive. Shade's house—mansion—was at the top of a hill. Lights were on, and a man was standing on the front steps. He was wearing a really nice suit, hands in his pockets. His casual stance made it seem like he'd been expecting them.

"Vampire business must be good." Darren stopped the car, then turned to Miranda and said, "Maybe you two should wait here."

Eden's pale face appeared between them. Her eyes were unfocused until she saw Shade.

She smiled faintly. "I need to introduce you."

"She's right." It was just an excuse, but Miranda didn't want to say what she was really thinking.

There's no time.

Miranda opened her door, then pulled her seat forward so she could help Eden from the back. As they emerged, Miranda realized both men were suddenly standing right next to them. She turned around to see them glaring at each other.

She let Eden push away and stumble toward Shade. He caught her up against his chest.

"Eden, are you all right?" he asked.

"I'm fine," Eden said.

She smiled so sweetly, it tugged on Miranda's heart. Miranda wasn't sure if Eden was trying to reassure Shade or didn't realize how close she was to death.

"You need to turn her right now," Miranda said.

Shade's eyes widened. "Excuse me?"

"Turn her into a vampire," Miranda said. "Now."

Shade laughed, but the sound was uneasy. "I don't know what you're talking about."

"We don't have time for this," Miranda said.

"This is Miranda." Eden's voice sounded breathless and her lips were tinged with blue. "She's an oracle. And my best friend. You can trust her."

Miranda's heart was in her throat. She knew that Eden was her best friend. She didn't know that Eden felt the same way about her.

"And what about him?" Shade asked.

Miranda shrugged. "He's a werewolf. And Eden doesn't have much time left."

"A werewolf?" Shade's smile faded. "Well, that's a surprise, Mr. Calverton."

"Wait, you two know each other?" Miranda asked.

"We met briefly," Shade said. "Amid talk of vengeance."

"Mr. Reece." Darren started to let out a low, steady growl. "So, you're a centuries' old vampire. Is that why you're interested in antiquities?"

"At the moment, I'm more interested in vehicles." Shade nodded toward Darren's car. "I can't help but notice you've had a little fender-bender. That's a very odd shape pressed into what's left of your grill."

Darren shrugged. It was a casual gesture, except his shoulders stayed a little hunched, his arms curved at his sides as if he was ready to launch himself at Shade.

At the park, she'd seen Darren's speed. And again just now as they exited the car. Shade must have seen it, too. He must know what he was dealing with.

"I hit an animal," Darren said.

Shade laughed again, but his smile didn't reach his eyes. He shifted Eden so that she was at his side, then angled his body to partially block her from view. "What kind of animal?"

"The kind that turns into a man." Darren was glaring at Shade. The tension between them building.

"That's a dangerous breed," Shade said. "When did it happen?"

"The night after the coins were stolen." Darren's shoulders hunched up further and his lips curled back from his teeth. Very sharp teeth. "But then, I'm guessing you already know all about that."

"These are my friends," Eden said. "You can trust them."

Shade's smile became more forced. "I'm glad you and Miranda worked out your differences, but you don't know what you're dealing with when it comes to her boyfriend."

"None of us do," Miranda said. "The werewolf he hit bit him. Darren is still figuring out how to manage the change. We need your help. But Eden needs you *now*."

"I'll take care of Eden." Shade glanced at her briefly, as if he didn't want to take his eyes off of Darren for more than a moment. "But that's all I can do."

If Shade refused to help them, Miranda didn't know where they would turn. Darren was handling his change okay at the moment, but they had no idea how the full moon would affect him. Eventually, Mr. Morrison would have holding cells available that could handle a werewolf, but that was months away.

"Afraid of what your boss would say about you helping us out?" Darren said.

Shade didn't rise to his bait. "As a matter of fact, I am. And you should be, too."

Crap. Shade *was* working for the Fairy Lord.

"You look like you're holding it together," Shade said.

"Congratulations on that. But the full moon coming up will be more than you can handle on your own. My advice to you is find the werewolf who bit you. You'll do less damage as part of a pack."

Darren shook his head. "That's kind of a problem, since the guy's dead."

"Dead how?" Shade's brow furrowed.

"Someone shoved one of those silver coins into him," Darren said. "And that was *before* I hit him with my car."

"You killed a werewolf two days ago?" Shade stepped away from Eden. Darren mirrored the movement.

Miranda didn't like where this was going. She wasn't sure if it would count in their favor or against them if Shade thought they had killed a Knight of Antares. It didn't seem wise to take credit for it, given that Forester was probably the one who had managed to capture Niall and put the silver coin in him.

"The fairy who put the silver in him killed him," Miranda said. "The werewolf was doomed before Darren hit him."

"I don't suppose you know the name of this mystery werewolf?" Shade chuckled, but the sound made her even more uneasy.

"Niall," Miranda said.

Shade's lips peeled back from his teeth. Miranda hadn't remembered his canines being so long and pointed.

"You killed Niall." Shade let out a roar and leapt at Darren, hitting him in the chest and slamming him back into his car. The car slid a few feet across the drive.

Darren looked dazed, but only for a moment. He shook his head, then growled.

"Oh no," Miranda said.

Darren grabbed Shade by his arms and threw him over the car, then leapt onto its roof. Shade must have not missed a beat when he hit the ground on the other side.

It seemed the moment Darren reached the roof, Shade impacted him again. They both flew through the air, hitting the ground and digging a deep groove as they landed.

Miranda ran to Eden. They held onto each other.

Shade was pounding on Darren, driving his head deeper into the earth. Darren reached out and slashed Shade across the chest. Blood sprang from the wounds. Shade staggered back and Darren leapt to his feet.

His skin turned gray, his teeth lengthening as his face started to morph. Fur sprouted everywhere Miranda could see. His fingertips ended in long claws, blood dripping from them to the ground. The change was happening faster than the last time. Darren didn't seem to be fighting it.

"Oh my God," Eden said. "They'll kill each other."

Punctuating her statement, Darren leapt at Shade, striking out with those deadly-sharp claws. Shade seemed to vanish.

One moment, he was right in front of Darren, the next he was landing in a crouch behind him. It was like watching a live-action anime.

Miranda had no idea what to do. With the threat Shade presented, she was sure there'd be no reasoning with Darren, no getting him to back down from this. They had to figure out a way to reach one of them. Shade seemed the only option.

"Why did Shade attack him?" Miranda said. "How did he even know Niall?"

"Niall was his best friend." Eden seemed to pale even further as she spoke, turning almost to a dull gray. "I assumed they were both vampires, but…"

"He was the werewolf who turned Darren." Miranda led them to the porch, half supporting Eden.

Eden made a visible effort to draw in a breath to speak. "Did Darren really kill him?"

"Of course not." Miranda hoped that Shade was listening. "Niall was already dying when Darren hit him—and even that was an accident. Darren tried to help, but ended up being bitten. Before Niall died, Darren said he was horrified at what he'd done—that he'd turned Darren."

Shade had been fending off Darren's attacks to that point. When Darren lunged at Shade again and the vampire tried to leap away,

Darren lashed out and caught his ankle, yanking Shade back to the ground.

"We have to get them to stop," Miranda said.

"Get Eden into the house," Shade yelled.

Darren twisted Shade's leg around at an impossible angle. The sound it made—the way Shade screamed—made bile rise in the back of Miranda's throat.

"Shade!" Eden tried to run forward, but Miranda held her back.

It would be too terrible if Darren killed Shade. Aside from the fact that he was Eden's lover, if Niall and Shade were best friends, Shade was probably a Knight of Antares as well. He was their best hope of help for Darren.

The entire fight was based on a misunderstanding. Darren wouldn't be able to forgive himself if he killed Shade.

She hoped.

Because that was the flip side of this. If Darren killed Shade and *didn't* feel bad about it, it would mean part of his humanity had slipped away.

"Darren, stop," she yelled. "You have to stop."

Shade had seemed distracted when Miranda explained Niall's death. Maybe he'd been listening and understood what had happened. If she could just get Darren to back off and calm down...

"Stay here," Miranda said. "I'm going to—"

Something changed in Eden. Her breathing hitched as her legs buckled. Miranda had to struggle to keep her from falling. She helped her sit on the smooth wood of the porch, propping her up against the railing.

"No no no," Miranda chanted.

Shade was supposed to turn Eden. She wasn't supposed to die. What had changed?

The only thing Miranda could think was that she and Darren were here. If they hadn't come along, Eden would have called Shade and they would have handled things together. Instead, Eden was freaking out—for very good reason. It must be aggravating her symptoms.

Miranda would not be the reason her best friend died. She turned and ran toward the combatants.

Shade had managed to grab both of Darren's wrists, keeping his claws at bay, but Darren was snapping at him with those jaws. As she neared, she saw his ears and face extend farther, the change progressing even more.

She threw herself on his back. She knew she didn't have a chance of overpowering him, so she wrapped her arms around his shoulders and buried her face in his neck.

"Please, Darren, please." She sobbed. She couldn't stop herself. "Let him go. Please let him go to Eden."

Darren barely seemed to register her presence.

Shade dared a glance toward his house, where Eden had slumped to her side on the porch.

"Eden? Eden!" Shade yelled.

He turned back to Darren, eyes pinched tight as he took a deep breath. When he opened them, he seemed in control. Desperate, but in control.

"Darren, I need you to listen to me," Shade said. "I understand what happened with you and Niall. I heard Miranda explain. If we keep fighting now, Eden will die. And be assured, after that, I *will* kill you. And then you won't be around to protect Miranda."

Darren growled and flexed his fingers, still trying to reach Shade. The vampire seemed to be gaining space, though, slowly pushing Darren back.

"You are a neophyte. You're dangerous. I can help you. Help you *protect Miranda*. But you have to control yourself. Right now."

Throughout his change, Darren had talked about their bond helping him. It seemed Shade knew exactly what buttons to push to help Darren calm himself down.

She felt his muscles tense beneath her. He stopped trying to bite Shade, but was still growling.

"Darren, please," Miranda said. "You can do this. I know you can."

Darren shifted his weight, standing and pulling Shade halfway off the ground with him. Miranda kept her arms around Darren's neck, her feet dangling.

Shade's eyes were wide. He looked like he didn't know if it was a good sign or not. Miranda didn't either.

Darren released him. Shade grunted as he hit the ground.

She let out a breath, leaning against the back of Darren's head. He lifted one hand to her arm and touched it—so gentle it surprised her—then nuzzled her cheek.

Shade pulled himself onto all fours. The leg that Miranda was sure Darren had broken was still at an odd angle, but as Shade turned, it popped back into place. He let out a small grunt, then ran to Eden so fast he blurred. Darren followed at a slower pace, still holding Miranda's arm to keep her in place on his back.

"Eden, hold on," Shade said.

Miranda's stomach felt leaden. They couldn't have come so close to saving Eden and then fail. There had been too much loss already.

"You need to turn her right now," Miranda said. "If there's any chance—"

Shade cut her off. "Not without her permission."

He spoke so vehemently, she knew he wouldn't budge. But if Eden couldn't wake up, how could she give it?

"Then Darren will do it," Miranda said.

"No," Shade yelled.

Darren shocked Miranda by forming words in his mostly-changed state. His voice was guttural, but he said, "You'd rather lose her than have her be a werewolf?"

Her heart sank further. If Shade thought it was worth letting Eden die rather than having her become a werewolf, Darren might have second thoughts about turning Miranda.

"I wouldn't care if she became a chupacabra," Shade said. "But she has to give permission first. It has to be her choice."

"What if she's beyond that now?" Miranda said. "What if she can't?"

"She can," Shade said. "She will."

He lifted Eden to his lap, cradling her face in his hands. "Eden, sweetheart. I need you to open your eyes. I need you to talk to me. Just one word."

He bent to her ear, whispering so quietly Miranda couldn't make out the words. But Darren's grip on her arm tightened.

He sucked in a breath, then let it out slowly. As he did, the dark fur covering his skin retreated. His muscles and bones shifted back into place as he shrank to his normal proportions.

Miranda slid down his back, but couldn't bring herself to let go. She was terrified.

Darren managed to twist in her embrace, wrapping his arms around her and tucking her into his side. He still seemed tense, watching the intimate scene before them playing out.

Finally, Shade let out a sigh and lowered his forehead to Eden's. Darren squeezed Miranda closer against his side.

"It's okay," Darren said. "He got his answer."

Shade didn't waste any time. He lifted his wrist to his mouth and tore a deep gash with his...fangs. He pressed the wound to Eden's lips.

"Come on," Shade said. "Please."

Her brow furrowed at first, but then relaxed as she started to drink. Shade let out a breath, slumping a bit as he pulled her closer.

Miranda felt a little sick to her stomach. It was one thing to read about vampires biting people and sharing blood, or even to see it in movies. In person it was more...gruesome than she expected. Still, she was so relieved that Eden was going to be okay, she felt a little giddy.

"That's enough for now." Shade pulled his wrist away from Eden's mouth, then rose, lifting her into his arms. "You have my gratitude. And incredible respect. I seriously don't know how you managed to rein yourself in like that."

"I get that a lot," Darren said.

Shade cast a cock-eyed grin at them. "I was sure I was going to have to kill you."

"Yeah, I hear that a lot, too." Darren grinned back at Shade. It wasn't exactly what Miranda would call a pleasant expression. "Nobody's managed it so far."

She wasn't sure this was safe territory for them to be wading into. She didn't want Darren to be set off again, so she brought the conversation back to Eden.

"Is she going to be okay?"

"She will," Shade said. "My blood will keep her out of danger. She just needs some time for it to regenerate her system. As soon as she wakes up, we can proceed, but the rest of the change is going to take a while and is…a private matter."

"We'll come back tomorrow night," Miranda said.

"There are a few things we need to go over first." Shade turned and started toward the house. "Starting with you telling me everything you know about what happened to Niall."

Chapter Twenty-Two

Vampire business was better than good. It was fantastic, judging by Shade's home. Darren had been in some swank houses during his work with Ford Security. This one would hit the top ten.

Darren and Miranda followed Shade through a foyer that was two and a half stories high. A double-staircase wrapped around the edges of the room. He led them through a door beneath one that opened to a sitting room.

The walls were covered in yellow and white striped wallpaper. Flower-shaped sconces lit the room. A few chairs and small couches filled the space, with a coffee table in the center and a sideboard between two doors set in the wall on their right.

The cheeriness of it seemed odd to Darren. He'd expected a vampire's home to be gloomy and gothic. Then again, he could say the same about the vampire himself.

Shade seemed to be constantly smiling—when he wasn't worried about Eden, or trying to kick Darren's ass. After gently setting her on one of the couches, Shade sat on the floor next to her, holding her hand.

"You're sure she'll be okay?" Miranda's grip on Darren's waist tightened.

"Yes. Well…" Shade half-shrugged. "Pretty sure."

"*Pretty sure* isn't very reassuring," Darren said.

"Whatever illness she has is affecting her blood. Weakening it. I'm not sure how it will affect us."

"Us?" Miranda said.

"Turning for vampires is about mixing our blood. Whatever fate is in store for her, I'll share." He glanced over at them, then smiled. "I'm okay with that."

Miranda started to fidget. "Is there anything we can do to help?"

"Actually, it would probably help for me to be at full strength. Healing that broken leg took a little out of me." He stared at Darren, but was still smiling.

"What can we do?" Miranda said.

"I need blood." Shade spoke casually, as if asking for blood was no big deal.

Darren felt his hackles rise, even though he was in his human form. He stepped forward and growled.

"Not hers." Shade laughed. "Come on, we're not savages here. I have a supply in the fridge in the kitchen." He gestured over his shoulder at one of the doors next to the sideboard.

"You're just going to let a couple of strangers wander around your house?" Darren said.

"Friends of Eden's are friends of mine. Besides, if Niall turned you…" Shade's smile faltered. He looked down at Eden for a moment, as if collecting himself. When he looked back at Darren, he was smiling again, but his eyes glittered. "If Niall turned you, that sort of makes you family."

Something shifted deep in Darren's gut. Forester had tried to claim Darren as family, and the offer had sounded so hollow, it didn't affect him at all. The sincerity in Shade's eyes, in his voice… Darren could feel that he meant it.

He started to feel hope again. He had been afraid after their fight that he had ruined any chance that Shade might help them.

"We'll be right back." Darren led Miranda toward the door. It opened to a narrow hallway lined with several more doors.

"How will we find the kitchen?" Miranda asked.

Shade laughed. "Just follow Darren's nose."

"Very funny." Darren scowled back at Shade, but only half meant it.

"I'm a comedian," Shade said. "You'll get used to it."

Darren chuckled, leading Miranda down the hall. Finding the kitchen was easy. Just as Shade said, Darren followed the scent of food —and the sharper, metallic scent of blood. He opened the door to the kitchen and let Miranda go in first.

"Holy crap. This place is huge." She spun around in a circle, looking at the high ceilings, the tiled walls, and the rows of tables and workspaces.

"Do you like it?"

He remembered with a start that he still didn't have a job. With Scott and Mrs. Ford gone, there was little chance he'd be going back to the security company.

If Miranda wanted a house with a kitchen as big as her apartment, he didn't know how he'd swing that. How the hell did werewolves provide for their pack?

She shook her head. "It's completely impractical. I mean, maybe if you were entertaining a bunch of people or threw lots of parties. But I like my little kitchenette. Everything is one step away."

"My apartment has a small kitchen. It's a little roomier than yours, but nothing like this."

"Sounds perfect."

He let out his breath. As soon as he had this whole werewolf thing squared away, he'd find another job. They would figure out how to make it work.

He started to lead her deeper into the huge room, but she stopped. She put her hands on his face and stared into his eyes for a few moments.

"Are you okay?" she said.

"Yeah. Shade barely touched me."

"That's not what I'm talking about."

Darren was aware. He was just trying not to think about it.

The fight had been terrifying. Primarily because it had been…fun.

He'd been focused on protecting Miranda at first, but the longer it went on, the more the violence sang to him. He'd ended up wailing on Shade just for the hell of it. The power in his limbs, in his claws and teeth, had made him feel invincible.

It scared the hell out of him.

The only thing that was anywhere near that rush was when he was making love to Miranda. Thank God Shade had reminded Darren of her, brought his focus back to her. It had helped him to pull himself out of it.

"I thought I was going to lose you." Her eyes filled with tears again. They were still red from crying earlier—when she'd thrown herself on Darren's back to try to get him to calm down.

He dusted his fingertips across her cheek. "That's never going to happen."

Then he kissed her. He needed it as much as she did, probably. The reassurance, the connection. He let his tongue slide into her mouth, feeling her embracing him, welcoming him into her body. She wrapped her arms around him, holding him close.

He lifted her from her feet, encouraging her to wrap her legs around his waist. Once she did, he walked them to the nearest table and sat her down.

Dammit, she was wearing jeans. He could tear them off easily enough, but then what would she wear after they were done?

"Do not have sex in my kitchen," Shade said.

Darren broke off the kiss, wheeling around and expecting to see Shade right next to them. But they were alone.

"What is it?" Miranda said.

"Shade."

"You're kissing me and thinking about Shade?" She cocked an eyebrow and smirked at him.

Darren scowled in return. "No, I heard him just now."

"She can't hear me," Shade said. Darren realized his voice was coming from the sitting room.

As if confirming Darren's thought, Shade said, "Vampires might not be able to smell things as well as werewolves, but we have great hearing."

Darren shook his head and slowly backed away from Miranda. Picking her up by her hips, he set her feet on the floor.

"Shade says we're not allowed to have sex in his kitchen," Darren said.

Miranda's eyes widened and she blushed. "How did he know what we were doing?"

"He heard us." Darren smiled at her. "Let's hurry up and get him his blood."

She nodded and followed Darren as he led her to the fridge where the metallic scent originated. When he opened the door, he saw that most of the fridge was filled with vegetables, drinks, meats—things you'd find in anyone's kitchen. But the bottom two drawers were filled with bags of blood.

He barely raised his voice as he said, "How many do you want?"

Miranda glanced around the kitchen.

"Three should do it," Shade said.

Darren plucked three bags from the drawer and closed it along with the doors to the fridge. "Big eater."

Shade chuckled.

"You could hear him from in here?" Miranda said.

"Yeah."

As they headed back to the sitting room, she said, "How does anyone have sex in the house without hearing each other?"

Shade didn't reply until they'd returned. "We don't."

He stared at them intently as Darren handed over the bags of blood.

"Thanks," Shade said.

His fangs descended again and he bit into the first bag, draining it in seconds. When they were all empty, he tossed them on the coffee table and sat back with a sigh.

"That is much better."

"Sorry about the leg," Darren said.

"No you're not. You loved every minute of that fight."

He stammered, wanting to deny it, but not wanting to lie.

"It's okay," Shade said. "It's a werewolf thing. Fighting is like catnip...or something that makes more sense for werewolves."

"You're really okay?" Miranda said.

Shade smiled at her. "I'm fine. It's one of the benefits of being a vampire—or a werewolf. We're very resilient." He gestured toward a nearby chair. "Please, have a seat."

Darren chose a small chair and pulled Miranda down onto his lap. Having her close would help him keep a lid on his temper if Shade said or did anything that upset him.

Darren had a feeling they'd be wading into some murky waters in their conversation. It didn't take long for Shade to start up.

"Eden said you're an oracle," Shade said. "Does that give you special strength or healing powers? Maybe mind control?"

Miranda laughed. "I wish. Aside from the visions, I'm a garden-variety human."

Shade let out a thoughtful sound. "I somehow doubt that."

"What do you mean?" Miranda said.

"You seem to be a pretty 'well bonded couple'. Not to be crass, but I've never heard of a werewolf having sex with a human without..." Shade seemed to be struggling to find words. Given what Jack had said back at the restaurant, Darren couldn't blame the guy.

Miranda pulled Darren's hand onto her thigh, holding his wrist. "Darren would never hurt me."

"That's what I thought about Eden." Shade's smile fell as he turned to look at Eden, smoothing some hair away from her forehead. "I still was so carried away that I..." He shook his head, his voice trailing off.

"You bit her," Miranda said. "That's what sped up her descent."

"If she had died, it would have been my fault," Shade said. All traces of playfulness left his tone. "I can never repay you for helping me save her."

"Saving her is good enough for us," Darren said.

Shade let out a soft laugh through his nose. "We've always known it was dangerous to be with humans. I thought I could control myself when we..."

He shook his head. "It was so natural, though. As soon as I realized what I was doing, I stopped. I caught myself so quickly. For a normal human, it wouldn't have harmed them at all."

"You didn't know she was sick, did you?" Miranda said.

"Not until I tasted her blood. Niall must have known. He kept trying to warn me away from her. I thought it was just because of—" He shook his head again.

"Listen, you want information from me," Darren said. "I need information from you, too. We've been fumbling our way through this blind."

Shade laughed. "Fumbling? I'd say you're navigating these waters with amazing skill, my friend."

"It helps that he has an oracle as a guide." Miranda smiled and leaned into Darren.

He wrapped his arms around her waist. "That's true. I guess we haven't been completely blind."

"Remarkable."

They both turned to Shade.

"I'm just stunned to see you in such control," he said. "We've always thought that we couldn't have that kind of... intimate contact with humans without harming them. That's why it's forbidden."

"Forbidden?" Miranda said.

"Niall fell in love with a woman from one of the villages we were protecting back when we had all just changed. It didn't end well."

"Did he turn her?" Darren didn't want to ask, but had to know.

A haunted expression passed over Shade's features. He took a deep breath, and said, "He killed her."

Darren's heart started to pound. That didn't make any sense. Darren loved Miranda. He would never hurt her. He was sure of it. But if Niall loved that woman, he might have thought the same thing—and been wrong.

Miranda turned to Darren and lifted her hand to run her fingers through his hair. He closed his eyes and focused on the sensation, letting it calm him.

They'd already made love, and she was fine. He hadn't come close to hurting her. But what if things changed? What if the full moon was more than he could handle?

He felt her hand on his cheek. She tilted his face toward hers and said, "Stop."

Darren opened his eyes again. She looked so determined. There was a fierce confidence in her gaze.

"That is not our future," she said. "Remember?"

He nodded. Still, he'd feel a lot better once she had turned as well —when she'd have the same strength coursing through her that he'd felt during his fight with Shade.

"In six hundred years of existence, I've never met an oracle," Shade said.

"I've never met a vampire." Miranda smiled at him. "But I'm...not that old."

His grin returned. "Well, I'm very pleased to make your acquaintance. Even under such circumstances."

"I'm glad to hear it, because we need your help," she said.

Shade turned to Eden and dusted a lock of hair away from her forehead. "You brought Eden to me and helped me to save her life. Anything in my power to give is yours."

Darren let out a breath. "The full moon is in two nights. I'm doing okay controlling myself so far, but we've heard it'll be worse on that night."

Shade nodded. "You heard right. Niall and the other werewolves among us have been living with this for hundreds of years, and they still lose control on full moons."

Hundreds of years? The reality of that started to hit Darren. He was immortal now. But it only meant something if Miranda could share that with him.

"What do you do to keep people safe from them on those nights?" Darren said.

Shade's smile broadened. "And with that, you've passed the first test."

"What test?" Darren asked.

"Niall and I are—" Shade winced as he corrected himself, "*were*— part of a group of warriors who have pledged ourselves to protect humans from the fey. Your focus wasn't on keeping yourself safe or even Miranda specifically. You want to protect everyone."

What he was describing sounded an awful lot like Darren's idea of the Knights of Antares. But if he asked and was wrong, what would that mean for his new relationship with Shade?

A wrong assumption could be deadly in this case. Fey beings didn't seem very fond of the "traitors" among them. Darren kept his thought —his hope—to himself, waiting for Shade to bring it up. It was enough that they all seemed to have similar goals.

"I don't want to hurt anyone," Darren said.

"I can see that." Shade nodded. "Niall has a safe room in this house. One that even a full-powered werewolf can't escape from. We'll get you settled in it before your first full change."

"Thank you." Darren felt as if a weight had been lifted from his chest. He let out a huge breath, pulling Miranda closer against his chest.

She leaned over and kissed the top of his head.

"Of course," Shade said.

Darren laughed. "That doesn't seem like much of a test, though."

"It's better than you think." Shade shook his head. "Most people become raving psychopaths after they're bitten. The ones that survive, anyway."

"As if I wasn't worried enough about Miranda," Darren said.

When Shade looked at them quizzically, Miranda said, "He's going to turn me."

Shade's smile faded again. "That's a very bad idea."

Darren felt a growl bubbling up in his chest. He choked it down. His voice was still a little lower than usual when he said, "Why?"

"I'm not saying she shouldn't be turned," Shade said. "Just that you don't have enough control to do it safely. You could easily lose control and kill her."

"Also not reassuring," Darren said.

Miranda let out a sigh. "How about this? I've seen us together, turned, helping people. Is that reassuring?"

He smiled up at her. Her visions hadn't led them astray so far. He believed in them.

"Are you alone in these visions, or are there other werewolves and vampires with you?" Shade said.

"The visions I've seen so far are just of Darren and I with our pack."

Hearing her talk about it so casually, as if it had already happened, was the most reassuring thing of all. Darren felt he could breathe easier. They were going to make this work.

"Then it's even more important that Lev is the one who turns her," Shade said. "He's the pack leader. It should make both of your integrations easier, especially since technically Darren is part of Lev's pack already. It'll be a bit tricky getting Boden on board. He and Niall were brothers before they turned, and... Let's just say he feels Niall's loss keenly."

"What about the others?" Miranda said.

"Others?" Shade looked confused.

"I've been studying Darren's future pretty closely," she said. "There are four other werewolves with us in my visions."

Shade's face fell. "Lev's pack is just the three of you."

"Our pack will have six werewolves," she said. "I'm sure of it."

Shade shook his head. "Not if it's Lev's pack."

Darren felt the tension pick up in the room. If Miranda's visions were about them joining a different pack—a pack that was at odds with the one Shade was talking about—things could get ugly again quickly.

"If they'll accept me, they might accept others," Miranda said. "I don't know how far into the future I was seeing."

That was a white lie. From what she'd told Darren, it wouldn't be long. She might not have an exact date, but she knew it would happen soon.

"Look, these are all really big *ifs*," Shade said. "I'm not even sure they'll accept Eden after I change her."

"Is that why you told her you might have to run?" Darren said.

"Yes. I'm still not sure which path is safest for her."

Miranda stood. "I can help with that."

Darren was reluctant to let her go, but she was right. If she could read Shade, it would help them all.

"May I read you?" Miranda said.

Shade looked over at Darren. It was almost like asking permission —or checking to see if it would set Darren off. Darren nodded briefly.

"Of course," Shade said. He held absolutely still as Miranda walked over to him. She touched his shoulder, then walked back to Darren and sat on his lap again.

"That's it?" Shade said.

"Not quite." Miranda turned her hand over and stared at it, as if she was watching a video. She let out a huge sigh and then her lips pulled into a broad smile.

Shade leaned forward, but kept his grip on Eden's hand. "What do you see? Is Eden going to survive the transformation?"

Darren had wondered if Shade was hiding worry behind his smile. It was clear as day when he asked his questions.

And like Darren had unwittingly passed Shade's earlier test, Shade had just shown his own true nature. All he cared about was that Eden was safe.

"You don't have to worry," Miranda said. "I see you and Eden together. She's going to be fine."

Shade let out a huge breath and sat back. "Thank you." He gazed at Eden, his smile tender, then turned back to them. "That's a very cool power you have there."

Miranda leaned into Darren. "A vampire thinks my powers are cool."

Shade jumped in before Darren could even formulate a thought. "And so does a werewolf, which is even cooler than a vampire." He cast a comical grimace at Miranda and said, "Werewolves can be territorial. Best not to make him jealous."

Miranda laughed again. "Thanks for the tip."

"What else did you see?" Darren knew she was relieved about Eden, but her reaction was so strong, he suspected there was more.

"That Shade is one of the Knights of Antares." She smiled down at Darren. "We found them, just like Niall said."

"Niall told you to look for us?" Shade's voice had a pensive tone.

"Before he died," Darren said. "He told me to find you. That you'd help."

Shade nodded. "He was a good man. That he bit you… I can't really bear to think of what he must have been going through to do that."

"Then don't think about it," Darren said. "Don't remember him that way."

Shade gave them another cock-eyed smirk, but there was a sad cast to it. "Thank you." He seemed to collect himself, then turned to Miranda. "So, we're all going to be happily fighting fairies for years to come?"

He had mentioned not being sure if his boss would be okay with him turning Eden. Shade had a vested interest in knowing what Miranda had seen.

"Eventually," she said. "We'll all be part of the Knights of Antares while we fight the impending apocalypse together."

"That's great," Shade said. Then his smile fell. "Wait... Did you say *apocalypse?*"

"There are some things that we need to fill you in on," Darren said.

Eden stirred and Shade turned to her. "It's going to have to wait. Eden needs my full attention now. We'll probably be...occupied...for at least tonight and possibly tomorrow as well."

"Isn't that cutting it a little close?" Darren wanted to be locked up in Niall's safe room before the full moon rose.

"It'll be fine," Shade said. "Michelle is staying with me. She and her sister, Stacey, are humans who help us out."

"What kind of help can humans provide the Knights?" Miranda asked.

"Oh, you know. Sharpening pencils. Polishing the silver." Shade looked at Darren and grinned.

Darren just scoffed. He really was getting used to Shade's sense of humor.

Shade's smile faded a bit. "All of the Knights are paired with a vampire and a werewolf. Niall watched over me during the days and I watched over him on full moon nights. Since he's gone... Well, Michelle volunteered to stay with me while the sun's up and I'm dead to the world. She can let Darren into the safe room if necessary while Eden and I are in our day-sleep."

That was a lot more reassuring.

Eden stirred again and this time Shade stood and picked her up from the couch. Miranda and Darren stood as well.

Shade turned back to them and said, "Michelle's sleeping right now or I'd have her show you out."

"Not a problem." Darren put his arm around Miranda. "We can find the way."

"Thanks." Shade walked with them into the foyer. He paused before one of the staircases. "And Darren, I'm glad you found your way to me."

"Me, too."

Shade nodded, then headed up the stairs.

Chapter Twenty-Three

Miranda felt like she could float away as they stepped into the warm night air. Her heart was so much lighter.

Eden was safe. Darren had a place to stay during his first full moon —and an ally who could help him through it. Things were looking up.

Now they only had to deal with a homicidal elf and the zombie apocalypse.

One thing at a time.

Darren didn't look quite as relaxed. His shoulders were hunched and he kept shifting his weight from one foot to the other.

"Are you okay?" she asked.

He shook his head. "It's been quite a night."

"Mostly good, though. We need to celebrate our victories."

"What did you have in mind?"

Something that got him moving. A way to siphon off his obvious restless energy.

Miranda hooked her arm through Darren's elbow and pulled him along with her down the steps. Instead of heading for the car, she walked around the side of the house.

"Where are we going?" Darren said.

"Eden made a moon garden for Shade. That's how they met—he contracted her to do a landscaping project. She wanted me to see it, so I'm taking advantage of this opportunity."

"I don't know if we should be prowling around a vampire's yard."

"We're not prowling. We're strolling."

Darren let out a little chuckle and the muscles of his arm relaxed under her hand. They followed a well-worn path through the grass that led down toward some trees at the side of the yard.

Shade's house felt like it was out in the country, even though it was really on the outskirts of town. The privacy all that land surrounding his home lent must be really useful—especially on full moon nights.

The path was a dark ribbon in the pale grass on either side of them. Even without the lights from the house, Miranda could find her way. Darren could probably see perfectly well.

She looked up at the dark, starry sky. The moon was right above them, nearly full and gleaming silver.

"It's beautiful," she said.

Darren didn't look up. His arm tensed again.

"Is it affecting you?" she asked. "Should we go back inside?"

"No, it's okay. I mean, I can feel it. A pull like the tides. But I'm starting to get used to it."

"Eventually, you'll enjoy it."

He scoffed. "Did you see that in one of your visions?"

"Not exactly. It's more a feeling I have."

They rounded a corner of the small hill they were walking down, and she froze. Darren sucked in a breath beside her.

"Oh my God," she said.

The hillside before them glowed.

Huge flowers stretched their petals along lattices that hovered over paths of milky stone. Plants with soft white leaves caught and reflected the light like tiny hands bending at a stream for water. The rice paper walls of an Asian-styled tea house gleamed in the center of the space.

They walked forward into a sea of a thousand different shades of silver.

"This is amazing," she said. "Even the ground cover catches the light."

Darren wrapped his arm around her waist and pulled her closer as they ducked beneath a low-hanging vine. She glanced at his face to see him staring at the garden, his eyes wide and lips parted.

As subtle as the colors were, it was still a feast for her senses. She couldn't imagine what it was like for him. They sat on one of the benches and looked around.

He took a deep breath and let it out, his body relaxing next to hers. "This is the most peaceful place I've ever been in."

"I feel it, too."

After everything they'd already been through and what still awaited them, it was a welcome respite. It didn't last long.

"Do you think Forester is still alive?" Darren said.

She let out a sigh. "It depends on how much iron was in the bullet

Mr. Morrison used."

"Probably not much."

"It's safest to assume Forester is still alive, then."

Darren was quiet for a moment, then said, "Good."

"Good?"

"I want to be the one who kills him."

If he'd growled as he said it, she would have been less unsettled. But he was absolutely calm. It didn't seem like he was struggling with his new nature or being influenced by it at all.

He *wanted* to kill Forester. And she couldn't really blame him. That didn't mean it was safe to hold on to those thoughts.

"I don't think revenge is a good thing for you to be focusing on," she said.

"I disagree. It gives me a direction for the anger. The rage. You have no idea what it's like."

"I don't. But I will." She put her hand on his cheek, turning his face to hers. "Someday soon, I'll be going through this. I need you to show me that I can handle turning without it changing who I am."

"It's getting harder to remember who I was before this."

"Let me help you. You're a man who will drop everything to help a stranger. You'll risk yourself for others without hesitating."

He let out a little snort and said, "We have that in common. What you did to save that family…"

He shook his head and she felt him tense again. He shouldn't be thinking about her accident, about her being in danger. That wasn't a good way to stay calm either.

"My visions told me I'd be fine," she said.

"Don't downplay it. What you did took courage. Seeing what was going to happen must have been terrifying. But you still got behind that wheel."

Warmth spread through her chest. She hadn't talked to anybody about what it was like, but he was right. In some ways, seeing what would happen actually made it more terrifying.

"You would have done the same thing," she said. "That's who you are. Who *we* are. We're going to work together to make the world a safer place."

"And stop the zombie apocalypse."

He let out a dark chuckle and she joined him.

"It sounds ridiculous when you say it out loud," she said.

"Thinking about it makes my skin crawl. And there's a lot more significance to that feeling now."

"I can imagine. But thinking about *that* is probably as bad as thinking about revenge."

"I know." He closed his eyes and leaned his forehead against hers. "I need something to hold on to."

"Hold on to me."

He opened his eyes again. Tiny lights were flickering in them, making the gray of his irises even more beautiful. He leaned in and kissed her.

She brought her hand to the back of his neck, pulling herself closer as he deepened his kiss. His tongue slid into her mouth and she sighed, burrowing her fingers through his hair.

If he needed her to be his anchor, she was fine with that. He might not realize it, but he was doing the same for her—grounding her among these extraordinary events. Giving her a feeling of solace.

He knelt in front of her and started taking off her shoes.

"What are you doing?" she asked.

"I need you naked. Right now. Are you up for it?"

He paused, one of her socks in his hand. The night air felt good on her bare feet.

She shrugged. "Warm air. Soft grass. Sure."

He smiled broadly, rising on his knees as he undid her jeans. She stood so he could shimmy them down her legs, along with her panties. She helped him out by pulling off her shirt and throwing it on the pile, along with her bra.

Darren knelt in front of her, a look of wonder on his face. She had a pretty good opinion of herself, even though she didn't quite fit society's expectations. But she'd never had anyone look at her the way he did. Like she was a goddess.

His hands actually shook as he reached toward her stomach and gently traced his fingertips over the roundness of her belly, then further down.

"You are so beautiful," he said.

She ran her fingers through his hair. It was pitch black in the dim light of the moon.

"That's nice of you to say."

"It's fact. I'll gut anyone who says otherwise."

She laughed. "You sure know how to sweet talk a girl."

"Sorry. I'm still getting those surges."

"I can think of better ways you can expend your energy."

He smirked up at her, then ran his hands up along her sides. He cupped her breasts, kneading them, running his fingertips over her nipples till they were tight buds. He let his hands drift down to her backside when he was done and pressed a kiss to her stomach.

"You smell so good," he said.

"Coming from a werewolf, I guess that's—"

Her voice cut off as he moved his lips to the curls between her legs. Waves of pleasure flooded her senses. He kept one arm wrapped around her backside, holding her up, while the other joined his exploration.

He spread the soft folds of her skin, sucking her clit into his mouth. She gasped as his fingers traced along her slit, finding her pussy and sliding in deep. The rough skin of his fingers pulled against her skin, stimulating her further.

"Darren…"

He growled, holding her close, his tongue laving her relentlessly, fingers moving in and out, stretching her, preparing her for him. Her knees were starting to weaken as the pressure between her legs built.

He broke away from her suddenly, grabbing her waist and pulling her down to the ground. She wasn't sure what he was doing, but was already dazed from the pleasure winding its way through her body.

The soft grass tickled her skin, the cool earth pressed against her back. She looked up at the round moon and the stars surrounding her.

Darren lifted her thighs, draping her legs over his shoulders as he practically dove back to her. This time, he found her core with his tongue. Arcs of pleasure flowed through her body. Her nerves were on fire, her pussy clenching with need.

He kept her hips off the ground, arms wrapped around her legs to keep her pressed to him so he could drive his tongue in deep. He found her clit with his fingers, circling it, his other hand clutching at her stomach with a desperation that somehow heightened every touch.

Her heart was pounding, her body aching for more, until finally the pleasure thrummed out through her body. She dug her heels into his shoulders, her back arching from the intense sensations. He kept thrusting, his fingers working her, pulling every drop of ecstasy from her climax that he could.

The moment she started to relax, he released her, easing her down. She had barely touched the ground when he gripped her hips and flipped her over onto her stomach. He pulled her onto her hands and knees. She heard his zipper, and felt him at her core for a brief instant before he drove himself in deep.

Her pussy stretched as he filled her, the pulsing of her orgasm intensifying as her body quickened again beneath his thrusts. He held onto her hips with an iron grip, ramming himself into her over and over again.

He let out a frustrated grunt, releasing her for a moment but keeping their hips locked together. The respite let her body finally start to calm a bit.

She looked over her shoulder and saw him pull his shirt over his head and toss it aside. He fell across her back, the warmth of his chest covering her. He put his hands on top of hers, their arms flush against each other's.

And then his hips started to move in earnest.

He crashed into her, the hair of his chest rubbing against the skin of her back. He buried his face in her neck, as if he was intent on keeping as much of their skin touching as possible.

She'd never known her body could take—or give—so much pleasure. Her pussy contracted around him, pulsing as the stimulus sent her over the edge into another climax. It went on and on as he pounded into her. He threw his head back and let out a guttural yell, spilling himself deep.

He didn't seem to want to stop. His breath tickled the hair around her ear. He pulled himself out slowly—almost all the way—then sank back into her with a sigh. He kissed her neck and shoulders, nipped her earlobe.

He was savoring the feel of her, of their skin pressed together, so much of their bodies touching. He finally slid from her pussy, but kept holding her close.

"Darren, that was—"

"Not yet. Please. I need this." He kissed the side of her neck again.

If he needed to hold on to this sense of connection, she was happy to help. Even if she sort of wanted to melt into a puddle on the ground with a Darren blanket on top of her.

He shifted his weight, gripping her hips to keep her where he wanted her. He sat back on his knees, holding onto her so that she was straddling him even though they were facing the same direction. She leaned against his chest, soaking in his warmth.

"Hold onto me." He lifted her arms so they were wrapped around his neck and she could hang from him. Then he moved his hands to her body.

After two amazing orgasms, she thought her body would be content. She was wrong. His hands cupped her breasts, rolling her nipples between his thumbs and forefingers until the pleasure was so intense it almost hurt. He lifted their weight, massaging them, as he trailed kisses along the side of her neck.

His lips latched onto her skin, suckling it, leaving a mark. One hand stayed at her breasts while the other drifted over her stomach, lovingly tracing it before delving between her legs.

Instead of her nerves feeling sated or overloaded, it was like he had primed her for even more pleasure. Heat tore through her nerves and her skin erupted in gooseflesh everywhere. She felt his dick prod at her again, slowly parting her flesh as he eased it into her pussy.

He rose up on his knees, pushing her body with him, crossing one arm over her chest to help her keep her balance as he started to thrust into her again. He never let up with his fingers on her clit.

She gyrated her hips on his dick, taking in more, wanting to him to feel as much pleasure as he'd given her. Her arms were still around his neck and she used that as leverage to pull her body up along his shaft and slide back onto him.

She turned her head to try to kiss him and saw him staring up at the moon. The silver light splashed over his features, emphasizing his strong cheekbones and straight nose. His eyes were glowing.

She tried to imagine what this must feel like for him. The pull of the moon, his heightened senses making everything more intense, the friction of their skin touching, the bond of their love strengthening as they experienced all of this together.

He looked back to her, his lips parting as he saw her staring at him. Then he claimed her mouth with his.

His tongue thrust deep, mirroring the movement of his dick buried inside her body. She let herself soak in the sensations, drinking in all of him, as much as she could with her human senses.

It wouldn't be much longer until they had both turned. She made a promise to herself that afterwards they'd return to this spot again when the moon was almost full.

She broke off the kiss, tilting her head so that her neck was exposed for him. She hadn't missed what a turn-on it was for him. Werewolves were predators. It made sense that the gesture would reach him on a deep level.

He sucked in a breath, then lowered his lips to her. He ran his lips, then his tongue along her skin before nipping and suckling it. His hands picked up momentum, his thrusts coming faster.

She let herself relax further against him, just taking everything he was offering. The pleasure of his hands, his mouth, his shaft. The knowledge of his love and how much he trusted her.

This was their 'forever'.

The heat that had been slowly pulsing through her body coalesced, building to a flashpoint that radiated out from where they were joined. Her entire body vibrated with it, thrummed with pleasure as her pussy pulsed around him.

He groaned against her neck, increasing his pace again, moving his hands to her hips to keep her steady as he pounded into her. She held his neck tight, focusing all her attention on his dick spilling into her, filling her with his seed. He pressed himself in as deep as he could and held himself there.

This time, when he started to soften, they both fell forward onto the grass. He let himself slide from her, but kept his arms around her, pulling her next to him. They lay on their backs, catching their breath, as they stared up at the growing moon.

Chapter Twenty-Four

The moon did not control him. Being a werewolf did not define him. He was in control. After making love to Miranda all night in the moon garden, Darren was sure of it.

He could still feel the change in him, sense the pull of the moon. But now when the urge toward violence rose in him, he had one purpose only—to protect Miranda. And part of that meant protecting the world she lived in.

She let out a little sigh in her sleep. Darren had carried her to the car just before dawn, after they'd both dressed. She'd passed out before they even reached the end of Shade's driveway.

They hadn't slept much.

The memory of the wind on his skin—the moonlight bathing every inch of him as he buried himself in Miranda's body over and over again—was strong. But if he thought about that, things could get a little awkward.

They were sitting in the parking lot of Ford Security. He was just waiting for her to wake up.

She let out a sort of purring sound and stretched, her head flopping toward him. Her eyes opened, rich brown like the earth. She smiled.

"Good morning," she said.

"Good morning."

She sat up and looked around. "Where are we?"

"Ford Security. You said you wanted to talk to Morrison. I'm pretty sure he's inside."

"Do you think he'll agree to see us?"

Yesterday, Darren would have growled and felt his hackles rise. Today, he smiled. He was pretty sure it wasn't a nice smile.

"He will."

She gave him a skeptical look. "What do you have in mind?"

He felt his smile widen and let his gaze slowly caress her body, lingering on her breasts and the apex of her legs. Her scent shifted. She had definitely received his message. He looked back at her face and noticed her throat work as she swallowed.

"I meant for Mr. Morrison." She opened her door, letting in a gentle breeze. "Geeze, it just rose like ten degrees in here."

Darren laughed. "I guess we should take care of him first. But don't worry, I won't kill him."

Unless he threatened Miranda. Then Darren would tear the building apart and burn it.

In a very controlled manner.

She started to unbuckle her seatbelt. By the time she was finished and had her feet on the ground, Darren was already at her door offering his hand.

Werewolf speed and agility was really useful. He helped her to her feet, which was good, because she swayed a little.

"I guess my knees are still a little weak." She smiled up at him almost shyly.

After everything they'd done last night, he was a little surprised and absolutely charmed. He leaned in to kiss her, but she stopped him with a finger on his lips.

"If we start that again, I don't know when we'll stop," she said. "And you're right, we really need to take care of this."

He sighed, but nodded. "Okay. But afterwards, we're going back to my place. I have a huge bed and a bathtub that can easily fit two. And it has jets."

She groaned and rested her forehead against his chest. He stepped back, pulling her along with him, and shut the door to the car. With her arm wrapped around his waist, he tucked her against his side and they headed for the building.

Darren wasn't sure what sort of reception they would get. If he still worked for the company, he could probably talk Miranda past the guard. As it was, whoever was on duty might call the cops the moment they saw Darren approaching. His skin prickled as he opened the door.

Terry was sitting behind the desk inside. He jumped to his feet and headed for them as soon as they stepped into the lobby.

Darren tensed. He didn't want to hurt anyone—least of all Terry. But the guard was approaching fast. He was armed.

Darren clamped down on the violent thoughts that rose in his mind.

He willed his muscles to relax, his skin to stop itching. If he needed to change, it would happen fast enough. If he needed to protect Miranda, he could.

Luckily, it wasn't an issue. Terry stopped an arm's length away and smiled broadly.

"Mr. Calverton! I am so glad you're back."

He reached out to shake Darren's hand. Darren flexed his fingers a few times to make sure there were no claws sprouting from them, then shook it.

"That's nice to hear," he said.

"I have your badge for you." Terry gave Darren the small plastic rectangle. "Mr. Morrison gave it to me as soon as I came on duty. Looks like it's been upgraded."

Darren turned the badge over in his hand. His old badge had been a deep green. This one was silver. He would have laughed at the coincidence if he wasn't floored by what it meant.

Full-access.

Silver was the highest clearance anyone at Ford Security could get. As far as he knew, only Mrs. Ford and Morrison had silver badges.

"It's a shame about the Fords," Terry said. "I suppose it goes with the territory, though, working security. I still can't believe they were blackmailed into aiding with that theft. Morrison said you helped with the case on the down-low and that's why they had to make it look like you were fired."

Darren played along. "Yeah. But I think we're trying to keep that information in the company."

"Right. I'll keep it to myself. Don't worry." Terry looked at Miranda for the first time. He was probably wondering if he'd stepped in it by saying that in front of someone else.

"I'm Miranda."

Miranda offered her hand and Terry took it. She held on, shaking it for long enough to make the moment awkward. Terry cast a look at Darren, and Darren shrugged. She finally let Terry go and smiled.

"Miranda Lennox," she said. "I helped Darren with his investigation."

Darren didn't know what she'd seen, but he played along. He didn't even have to lie. "Ms. Lennox was invaluable in figuring out what happened."

"Are you with law enforcement?" Terry asked.

"I'm an independent consultant," she said. "You'll be seeing me around quite a bit."

Terry smiled at her. "Well, then, let me get you a badge."

He trotted back to the front desk. After scribbling something down, he opened a drawer and returned with a beige piece of plastic on a clip.

"It's just a guest badge," he said, "but I'm sure Mr. Morrison will hook you up with something a little more permanent soon."

She grinned at Darren. "I'm sure he will."

"Well, I won't keep you," Terry said. "Mr. Morrison is in Mrs. Ford's office."

"Thanks, Terry." Darren nodded to the taller man as they stepped past him.

Darren led Miranda deeper into the building. He held his breath when he passed his badge over the scanner and didn't relax until the door beeped and he heard the latch retract.

Miranda leaned in close and said, "That went better than expected."

"No kidding."

The door to Mrs. Ford's office was open when they arrived. Morrison was inside, standing at the desk and sifting through piles of paperwork.

Darren's chest suddenly constricted. Rage flooded him. It came on so fast, he couldn't think himself out of it.

Seeing Morrison here, it brought back everything that had happened at the park—and before. Losing his job, Miranda's accident, watching Scott die. Darren wanted to leap into the room and snap Morrison's head off of his body.

Until Darren felt Miranda's hand on his chest.

She was staring up at him, her eyes were so warm, so full of concern. He let it soak into him, used it to bolster his strength as he fought back the rage. He closed his eyes and took a few deep breaths.

"Whatever you're going to do to me, you need to come in and close the door first." Morrison's voice was rough and lower than usual. "Honestly, if you're here to kill me, you'd be doing me a fucking favor."

The last traces of Darren's rage evaporated when he finally really looked at Morrison.

His eyes were red. He smelled of saltwater and there were stains around the collar of his shirt from where he'd cried. A lot. His scalp and face were covered in stubble and his tie was loose, the top button of his shirt undone. He was a wreck.

Miranda pulled Darren into the room, then closed the door behind them.

Morrison stared at them expectantly. After a few moments, he dropped the papers he was holding back onto the desk. He actually looked disappointed.

"I don't suppose you owe me any favors," Morrison said.

"He doesn't." Miranda's voice was stronger than Darren had ever heard it. "But *you* owe *us*."

Morrison turned around to face them. He didn't say anything.

"Mrs. Ford left everything to you," Miranda said. "Because Scott —"

She stopped herself, casting a quick glance at Darren. He worked harder at holding it together. He could always kill Morrison later. Darren chanted that in his mind to keep from jumping over the desk and sinking his teeth into Morrison's neck.

"You run the company now." Darren could hardly believe it.

"Yeah," Morrison said. "So, what do you want? Money? Access to information?"

"We want you to shift the company's resources into Research and Development," Miranda said.

Morrison's brow furrowed. "What kind of R&D are we talking about?"

"The kind that kills things like Forester," she said.

Her voice was like steel. A frisson of pleasure shot down Darren's spine from the sound.

"I thought you were calling in a favor," Morrison said. "If you know how to kill him, I'll gladly help."

"Good. Because this is only the beginning." Miranda nodded curtly, a General marshaling her resources. "We're going to need holding cells that can contain powerful beings. Cells lined with iron and silver to start. And we'll need weapons and armor to support the fairy-fighting community that already exists."

"Fairy fighters?" Morrison let out a harsh laugh and shook his head. "If I hadn't seen with my own eyes…"

"You *did* see it," Darren said. "And if you ever need a reminder, I'm right here."

Morrison's heartbeat picked up and his scent shifted with the sharp tang of fear. Morrison might say he was ready to die, but on some level, he would fight it. That was good. From what Miranda had said, they needed him. Not just his resources, but his commitment.

Morrison cleared his throat. "Is that all?"

"No," Darren said. "I want an apology."

"I'm genuinely sorry we framed you—"

"Not for me. For Miranda. You almost killed her with that stunt you pulled to get me away from the package."

Morrison actually paled. His lips pulled into a tight line.

"That wasn't supposed to happen. I was going to pull into the intersection and let somebody hit the passenger's side of the SUV. You came out of nowhere."

"It was me or a family in a minivan," Miranda said. "A family that would have been killed."

"Christ." Morrison ran a shaking hand over his head. "Edith was set on getting this done. I hadn't driven anything other than the company cars in so long. The brakes and the response were—"

He shook his head. "That's just a lame-assed excuse. We never meant for anyone to be hurt. I am truly sorry for putting you and others in danger."

"I accept your apology," Miranda said. "And I apologize in advance for doing the same to you. You're going to be working with very dangerous individuals. Both as targets and as colleagues."

"I can handle myself," he said.

She smiled. "I know. Forewarned is forearmed. I'll take care of the warnings. You take care of the armaments. Deal?"

He let out a snort. "Deal. But you need to go after Forester first."

"You don't choose our targets," Darren said. "Miranda does."

If they were going to stave off the apocalypse, they needed to follow her visions.

Morrison shook his head. "I'm not talking about revenge. Yeah, it kills me that he's walking—or teleporting—around out there. But he's also plotting, regrouping, getting ready to strike. I heard what he said about Miranda. He's going to come for her, and soon. You need to take the fight to him, strike while he's still weakened."

Shit. That made a lot of sense. Morrison was going to be a better ally than Darren thought.

"He's right." Miranda's gaze was unfocused. He'd seen that look before when she was thinking things through or concentrating on a vision.

"Do you know where we can find Forester?" Darren said.

"No idea." Morrison shrugged. "The only place we ever met him was that damned park."

"We don't need to find him," Miranda said. "He'll find us."

Darren didn't like the sound of that. But Miranda was smiling.

"We can use the coin to lure him into a trap," she said. "If we take it out of the iron box, he'll come to it, like he did before."

"We don't know that for sure," Darren said.

"It's the best chance we have."

"If you can draw him out, that means you pick the terrain for battle," Morrison said. "You can choose a location that gives you an advantage. But I'm going to need time to develop weapons for you."

"I'm all the weapon she needs." Darren relaxed his hold on his change a bit. He felt his teeth lengthen, his skin prickle. Most gratifying of all, he saw Morrison's eyes grow wide and his mouth fall open.

"Darren, stop showing off," Miranda said.

Darren took a deep breath and willed the change to recede. It was getting easier, not harder. Maybe it was because the moon wasn't out. Maybe it was because he had spent the entire night making love to

Miranda bathed in its glow.

"If Forester hadn't had home field advantage..." Morrison shook his head. "Things might have ended differently."

"They'll end differently this time." Forester's immortality would end the next time Darren saw him.

"I just wish I could be there when it happens," Morrison said.

Darren didn't doubt it. He wanted to rip Forester's head off for threatening Miranda. Forester had *killed* Mrs. Ford—the woman Morrison loved.

Darren actually started to feel sorry for the guy. It was a hell of a lot better than murderous rage.

"Could you give us a moment, Mr. Morrison?" Miranda asked. "I need to speak with Darren in private."

Morrison nodded. "Sure."

He kept his distance as he headed out the door, closing it behind him.

As soon as he was gone, Miranda said, "The Red Thread. That's where we should spring the trap. We make sure Jack's friends aren't around, load ourselves up with skillets, and—"

Darren's skin started to crawl again and his shoulders bunched. "Hang on. You're not going to be anywhere near where this goes down."

She glared at him with an unmistakable challenge. Even in her frail human form, she was willing to take him on. Part of him wanted to lock her up somewhere to keep her safe. Another part wanted to bend her over the desk.

"You need me there to help you come back from the change," she said.

Darren stepped closer, towering over her. "I'm better at controlling it. I was able to come back after fighting with Shade."

She wasn't impressed by his posturing at all. "I still helped. Besides, we don't know what sort of spells are on that coin. When we're done using it, we need to put it back in the iron box, and you can't touch it."

"Jack can help me."

"Jack is still considering killing you."

"I can take him."

"He's our ally. You might kill him accidentally or he might kill you on purpose. He's an experienced werewolf hunter. And he's my friend. He's the closest thing I've had to family since my mom died."

Shit.

Okay, fighting Jack was definitely a bad idea. But so was having Miranda on site when they lured in Forester.

As if she could read his thoughts, she said, "Forester doesn't want to kill me. He wants to capture me. I have faith in you. You won't let that happen."

"It's too much of a risk."

"And it's my risk to take." She took a deep breath and let it out slowly, visibly calming herself down. "This is turning into a pivotal moment in our relationship, Darren. I know your instinct is to protect me. But you have to let me make my own decisions. If you can't do that, if we can't be partners in this—"

"I get it," he said.

He couldn't let her finish her sentence. Couldn't even think it. To lose her over this would be...something he couldn't handle.

And she was right. She had risked her life before to protect people. Given what she'd seen—the apocalypse they had to fight, together— she would probably have to do so again. She'd *choose* to do so. It was part of why he loved her. He had to be strong enough to live with the fear that came along with it.

"Let's call Jack and set it up," he said.

Chapter Twenty-Five

Walking back into The Red Thread was surreal. The place looked the same, smelled the same, but everything was slightly off.

Miranda had spent so many hours there, thinking she had the world mostly figured out—especially with her powers giving her an edge. She'd had no idea what the world was really like.

The silver bell above their head rang frantically as Darren followed her inside. Jack limped out from the kitchen. He was wiping his hands on a towel. He tossed it on the counter as he approached them. When he was close enough, he reached up and touched the bell, silencing it.

In his deep voice, he said, "Welcome to The Red Thread."

"Thanks for having us." Darren smirked at him.

"You said you needed to talk," Jack said.

"Could we sit down?" Miranda had noticed Jack wince when he'd turned off his alarm system. She wanted him to rest if he could.

"Yeah." He turned around and led them to the back room again.

The smashed furniture had been cleared and a collapsible card table sat in the middle of the room. The cabinets along the counter were gone, along with all the weapons that had been on the walls.

"What happened?" Miranda said.

"Forester happened." Jack shook his head. "A fairy found our base. We had to move it."

"The energy's gone too," Darren said. He sniffed the air.

"We left the bells in place for now and are going to plant a booby trap for any fairies that might come poking around." He smiled at Darren. "I recommend you find another establishment to patronize."

"Wait, are you shutting down The Red Thread?" Miranda's chest constricted and her stomach lurched.

The Red Thread wasn't just where she worked. It had been like a second home to her for years. And if Jack was leaving it behind, did that mean he was leaving her too?

She knew she had another family to go to now, even though it hadn't quite formed yet. But Jack was family, too. She didn't want to lose him.

"It's too dangerous to stay," he said. "I'm a sitting duck now that the Forester knows where I am."

Miranda was desperate to give Jack a reason to stay.

"Forester doesn't seem the type to share information," she said. "If anything, he'll come back by himself and try to capture or kill you."

Jack nodded. "I agree. That doesn't make it any less dangerous to stick around."

"But we came here to kill him," she said.

Jack's eyebrows hiked up his forehead. "You have my attention."

"Please, sit." Miranda pulled out a chair for him. He sighed and sat down, then she and Darren joined him at the rickety table.

"I'm listening," Jack said.

"We have a plan to lure Forester here." Miranda took the iron box out of her purse and set it on the center of the table. "We're going to open the box."

Jack glanced at the box. "You think he'll show up again when the coin comes back on his radar?"

"Fairies are vindictive," she said. "After what we did to his pocket of Faerie, I think he'll come to kill us the moment he knows where we are."

Jack picked up the box and turned it over in his hands. "You're probably right. But he'll be at full strength. If you didn't kill him, he'll be healed by now."

"That's okay," Darren said. "I'm pretty close to full strength at this point, too."

Jack was quiet for a few moments as he stared at Darren. "You look like you're holding up pretty well."

"I am."

"Looks can be deceiving," Jack said.

Miranda shook her head. "I thought we were past this. Darren is in control. I just watched him kick a vampire's butt, then back off from the fight and turn himself back, almost entirely on his own."

"A vampire?" Jack's brow furrowed.

"It was a long night." Miranda felt a blush creep over her face.

"Apparently so." He stared at her neck, which was probably

covered in love bites. At least they weren't vampire bites.

Miranda quickly went on. "The vampire is one of the Knights of Antares, and he's an ally now. He has a safe room where Darren can spend his first full moon."

Jack let out a chuff of air. "There are no Knights, Miranda. They're a legend, like I said. And if that guy was a vampire, he's yet another fey being. He'll say anything to get you to lower your guard. You can't trust them."

"I can and I do," she said. "I'm going to have to if we're going to make it through this apocalypse. And if you're going to help me, you have to come around on this point."

He shook his head.

"I'm going to turn," she said.

Jack's dark eyes locked on hers.

She went on when he said nothing. "I've seen it in my visions. I'm joining Darren's pack within the next few months."

The lines at the corners of Jack's eyes deepened. Moments stretched on.

"Why not sooner?" Jack's voice sounded thin.

"I'm not sure," she said. "I have a feeling there's something I have to do first as a human. I'm trusting my instincts, like you told me to."

Jack kept staring at her. She reached under the table and rested her hand on Darren's thigh.

Her mouth went dry and she had to swallow before she could force out the words, "Will you still trust me after I've turned?"

"Honestly?" Jack said. "I don't know. But I won't be around to find out."

"What?" Her heart was pounding in her throat.

"When I said we were relocating, I meant in another city," he said. "You were right about the Fairy Court setting up shop in Olympus. My old team and I talked it over and agree that this place is a lost cause. It's too dangerous to stay."

Darren let out a huff of breath. "How can you just leave?"

"Because we've been doing this for a long time," Jack said. "We've seen… Things I wish I could un-see a thousand times over. We've lost too many of our people already. And all of that was nothing compared to what's coming. This new Fairy Lord is behind some of the worst catastrophes in human history."

"Then it's even more likely that he's the one behind the impending apocalypse," Miranda said. "I need your help to stop it."

"This guy might be the thing behind what happened to Pompeii." Jack's voice had a frustrated edge to it that she'd never heard before. "Now, he's gathering all kinds of fey to his banner—not just High Court Sidhe, like elves. He's bringing in the Low Court. Vampires, werewolves, ghouls—*created* fey that are usually left to their own devices. He's gathering them together and leading them in numbers that we've never had to face before. How are we supposed to stand against that?"

She shook her head. Losing the fairy fighters she hadn't met yet didn't bother her that much. Losing Jack? That was a blow.

"There isn't going to be a safe place on the entire planet when this guy is done with it," she said. "What part of *apocalypse* are you not understanding?"

"Have you had another vision about it?" Jack asked.

She shook her head. "The details are still fuzzy. It's like the exact path to that future hasn't been decided. But I'm clear on one thing. There will be nothing left when this guy is done. It's like he wants to stamp out every living thing on the planet. Why would he do that?"

"Immortality lasts a long time," Jack said. "This guy has been around forever as far as we can tell. Fairies get bored, and the most entertaining thing for them is watching others suffer."

"But if he kills everyone, won't it be even worse for him?" Darren said.

Jack shook his head. "You can't attribute reason to an irrational being. Fairies have minds that are alien to us—especially the High Court."

"That's all the more reason for us to figure out a way to stop him," Miranda said.

"Look, I believe in your visions. My colleagues…" Jack shrugged.

"The battlefield has changed," Darren said. "And there's more change coming."

"We don't stand a chance—" Jack began.

Miranda finished for him. "*If you run.* You don't stand a chance if you run. But if you stay, we can work together."

"If your human friends want to run, that's fine," Darren said. "But Miranda needs you. You've been like family to her."

He wasn't wrong. The thought of losing Jack was almost more than she could bear. She'd been anchoring Darren to his humanity through his change. Jack would absolutely an anchor for her as well. She needed that foundation. She needed him.

Growing desperate, she said, "Have you ever once fought *with* a werewolf instead of against one?"

That caught Jack's attention. He stared at Darren for a while.

"I can't say I have."

Miranda felt hope flutter in her chest. "Give it a try. We can take down Forester together, then you can decide what kind of chance you think we stand against the Fairy Court that's in town."

Jack let out a rumble that almost sounded like one of Darren's growls. "I would really like to see that Forester taken down."

Darren grinned at him. "It can be a parting gift—or an incentive to stay."

"We're going to need some iron," Jack said. "Skillets are in the kitchen."

Miranda closed her eyes and let out a huge breath. She was sure Jack would stay after they defeated Forester. She just had to be sure they won.

"When is the best time to lure him here?" she asked. "Will Darren be stronger at night?"

"Darren will be stronger the closer we get to the full moon—but also less in control," Jack said. "At least, that's what I've always been led to believe. But Forester will be weaker during the day."

"Then let's get to work." Darren stood up and looked around. "Do you still have those guns handy?"

"I kept a few around," Jack said.

Miranda wanted to give Jack more to think about while convincing him to stay. "The new head of Ford Security is working on R&D for us and will be coming up with better weapons to use against the fey."

"Now *that* is intriguing," Jack said. "My guy's been working out of his garage."

"Mine has access to the most cutting-edge technology available." Miranda smiled. "It's like Darren said. The battlefield is changing."

"Yeah, but not the scenery." Jack looked around the room. "This place is as good as any for the first fight. It'll limit the Forester's ability to teleport."

"We'll go get a couple of skillets," Miranda said. "But while we're gone, I want you to think about one thing. You say you believe in my visions. You can't pick and choose which ones you want to be true. Like it or not, Darren will prove himself to be a powerful ally for humanity. And the Knights of Antares are real. They're here in Olympus. And we can't afford to turn away any potential ally in this fight."

Jack's skin turned ashen and his lips pressed into a thin line. When he leaned forward to set the iron box on the table, his hand was shaking. He stared at it intently for a few moments.

"Good-guy werewolves," he mumbled. "The Knights are real. The *Knights*..." He ran both hands over his face, then shook his head. "This is my own private apocalypse. I thought I had things figured out, but the world as I knew it is just shattered. I don't know what to make of this. How to put it all back together."

"I'll help you." She reached across the table, remembering just in time to grip his wrist instead of his hand. "*We'll* help you."

Jack snorted, then nodded, resting his hand briefly on top of her forearm. He would stay. All they had to do to convince him he should stay was fight together to take down Forester. They could do that. She had to believe it. The thought of Jack leaving and shutting down The Red Thread was more than she could bear.

"You rest for a moment," she said.

She stood and waited for Darren to join her before they headed out of the room. It wasn't hard to find the weapons she was looking for. Skillets were still stacked all over the kitchen.

"Are you okay?" Darren said.

"Yeah. There's just so much riding on this."

"Are you worried I can't take Forester?"

She smiled. "After watching you beat the crap out of Shade? No."

"Good." He put his hand on her waist and gave her a quick hug.

"I wish I could say I feel sorry for Forester." She lifted a heavy skillet. "But I don't."

"That's also good. Because I'm going to tear his arms out of their sockets and beat him to death with them."

"Wow. Full Beowulf, huh?"

"Who?"

"Forget it," she said. "But we're going to spend part of your new immortality expanding your reading."

He grinned at her. "Maybe the Knights and I can start a book club."

Miranda laughed as she picked up another skillet for Jack. She was pretty sure neither of them would get a chance to use them.

The fight wasn't as worrisome as Jack's reaction to it. Her visions had helped her be prepared for seeing Darren in his other form, and it had still been terrifying. What if they won but Jack was still too freaked out by Darren to stay?

One way or another, it was time to find out.

"Are you ready?" she said.

"I just need one thing first."

"What?"

Darren pulled her close, bending down to kiss her. His heat soaked into her, the hard planes of his chest a barrier that she knew would keep her safe.

After a long while, he released her. His eyes were glowing.

He smiled and said, "Let's do this."

Chapter Twenty-Six

Letting loose on Shade had been cathartic. Having a place for the full moon was reassuring. But spending most of the past two days and nights making love with Miranda had been transformative.

Instead of bursts of rage that took Darren by surprise, there was a simmering pool of lava deep inside him. He was still watching out for spikes, curtailing them and keeping a tight hold on his behavior, but he wasn't afraid of them anymore. He was going to harness that power and use it to defeat Forester.

Darren handed Jack a skillet as they walked back into the room. The silver bell sounded as always, but Jack was right there to silence it.

"Miranda, why don't you stand opposite me," Jack said. "Forester doesn't have many options for where he can appear in a space this small. If we spread out, we can cover more area."

She nodded, then leaned in and gave Darren a quick kiss on the cheek before taking up her position.

"Where do you want me?" he said.

"Opposite the door." Jack leaned in and murmured, "You should know I'm armed with silver. If something goes wrong, I will put you down. Don't make me—for Miranda's sake."

Jack picked up a wicked looking knife that he had laying on the counter behind him. Darren took a quick sniff of the air. Iron. That blade was meant for Forester. But there were hints of silver around Jack. Enough to burn Darren's nose.

Darren shook his head to get the smell out. The now-familiar rage rose up in him.

How dare he threaten me? How dare he think I'm a danger to Miranda?

Darren curbed the instinct to growl. Instead, he smiled.

Jack's brow furrowed. His scent shifted. Somehow, the smile made him *more* afraid.

Instead of letting himself laugh at the thought, Darren said, "Thanks for looking out for her."

Before Jack could say anything more, Darren walked to the wall opposite the door—not that Forester would need to use it.

The iron box was sitting in the middle of the floor. Jack had moved the folding table out of the way. They had a big empty room, perfect for fighting. Darren couldn't wait.

He pulled his shirt over his head, remembering the fight with Shade. Darren's clothes had inhibited his movement. He'd felt seams start to tear.

Every time he changed, he was bigger. The ground was farther away and the world felt smaller, his clothes tighter. He was going to have to invest in some stretch pants at this rate. He tossed his shirt on the counter and kicked off his shoes.

"I'm going to need you to look away, Miranda," Darren said.

"What? Why?" she said.

She was staring at him with her lips slightly parted, her gaze telling him almost as much as her scent. It was too much of a distraction.

"Because, we're supposed to fight, not…" He glanced over at Jack, then back to Miranda. "If you get worked up like that, I'm going to get worked up like that, and this whole thing is going to go in a very different direction."

"Right. Okay." She grinned, her cheeks turning red, then covered her eyes with one hand. "I'm not peeking."

Darren chuckled, then he pulled off his socks and pants and threw them on top of his shirt.

Jack's scent changed, deepened with a rich almost sandalwood tone. When Darren turned to him, Jack quickly looked away.

Oh… Uh… That was unexpected.

Hearing Jack talk about Miranda's dad, Darren had felt there was something left unsaid. Now he wondered just how close they had been.

"Leave it," Jack said.

"Leave what?" Miranda still had her eyes covered.

Jack and Darren both said, "Nothing," at the same time.

"O…kay," she said.

Darren had other things to focus on at the moment. He pushed that mystery aside for another time. Jack looked away as Darren took off his boxer-briefs.

He flexed his fingers, felt the prick as his claws extended. His skin started to itch. He didn't fight it. Shaking his head, he stretched his lips as his face changed. He rolled his shoulders, feeling the muscles and bones pop as they shifted.

It felt…good. Incredibly good.

Energy coursed through him. He could feel his blood pulsing in his veins. The room shifted into shades of blue and green. Miranda and Jack were glowing yellow-orange-red silhouettes. He could see their hearts through their chests, both beating faster as they finally looked at him.

Jack was afraid.

Miranda wasn't.

She stepped forward and knelt by the iron box. "Everybody ready for this?"

"Go for it," Jack said.

Darren nodded.

She opened the box, then returned to her spot by the wall.

Darren stretched his mouth again. He could feel a kind of wall stopping him from changing completely, something limiting his strength. He wondered what it would be like to let go after his first full moon.

What was available to him now would be enough. It had to be. Forester wasn't leaving this room alive.

He thought about having the elf's blood in his mouth and growled.

"You okay there, Darren?" Jack's voice grated on Darren's sensitive ears.

Another sound was vibrating beneath it. A keening that made his head hurt. The air in front of Jack rippled, a line of white appearing, then widening.

Darren leapt forward. Jack reached behind his back—probably going for that gun loaded with silver. He seemed to be moving in slow motion.

Forester stepped through the rippling air. At least, Darren assumed it was Forester. He was completely covered in armor. Vines were engraved in the gleaming metal. The pattern looked like it was moving.

The sword in Forester's hand was of greater concern. In a graceful arc, he swung it at Jack's head. The bamboo bell above the door began to ring.

So much for Jack's alarm system.

The human was just starting to register Forester's appearance when Darren landed between them, grabbing the elf's sword arm. A slit in the faceplate of his armor let Darren see the glowing green eyes he'd come to hate so much.

Jack scrambled out of the way the moment Darren registered the blistering pain in his hand.

Forester's armor was made of silver. At least in part. Enough to burn Darren's skin. He let go of the elf's arm and jumped backwards onto the counter.

"We've battled the Knights for hundreds of years," Forester said. "You think I wasn't prepared for this?"

He slashed at Darren. Darren leapt over Forester's head to avoid the blade.

Jack ran at Forester from the side, swinging his skillet. Another line appeared in the air between Forester and Jack. Darren didn't know what would happen if Jack fell through it.

He leapt at Jack, catching him under his ribs and spinning him in a different direction. Forester disappeared through the crack in reality.

"What the fuck was that?" Jack yelled. Apparently, he was getting over his fear of Darren.

Darren suppressed the urge to rip Jack's head off. "You were heading right for…whatever he uses to teleport. I didn't know what would happen if you crossed through it."

"Oh," Jack said. "Thanks."

"Don't mention it."

Miranda was shifting nervously back and forth, looking around the room. "I didn't foresee the armor. He's too fast. This was a mistake."

She was right.

Forester could appear anywhere at any time. And he was covered in silver. How the hell was Darren supposed to protect Miranda? He couldn't even touch Forester without feeling excruciating pain.

Another line appeared, widening to let Forester through. Time dilated again. Even if Darren could warn Jack and Miranda, their weapons were useless. There was nothing they could do.

But *he* could.

He took several deep breaths, working up his nerve. The moment Forester stepped through the opening, Darren rushed him. He rammed his shoulder into Forester's gut, lifting him from his feet. The elf's sword clattered to the ground.

Darren kept running forward, crashing into the wall and pinning Forester there. Forester struck at Darren's back. The pain was nothing compared to the agony of his shoulder. Darren could feel blood running down his arm and back. He tried to bite at Forester's neck, but his armor had a neck guard Darren couldn't get past.

There had to be weak points—joints where the parts connected. If he didn't find them quickly, it wouldn't matter. The pain was making Darren's vision turn red. The lava pool of rage deep inside was bubbling up to the surface. He could barely keep himself from letting Forester go. Darren wanted to destroy something—anything. He wanted to make others hurt as he did.

"Hold his head." Miranda appeared at Darren's side.

It didn't calm him. Instead, he felt the rage build even more. He had to find a way through Forester's armor. He had to kill him to protect Miranda.

"Darren!" She lifted Forester's sword. Was she turning on him?

No. She wouldn't. She needed him to do something. Darren focused past the pain. He grabbed onto Forester's helm and held on. His hands blistered, blood running down his arms.

Miranda made a sort of choking sound, then she lifted Forester's sword and held it in front of the slit he used to see through.

Forester started to scramble frantically in Darren's grip. Weakened skin tore, sloughing off as the muscle beneath started to melt.

Darren didn't care. He was going to do this.

Jack appeared at his back, holding Miranda's arms steady. Together, the leaned forward, driving the sword deep into Forester's head. Green blood gushed out over his armor.

His body kept on with its frantic movements for a few seconds, but then the movements became twitches. Death convulsions? Darren wasn't sure. And until he was, he couldn't let go.

"Darren, please. You have to let him go." Miranda was tugging on his arm. She couldn't get purchase.

Jack joined her, grabbing Darren's other arm.

Darren wanted to...bite them. He clenched his jaws shut tight.

He let them pull him away from the elf. Forester fell forward onto his knees and stayed there. Darren took another step forward, but his legs gave out. He landed on all fours, letting out a howl as his hands hit the floor. He reared back on his knees, a macabre mirror of the elf in front of him.

Forester was still alive.

He started to reach for his sword, but Miranda was already there. She used her skillet like a hammer, pounding the sword in deeper. It burst through the back of Forester's helm.

She retched, then let out a horrible sob. "His sword is silver. Use your knife. The iron one. It'll make it past his defenses now. Hurry, while he's weakened."

Jack picked up his knife from where he'd dropped it. Without hesitating a moment, he lined it up next to the sword already sticking out of Forester's face and drove it in deep.

The green blood turned black. Forester's body jerked again. His blood thickened, then dried into ash that poured out from spaces in his armor under his chin, down his sides. His armor collapsed on itself until it was just a pile of gleaming metal laying on the floor.

Miranda dropped to her knees next to Darren and wrapped her arms around his neck. She buried her face in the fur covering his intact shoulder.

"God, Darren. I'm so sorry."

"I...wanted..." Darren coughed. His hands and shoulders itched like crazy. "*I* wanted to kill him."

"You couldn't," Jack said. "We had to work together to take him down."

Darren started to growl. He wanted to taste blood. Jack's would do.

He started to rise, but Miranda was still clinging to his neck.

"Jack, don't move," Miranda said. "No matter what, don't move."

The scent of fear joined the blood and ash of the room. Jack's fear. It numbed some of the pain Darren felt. His vision was totally red.

He would slash open Jack's stomach and soothe the pain in his hands with the human's blood. And then he'd bite Miranda and turn her —*make her* join him. Nothing and no one would stop him.

"I can see what you're planning." Miranda held on tighter. "If you kill him, I'll be next. You won't be able to control yourself."

What? He would never hurt her. Ever.

Except to bite her. To turn her. Hadn't he just been thinking of that?

"I'll try to stop you if you go after Jack," she whispered.

How could she side against him?

"No," he said.

"You know I will. And it will send you over the edge. You're too hurt. In too much pain."

She pressed a kiss to his cheek—actually kissed him when he was in this form, covered in blood, ready to turn her, whether she wanted it or not. Ready to kill…the closest thing to family she'd had since her mother died.

And Jack was so much closer to Miranda's family than she realized. He had loved Miranda's dad. Darren was sure of it. Jack probably thought of Miranda as a daughter. If he stayed, he would protect her like Darren would. And whether that happened or not was all on Darren.

Darren stood up. Miranda dangled from his neck. He lifted an arm to hold her against his side, keeping his regenerating hands away from her.

Jack was normally taller than Darren. In this form, Darren stared down at him.

"You're not leaving," Darren said.

He felt them both suck in a breath, preparing themselves for whatever would come next. Jack looked ready to fight. Miranda was trembling.

Darren wouldn't force her to make that impossible choice. Instead, he forced himself to calm, pushed down on the rage surging through him. He didn't care that his vision was red. He was still Darren. He was still in control.

He took a few steps toward Jack.

Darren had felt so invincible the other times he'd changed. But Forester had taught him a painful lesson. Even outside of Faerie, he had been powerful enough to nearly kill them all. Silver armor was all he needed. If it hadn't been for Miranda and Jack...

Thinking about that was too dangerous. Darren thought about the weapons Morrison was making—thought through new permutations of what was needed. As much as Darren loved the idea of using his hands and teeth to rip Forester to shreds, he would have needed a fucking can opener to get to the elf's flesh.

If he'd thought to have a weapon handy, he might not have been hurt at all. He might not have come so close to killing his allies—allies he needed.

He'd been wrong about being able to take Forester on his own. And if he'd been wrong about this, he could be wrong about other battles in the future.

"You're not leaving town," Darren said. "Not leaving Miranda. You will stay and help me protect her."

Jack swallowed hard, then nodded. His voice was barely audible.

"Yeah." He cleared his throat and spoke again more strongly. "Yeah. I will."

Darren wrapped both arms around Miranda and pressed his cheek against the top of her head, waiting for the pain to pass. The red slowly faded from his vision.

Chapter Twenty-Seven

Blood was everywhere—Darren's blood. Miranda could feel it sticking in her hair, coating her arms.

Jack had said Darren could only turn someone by biting them in his fully transformed state. If he was wrong and blood was a factor...

She didn't care. She needed to be close to him.

It wasn't just about feeling him, it was about *not seeing* him. His wounds were horrific. She felt bile rise in the back of her throat every time she looked at him. There was bone visible in his shoulder.

She was careful to keep her arms up around his neck. He seemed to be taking care not to press his hands against her either, which was good given how they had looked.

She pinched her eyes shut, willing the memory out of her mind. He would heal. Werewolves healed quickly, right?

She heard Jack shuffle toward the door.

"I don't know about you two, but I could use a drink," Jack said. "And you could probably use a little time alone."

She let out a breath as the door closed behind him. Jack finally trusted Darren. There was no other way he'd leave them alone when Darren was in this form. Darren seemed to relax a bit, too.

"Are you okay?" she asked.

Darren chuffed. Was that a chuckle?

"I will be," he said.

She forced herself to open her eyes, then slid down his chest. He released his hold on her so she could step back and look up at him.

God, he was a mess. His body was completely covered in thick black fur. It glistened and was matted with blood in so many places. But his shoulder looked better. Now it just looked like raw meat instead of gleaming bones sticking out of his flesh. She covered her mouth and looked away again, trying not to gag.

When she thought it was safe to try to speak, she said, "I'm going to need to develop a stronger stomach. You'll all laugh at me if I'm constantly barfing up the deer we hunt."

Darren chuffed again. Definitely a chuckle. He lifted a hand toward her, but quickly lowered it and hid them behind his back.

"You don't have to do that for me," she said. "It must be hurting you."

"I'll live. I'll heal."

"You'd better. But first, you need to turn back."

"I just need a moment."

"Let me help." She stepped toward him again, wrapping her arms around his neck and tucking her face against the less-bloody side of it. He held her, too—warmth and energy passing between them that helped to calm her racing heart.

His muscles rippled beneath her arms, the fur receding as he shrank to his normal size. She felt his hands against the small of her back and didn't notice him tense from pain. She buried her fingers in his hair, a shudder passing through her as she realized that he really was okay.

"I'm so sorry you were hurt," she said.

"You should see the other guy."

She paused for a moment, then broke out laughing, even more relieved when he joined in. She pulled back, wanting to see that he was well, that he was *him*.

Dark black hair, warm bronzed face, strong jaw, lots and lots of dark stubble, and those beautiful gray eyes gazing into hers.

Darren. *Her* Darren.

He leaned down to kiss her, lips tender in their caress. The kiss deepened slowly, as if he finally believed that they would have all the time in the world to enjoy each other. She would do everything she could to make that true.

Jack's voice broke through the heat building between them, as he shouted, "Don't you dare have sex in my office."

They turned toward the door, laughing again.

"How does everyone always know?" she asked.

"I guess I should get dressed," Darren said.

"Yeah. I don't want any delays getting back to my apartment." She smirked at him, and he responded with a low, sensual growl.

"Let's go back to the garden tonight," he said. "To check on Eden and Shade."

"Sure. To check on them."

Darren shrugged. "And I'd like to see the room where I'll be spending the full moon."

"That's a good idea. And we'll need to start to plan. There's so much to do."

"It'll be okay," Darren said. "As long as we're together."

She nodded. This was the future her visions had shown her. They would be happy together—eventually.

The light reflected off of something on the ground. She looked over at the silver coin lying where it had fallen nearby.

"It will be okay," she said. "Better than okay. But this is only the beginning."

About the Author

Cassandra Chandler has been obsessed with stories for as long as she can remember. A prolific writer, she has several Paranormal and Scifi Romance series that feature aliens, psychics, werewolves, and vampires—sometimes all in the same book. When she's not writing super-sexy love stories, you can find her knitting, chatting with readers, or making weird puppets.

If you want to talk to her, head over to Twitter (@CassChandler), or Facebook (CassChandlerAuthor), send her email at AuthorAtCassandra-ChandlerDotCom, or, of course, leave a review. Remember to sign up for her newsletter (cassandra-chandler.com/ newsletter) to receive exclusive content!

Enjoy this excerpt from Cassandra Chandler's next
Forbidden Knights novel,

Forbidden Pleasure

Coming Soon

June 15 — 11:02 PM

With a quick stab through the heart, the vampire Shade was fighting lurched to a stop. He didn't bother to watch his opponent's body blacken, turning to ash starting around the wound and spreading until nothing was left but a pile of gray soot. He'd seen it too many times to be impressed.

He turned to face his next opponent, swatting away the vampire's arm with the flat of his blade before bringing his sword back in an arc that took his head.

Amateurs.

The group of vampires probably thought they had Shade and Niall trapped, stuck in a dead-end alley. Instead, the walls made sure that the vampires couldn't attack in their full numbers.

From their clumsy attempts at engagement, none of them had bothered with any sort of martial training or combat strategy studies before they'd been turned or after. They were relying on their heightened speed and strength to win.

Big mistake.

"What do you call a group of vampires?" Shade said, engaging yet another foe.

"I don't know." Niall said. "What do you call them?"

From his tone, it sounded like Niall thought Shade was telling a joke. It happened often enough that Shade couldn't mistake it.

"No, seriously," Shade said. "Werewolves run in packs. Witches have covens. What about vampires?"

"I couldn't care less."

Niall's Irish accent always thickened in battle. The words sounded more like 'couldnae keer'. Shade wished his own English accent hadn't faded over the centuries.

"How about we call it a murder," Shade said.

He spun in a circle, his sword whistling through the air until it met the neck of another opponent. The razor-sharp edge and weight of the blade were enough that Shade barely had to add force to cleave the next vampire's head from his body.

Okay, it hadn't started out as a joke, but that was kind of funny. And dark. Really dark.

"Enough with the morbid humor," Niall said. "And this isn't murder. It's an execution."

Shade shrugged as he sidestepped another vampire's attack. "I don't understand why I have to be here. There are only a dozen or so of them. You could handle this yourself."

Niall scoffed, wielding his much heavier sword as if it weighed as much as a toothpick. Dust was gathered around his feet from the vampires he'd already killed. There were dark flecks of ash in his coppery beard.

"Some partner you are," Niall said. "We're supposed to have each other's backs."

Shade stopped for a moment, his sword arm lowering. "I do have your back. Always." With a grin, he added, "I just also have a date."

Niall scowled, pointing with his blade to a vampire who was just about to launch himself at Shade.

He was aware.

With a pivot and dropping his weight a bit, he held his sword parallel to the ground, letting his attacker decapitate himself with his own inertia. Unfortunately, the same inertia caused the cloud of dust that had once been the vampire to hit Shade in the chest.

"Dammit," he said. "Now I need a shower."

"It's not safe to be 'dating' anyone." Niall was still scowling.

"That's why it's forbidden."

"Relax, it was just a joke."

Mostly.

Shade kept that thought to himself.

Three vampires were circling Niall, but he paid them as much attention as he might a swarm of gnats. "You spend every spare moment with Eden."

"I'm helping her with putting in the garden," Shade said. "Which, I will remind you, is for both of us to enjoy. It's a *moon* garden, after all."

Niall let out a disgusted puff of air just as two vampires leapt at him. Moving almost too fast for Shade to see, Niall caught one on the tip of his sword and the other with his bare hand.

Shade grimaced as Niall pulled his sword up to the vampire's heart, cutting a line through the middle of his torso. It was hard not to feel a twinge of sympathy, even though this batch of was particularly nasty and seemed almost mindless. Shade still had trouble watching Niall gut the guy.

Light from the nearby streetlamps filtered into the alley, illuminating the twisted features of the vampire Niall had by the throat. He held him off the ground effortlessly. The third ran forward and started clawing at Niall's forearm, trying to free the one in his grip.

"That's damned annoying." Niall kicked the vampire off his sword —toward Shade—and said, "Be a dear, won't you?"

Shade nodded, then swung his sword, giving the vampire a quick end.

Niall was right. This was an execution—one among hundreds. Thousands. Just like every other night they hunted.

The vampire clawing at Niall's arm let out a frustrated grunt, then she bit down on Niall's flesh. Her eyes widened briefly and she let him go, staggering back and spitting.

"Werewolf?" she said. "You traitor!"

"That's rich, coming from someone who kills her own kind," Niall said.

"I feed on *humans.*" She managed to straighten, and even looked indignant.

"What do you think you were before you changed?" Shade said.

She bared her fangs at him, the amber glow from the streetlights yellowing their sharp points. Shade just laughed. The ring of opponents around them had widened, as if the vampires were finally starting to realize they were in trouble.

"The new ones always posture," he said.

Niall scoffed. "They're like fucking mosquitos. Squish one, and a bunch of others pop up and take their place."

He dropped his sword, then pulled the vampire he'd been holding up in the air closer, wrapping one arm around the vampire's head and the other around his shoulder.

"Oh, come on," Shade said. "Don't—"

Shade flinched as Niall pulled the vampire's head off. Dark ash fell around his feet, a streak of black running down his shirt.

"You're doing the laundry tonight." Shade hoped his humor would help to take the edge off for Niall. It usually did, morbid or not.

This close to the full moon, Niall was at nearly full strength. He was also at the limits of his self-control. Letting loose on the vampires would help him curb the violent tendencies that came along with the power. That was part of why Shade was hanging back.

The vampires had to be destroyed. If they weren't, people would die. Niall was all too happy to take care of the matter. The fighting would help him vent and keep himself in check. Probably.

Hopefully.

Niall rolled his shoulders. "As we were saying, this garden of yours —and mine, I suppose—is almost finished. Are you going to be ready when Eden walks out of your life forever?"

Absolutely not. Shade was working on ideas to keep Eden around. An expansion on the current garden. A new project. Anything.

He wished that he could turn her, but that would be...complicated. Beyond complicated. He would have to tell her what he was. She would see him as a monster.

Still, it was hard not to think about—to dream about. The two of them fighting side by side. Protecting humanity from the monsters in the dark. Other...activities...they could do when the stars lit the night sky.

"Stop thinking like that," Niall said.

"Like what?"

"Daydreaming about 'recreational activities' with your lady friend. You're stinking up the alley with it."

"Sorry. I forget your sense of smell is much better than mine."

A vampire feinted, as if he was going to attack, and Niall turned and glared.

"We're talking," he said.

The vampire scrambled back.

By Shade's count, they were down to six from the initial twenty that had chased them into the alley. The ones remaining weren't attacking, but they weren't running away, either. That was a good thing, because Niall and Shade would have to track down any who escaped, and Shade wanted to get home and cleaned up before he met Eden.

Niall picked up his sword, which was reassuring. He hadn't quite fallen so far into bloodlust that he was just ripping people apart. Well, except for that one. He gestured toward the vampires to come at him, but none seemed eager.

"Maybe if you attack him all at once," Shade said, stepping to the side to give them more room.

The nearest vampire looked at him strangely, as if he'd managed enough sanity to realize Shade was giving tips on attacking his partner. The others weren't sane enough to recognize the trap. Shade engaged the sane-ish vampire while the rest rushed at Niall.

"Something most new vampires never live to realize is, these kinds of fights go much better if you bring a weapon," Shade said.

The vampire pulled out a gun.

"Oh." Shade felt his smile fall. "I wasn't actually thinking about *that* kind of weapon."

Unless it was loaded with silver. And even then, that would only work on Niall. The vampire didn't realize that, of course.

He fired. Shade felt the bullet hit him in the stomach as he leapt forward, a sharp sting of pain that he pushed away from his thoughts.

He focused on his form, on the arc of his blade coming down on the vampire's arm, cutting off the hand that was holding the gun.

Ignoring the vampire's pained scream, Shade dropped his sword and grabbed his target by the back of his head and twisted, baring his neck. Shade registered the look of shock and confusion on the vampire's face as Shade's fangs snapped down. Then it was just the pulse pulling him forward.

Shade bit down, siphoning the vampire's blood into his body through the hollow channels in his fangs. It wasn't as potent as the human blood Shade procured from the local hospital, but it would be enough to heal his wound—especially since he planned to drain the vampire dry.

The influx of blood helped his body work the bullet out. It hit the pavement with a *'tink'.* Shade released his hold just before the vampire exploded into dust.

"So much laundry," Shade said.

The area had been cleared of threats. Niall wiped off his sword before sheathing it, then clapped his hands together. Clouds of dust fell from them.

The battle was over, but he seemed agitated. He was also still fixating on Eden.

"I understand that she's an amazing woman," Niall said, "but you need to let her go."

Shade laughed. "How can I let her go when I haven't even gotten my hands on her?"

Oh, that was a tempting thought, though.

"It's not possible for our kind to have relationships with humans," Niall said. "There's a reason Antares has forbidden his Knights from falling in love—and it isn't just because it opens us up to being ransomed and manipulated."

"I never said anything about love."

The conversation was irking Shade more than it should. There was no way that he was in love with Eden. His best friend of the last half-dozen centuries should know better.

Niall's voice gentled a bit. "You can't have a future with Eden."

"I know," Shade snapped. "Of course I know that."

But there was a pain in Niall's eyes that Shade couldn't quite explain. As if he was keeping something back. As if...

Shit.

"I am an insensitive asshole," Shade said.

Niall let out a snort and smiled. "I know."

"I didn't even think about..." Shade shook his head.

"You live in the moment. That's part of your charm." Niall's voice became rougher. "And it happened a long time ago."

Still, Shade couldn't believe he'd forgotten Margaret, the woman that Niall had loved. The *human* woman.

The woman he had killed.

"Niall—" Shade began.

"I accept your apology. Let's leave it at that."

Shade tried desperately to lighten the moment. He shrugged, and said, "Eden's probably not interested in me, anyway. I mean, the age difference alone would send any mortal running."

Niall laughed. "You're a fine catch, Shade. She'd be crazy not to see it. That's why it's on you to keep the pair of you apart."

"I know."

Niall shook his head again, a distant look in his eyes. "There's not a day that passes where I don't think of Margaret. It's been tearing me up for over six hundred years. Just know that I would spare you that pain."

A knot wedged itself in Shade's throat. He couldn't speak, so he nodded.

Niall cast a sad smile at him and started to turn away, but stopped suddenly. Shade felt the hairs rise on the back of his neck.

"A three count, on your six." Niall kept his voice low and steady.

One. Two...

Shade lifted his sword as if he was about to wipe it clean.

Three.

He turned and stabbed upward in a fluid movement, his sword finding little resistance in the form that had suddenly appeared behind him. Blue blood gushed over the blade.

Niall was at his side in an instant, ready to help fight the new attacker. But there was no need. His sword was heavily laced with iron.

Shade lowered the dying fey being to the ground, taking in as many details as he could before the body disintegrated. Large green eyes, delicate features, pointed ears.

"Shit," Shade said.

"Bloody hell," Niall whispered.

"An elf. This guy's an elf." Shade turned to Niall, wanting to be sure his partner was seeing the same thing he was. "What is a member of the High Court doing in Olympus?"

"The same thing they always do. Preying on humans." Niall let out a long breath through his nose. "Fucking fairies."

It might be Shade's imagination, but it seemed like the shadows under Niall's cheekbones had deepened. There was a rumble to his voice that might not be part of his Gaelic burr. His hair had grown longer and darkened to more of a reddish brown.

"Niall, you still with me?"

Niall shook his head, but said, "Yeah. Just… If the High Court has come to town, things are about to get ugly."

"We have the advantage of surprise. If he'd known the Knights of Antares were here, the elf would have been wearing full armor. He would have brought weapons and enchantments along on his hunt."

Which might have resulted in Shade or Niall—or *both* of them—being killed.

Elves were teleporters. Engaging them in battle was always dangerous. Shade watched the blackening body turn to ash and slide from his sword, exploding into dust as it hit the ground.

The Knights were trained to fight all manner of fey. High Court like the elves or Low, like vampires and werewolves—the 'made' fey as opposed to those born of bloodlines. Niall and Shade, along with their comrades-in-arms, had centuries of experience on their side. That didn't mean they could let down their guard.

"Why was he here at all?" Niall said.

"Antares always knows where fey activity is about to grow. He gets us there before it happens somehow."

Niall shook his head. "I mean in this alley. There are no humans near. The vampires are—*were*—the only living beings I sensed within half a mile. Not even any homeless."

"It's been a long time since we've seen an elf," Shade said. "And they've never worked with vampires before."

Shade looked around at the piles of ash scattering in the night breeze. Why would a High born elf be hanging around vampires? The two courts didn't interact. Hell, most members of the High Court couldn't stand working together. It was a big part of what helped humanity survive.

If the fey ever united against humans and revealed themselves in open warfare...

That line of thinking would freak Shade out. They needed to process the information they had, and get it back to the others.

"Come on." Shade bent down to pick up the vampire's dropped gun. He tossed it to Niall, who bent the barrel, then chucked it into an open trash bin.

"We have a stop to make on the way home," Shade said. "Antares needs to know about this."

www.ingramcontent.com/pod-product-compliance
Lightning Source LLC
Chambersburg PA
CBHW052027020726
47501CB00004B/1280